THE ATLANTIS STONE

The "Stone Collection" Book 1

NICK HAWKES

Hawkesflight Media

The Atlantis Stone

First edition published in 2019 *(v.1.0)*
by Hawkesflight Media

The characters in this novel are purely fictional.
Any resemblance to people who have existed, or are existing, is coincidental.

ISBN 978-0-6481103-5-4

www.author-nick.com

Cover Design by Karri Klawiter

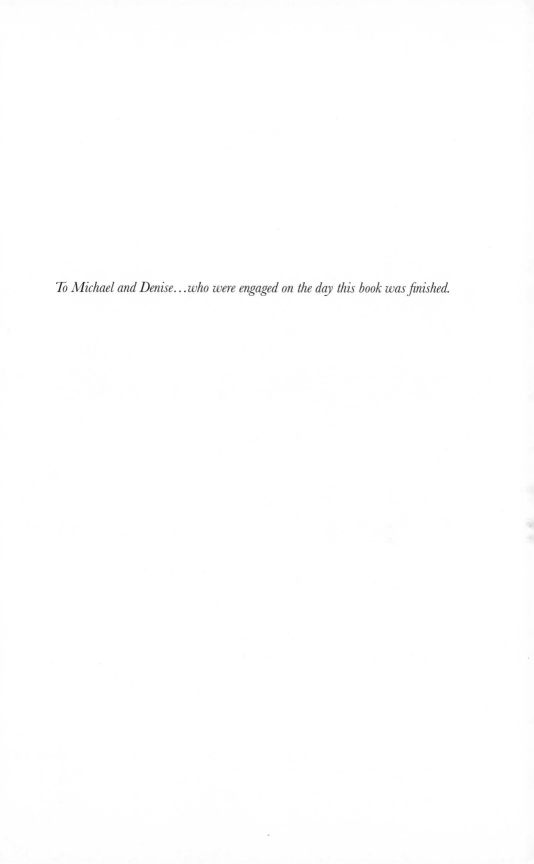

To Michael and Denise…who were engaged on the day this book was finished.

The Atlantis Stone

A novel

by
Nick Hawkes

Prologue

It was a single piece of parchment stamped top and bottom, and he'd signed it with his name. It was an agreement; a treaty…and he had no intention of abiding by it.

John II, king of Portugal and the Algarves, had studied it carefully. The first line was written in bold, decorated text, perhaps to give fair warning of the verbosity that was to follow. It was being read aloud by Fernando Alvareze, scrivener of the high court of justice, to all those gathered in the great hall.

The king had dressed carefully for the occasion, wanting to give the impression of understated power. He wore a red velvet cloak, over which he'd hung a gold chain with a diamond and pearl-encrusted pendant. This—together with his black cap and black beard—would, he felt, lend an appropriate air of severity.

He glanced across to the Spanish contingent. There was chief steward Don Enrique Enriques, chief auditor Don Gutierre de Cardenas, and Dr Rodrigo Maldonado. They were representing king Ferdinand II of Aragon and his wife, Isabella I of Castile…and they were looking altogether too smug.

The king was only half-listening as Fernando Alvareze continued to read.

Don Ferdinand and Dona Isabella, by the grace of God, king and queen of Castile, Leon, Aragon, Sicily, Granada…

Hell's teeth! He'd worked hard to reassert Portugal's fortunes and political dominance; he wasn't going to weaken now. He thought back to the early years when he inherited the throne from his father. The old king had fled to a monastery, leaving the nation in financial ruin. The resulting power vacuum was filled by the nobles, who'd run riot. King John curled his fingers into a fist. He'd needed to curtail their excesses.

They had protested, of course, and plotted rebellion—but the king had responded decisively. When his spies intercepted incriminating correspondence from the Duke of Braganza, he confiscated the Duke's lands and had him executed.

John's own cousin and brother-in-law had been equally truculent. The king recalled the night he had personally stabbed him to death—the agonizing retch, the look of astonishment.

He shouldn't have been surprised. *Fool.*

The Bishop of Evora had been the next to die. He'd assumed that his clerical status gave him license to agitate with impunity. He was mistaken. The bishop had been fatally poisoned in prison on his orders.

John was now satisfied that his hold on the nation was secure. Financial stability had been restored and he'd even earned a nickname from his people: *o Príncipe Perfeito,* 'the Perfect Prince.' He stroked his beard. But he wasn't satisfied; he wanted glory. He wanted to revive the dream of his great uncle, Henry the Navigator —to discover new lands, subdue them, and have their wealth flow into his kingdom.

He acknowledged to himself that his explorers had done well. Diogo Cao had discovered the great Congo River. Bartolomeu Dias had rounded the southernmost tip of Africa, which the king renamed the Cape of Good Hope. Even now, his explorers were readying themselves to push on to India.

But he'd heard tell of a land, a vast land in the southern seas—a land of gold.

In the name of God Almighty, Father, Son, and Holy Ghost, three truly separate and distinct persons and only one divine essence. Be it manifest and known to all who shall see this public instrument, that at the village of Tordesillas, on the seventh day of the month of June, in the year of the nativity of our Lord Jesus Christ 1494, in the presence of us.

King John looked covertly at his nemesis, Isabella I. He could expect trouble from that woman, "Isabella the Catholic." He glanced down at her feeble-looking son, John, Prince of Asturias. "My little angel," she was fond of calling him. But no amount of finery could disguise the fact that the boy was a weakling. He would pose no threat, but his mother was another matter. She was Queen of Castille and every bit as powerful as her husband, Ferdinand II, known (predictably enough) as "Ferdinand the Catholic." Both were religious zealots. Together, they had torn up the Alhambra Decree that protected Muslims and set out on a religious rampage, forcing both Muslims and Jews to convert to Christianity or face deportation—or death. They were strong.

The king gripped the side of his chair. But he was stronger.

Ferdinand and Isabella had sponsored Columbus's voyage in 1492. That had started the problem. It was only through good fortune that Columbus called in to Lisbon and reported his American discoveries whilst on his way back from the Americas to Spain. John remembered his anger on hearing of it. He had complained to the Pope that any lands discovered in that part of the world were promised to Portugal, not Spain. The Spanish had immediately organized a diplomatic solution for they were intimidated by Portugal's maritime might.

As well they might be, thought John sourly.

The Pope, Alexander VI, had moved quickly to organize the Treaty of Tordesillas. Its purpose was to divide trading and colonizing rights for all newly discovered lands between Portugal and Spain, to the exclusion of other nations. It decreed that all lands west of the meridian forty-six degrees west would belong to Spain, and all those east of the line would belong to Portugal.

That at least should protect my claim on Africa and India, thought the king—but he was hungry for more. He wanted to find new lands that were rich in gold, wherever they may be.

We renounce all fraud, evasion, falsehood, and pretense, and we shall not violate or oppose this treaty, or any part of it, at any time or in any manner whatsoever.

John shifted impatiently in his seat.

Drawn up by me, Fernando Alvarez de Toledo, secretary to the king and to the queen, scrivener of the high court of justice, and notary public in their court, who is witness.

It was done.

The king leaned back and growled to his secretary, "Fetch me Manuel. We must plan how to find new lands of gold before the Spanish find them. Manuel will soon succeed me as king, so I want those plans in place immediately." He banged the seat of his chair. "If he prevaricates, remind him that I executed his brother. If there is a great South Land of gold, Portugal must own it. A pox on the Spanish and their wretched pope…and damn this miserable treaty!"

Chapter 1

The doorknob turned very slowly, then stopped...and twisted back again.

Benjamin watched it in the darkness. His skin prickled as the familiar fear washed over him. He held his breath and waited. He must not—dare not move. His body screamed in protest and begged him to breathe. He allowed himself a shallow pant; it sounded like a sob. This couldn't be happening! The nightmare was being played out again. He'd sobbed in terror many times as a child...watching the door handle turn.

It turned again, testing. Benjamin expected to hear the labored breath and the drag of the crippled leg.

But there was only silence.

He waited. Moonlight streamed through the windowpanes of his workshop, highlighting the last of the wood dust that was still trying to settle. Everything was still—almost. With his cheek pressed against the splintered wooden floor, Benjamin watched the shadow of two feet through the crack under the door.

He felt trapped inside his canvas swag, the bushman's sleeping bag that he'd rolled out on the workshop floor. Only a moment ago he'd been snugged down, hiding in sleep from the chilly night air.

Benjamin drew his arms up and placed his hands on the floor, bracing himself to flee or fight. Which?

He glanced across the darkened room. His half-inch skew chisel was made of Böhler S700 high-speed steel. Its edge could shave the hairs off his arms; its long blade would be deadly. But it was well out of reach, nested neatly in the rack above the wood lathe on the other side of the workshop.

The shadows under the door disappeared. Silence.

A minute passed.

Then another. An eternity.

Suddenly, there was the crash of splintering glass. Benjamin ducked instinctively. Something large fell through the skylight above him. It ripped off the old sheet that he had tacked over part of the skylight and smashed to the floor beside him.

Shards of glass fell everywhere. Then all was still.

Benjamin removed his hands from his face. It took a moment for him to focus…and to realize that he was staring at the ruined remains of a human being. A corner of the sheet had tried to fold itself over the body like a shroud. It failed to cover an out flung arm. A pistol had spun away and slid across the floor. Moonlight gleamed on the dull metal of its silencer as it rested against the leg of Benjamin's workbench.

"What's your name?"

"Benjamin Bidjara."

"Spell it."

"B-I-D-J-A-R-A." Benjamin knew what was coming next.

"What sort of surname is that?"

"It's Aboriginal."

Detective sergeant Richard Anderson scowled. "You don't look Aboriginal."

"I know." When it was apparent that the inspector wanted more information, Benjamin added, "My mother was Kija, from around

Kununurra. Not sure of my father. Never knew him. I was told his family originally came from around here."

"Kununurra is northern Australia. That's a long way from Port Fairy here in coastal Victoria."

Benjamin shrugged and felt awkward. He didn't understand either. He reached across the workbench and picked up a block of mulga that he had prepared for turning. It was wood of uncompromising hardness from the desert regions of Australia. He stared at the dark wood and traced the ivory-colored streak that ran through it with his finger. *A bit like me*, he reflected sourly. *Black but not black.* "Throwback," they'd called him. "Hey, Throwback...you think you're better than us, eh? You gonna forget you're trash, like us? You gonna get a white man's job in the city?...Hey, Throwback, show us your white willie." Laughter.

"You don't even speak like an Aborigine."

Benjamin raised an eyebrow.

"You speak...formally, like a Pom: an Englishman."

"How should a blackfella speak, detective?"

The detective ignored the rebuke, remained impassive, and waited for an explanation.

Benjamin sighed. "The Christian Brothers offered scholarships to a few of us to attend Rostrevor College in Adelaide. I went to school there. They had a good English teacher." Benjamin pinched the top of his nose. "I haven't been back to Kununurra since I was twelve."

They were sitting on ornately carved stools next to the work-bench under the window. Behind them, a police photographer hefted a camera case over his shoulder and made for the door. Crime scene investigators in white overalls were still examining the scene, occasionally placing samples into specimen bags. The body had been taken away two hours earlier.

The detective looked at his notes. "Why would anyone be standing on the parapet of a wall next to your skylight with a silenced pistol?"

"I thought we'd been through this."

"Let me hear it again."

"No idea."

"You owe anyone? If it's drugs, we can organize some sort of protection…but only if you help us."

"As I've told you before, I don't do drugs. I don't owe money… and there's no one I can think of who would wish me harm."

"A bloke doesn't shin up to the parapet of a wall with a silenced gun for no reason. It's likely he was trying to get a clear shot at you. You'd only covered half the skylight with your sheeting. Why did you put the sheeting up, by the way?"

"I work in wood. I'm a wood-turner, so having the right light is important. Light needs to be even and diffuse. No deep shadows."

The detective swiveled to and fro on his bar stool, rubbing his hands along the side rails of the seat appreciatively. "Did you make this?"

Benjamin nodded and looked at the delicately turned spindles. He'd enjoyed making them. *Redgum. Strong enough to hold a one hundred kilogram policeman.*

"It's good." The detective continued on seamlessly. "We'll need to search this place thoroughly for…anything, and also your home. Where do you live?"

"I live here, in the workshop."

The detective raised an eyebrow. "All the time?"

"For the last eight months—ever since I've been in Port Fairy."

The detective looked at him disbelievingly.

Benjamin pointed around the room. "Shower in the cubicle over there. Potbelly stove for warmth. Electric fry pan by the sink…and a swag on the floor."

"So you've got money problems?"

Benjamin rubbed his forehead wearily. "Until my business gets going, I can either put petrol in my ute or rent a flat. Can't do both. I'm happy enough with the arrangement and in no hurry to get other accommodation."

"Well, you can't stay here. We've got another day's work to do at least. Your workshop has been taped off as a crime scene and we've put a tarp over the skylight to protect it. We don't want you traipsing around."

Benjamin was about to protest when the detective got to his feet and peered out the window. "Damn and blast. The press are here." He levered himself off his stool. "I suppose I'll have to speak to them."

Benjamin followed the detective's gaze out the window and frowned. An untidy figure was standing beside a car. His hands were deep in the pockets of an open coat that he was swishing around as he emphasized what he was saying to a policeman. There was something familiar about him. Benjamin turned the piece of mulga over in his hands and waited for the answer to swim into his consciousness. Lost thoughts, like trees, needed time to grow—and they grew more quickly if you didn't watch them too closely.

The man's untidy gait…standing by a lemon-scented gum years ago…wearing a black blazer with red trim. Aah, yes…the front gardens of the school. Then he had it. It was an old classmate from Rostrevor days. Benjamin hadn't seen him—or, indeed, any of his classmates—for five-and-a-half years. He looked out the window again to make sure. The angular figure jerked like a badly co-ordinated string puppet as he argued with the policeman. There was no doubt about it. Marcus O'Lauchlan was being as passionate and loquacious as ever.

Benjamin turned and called to the detective who was speaking with a forensic officer. "Detective, I think I know the bloke outside, the guy you said was the press…if that helps," he trailed off.

The detective scowled. "You're not to go blabbing to the press until I give you permission to do so. Is that understood?" He rubbed his hands through his hair, walked to the open door and ducked under the crime scene tape.

Benjamin watched the ensuing pantomime from the window. He wasn't surprised to hear raised voices. The detective put up a hand to forestall the torrent of words coming from the reporter and beckoned for Benjamin to join him outside.

Benjamin did so diffidently, unsure of what would transpire. He stood a few paces away, waiting to be invited into the other men's space—waiting to be recognized.

The reporter straightened up and looked at him with a puzzled frown before exclaiming, "Ben! What on earth are you doing here?" He stepped over to Benjamin and held out his hand. "Well, I never," he said, jerking himself upright. "Are you something to do with the drama that's happened here?" He nodded in the direction of the detective. "This fellow won't say anything other than that there's been a death."

"Don't beat up the local police too much, Marcus, they're only doing their job. Yes, I live here. Yes, someone has died in unusual circumstances. And no, I haven't a clue what's going on."

The detective interrupted. "That's quite enough. This is an ongoing investigation."

Marcus began to protest.

The detective turned to Benjamin. "Can you shut him up?"

"Probably not. I was never able to at Rostrevor."

The detective rolled his eyes. "You are not to say anything, d'ya hear? And I want you at the police station in Warrnambool tomorrow morning at 10am. Can you manage that?"

"Can I get my swag?"

"No."

"Then where do I sleep?"

"At a friend's. With a relative."

"I've pretty much kept to myself since I've been here. I don't know anyone."

Marcus began bobbing his head forward like a Jabiru looking for a juicy frog. "Am I to take it that you have no place to stay...and that you're actually living in Port Fairy now?"

Benjamin nodded.

"Well, that's easy, then," said Marcus. He swung around to the detective. "Benjamin can stay with me. I've got a flat in Warrnambool. It'll be convenient for Ben, only ten minutes from here...and it will mean he'll be on hand for your interview tomorrow."

"I'm not sure that's proper. You're a journalist."

"What's the alternative?"

The detective sniffed. "You're not to milk him for information. If I find anything in print before I give the okay, I'll arrest you every birthday for the rest of your life for assaulting my boots with your balls. Is that clear?"

Marcus jutted out his chin. "If you promise me an exclusive on the story when you release the details."

"Hmff."

Evidently satisfied that the detective had signaled assent, Marcus replied, "Brilliant. Grab your stuff, Ben, and hop in the car."

Benjamin had been feeling like a box of vegetables being bartered for at a market. He cleared his throat. "Um, thanks Marcus. I'll follow you in my ute." He looked up at the sky. The sun was hovering near its zenith. What on earth was he going to do with the rest of the day? He felt the need to get away from the barrage of questions that he knew would come from Marcus. He needed another world, a quieter place where strangers with guns didn't fall through the roof and die.

"Detective, can I get my wetsuit and fins from inside?"

"I'd have thought an overnight bag would be more useful."

"That too."

"Why do you want it?"

"Calm day. Good light. I thought I'd go for a dive."

Chapter 2

F elicity Anderson looked at the devastation around her and tried to fight down a wave of despair. The 'house' she had purchased was little more than a shed made of ugly cement blocks and a corrugated iron roof. However, its location meant that it had been horrendously expensive to buy. It stood just one street back from the Moyne River, which was very upmarket. The river was edged with luxurious modern houses, pontoons, and expensive boats owned by rich retirees from Melbourne. The rest of Port Fairy was very different; it was comprised largely of old houses built either of dark volcanic stone or weatherboard. Its gentle streets and cafés whispered of an age when time was kinder to people. The tourists loved it.

Felicity, or Flick as she was usually called, ached for that kindness. She needed it desperately.

She leaned on the shovel and stared at the pile of building debris in the middle of the shed. Ruined…like her marriage. She had invested her inheritance and her heart in a marriage and a townhouse in North Melbourne. The house had been a futuristic thing, minimalistic and clever but emotionally cold. He blamed her for the unreasonable demands of her job. She blamed him for having an affair.

The separation had been acrimonious. He was a lawyer, and she hadn't fared well in the divorce settlement. She had run away to lick her wounds, fleeing her job and her marriage to the country with just enough to buy an ugly post-war garage in Port Fairy. The garage had once been used as a car repair business—until it was trumped by the large steel and glass dealerships in the nearby town of Warrnambool.

Could this ugly shed ever be transformed into a place where Felicity could live and chase her dream of being a writer?

She was currently staying in the back room of her brother's home. He was one of the doctors in Port Fairy. His wife was pregnant again, so the arrangement couldn't be long term. Nonetheless, she was grateful to have had a place to hide for the last six months. Staying with her brother certainly had its perks. When he felt the need to flee the demands of his career, he took himself off with one or two friends in his twin-hulled Shark Cat and went scuba diving. It was a passion Felicity shared, and she often went with them.

She checked the weather forecast again with the app on her phone. The conditions at Thunder Point would be perfect today. It was a rare occurrence. Swells from the Southern Ocean usually threw themselves against the rugged cliff-line west of Warrnambool, causing the sea in the tiny coves to boil with deadly fury. Today, however, all would be calm, and she could continue to test out a theory, a theory she was not yet prepared to share with anybody. She would explore it alone.

But first, there was work to be done. She kicked at the broken pieces of plasterboard and metal off-cuts on the floor, sighed, and began carrying them to the trailer that was parked outside. She wanted the debris cleared away before the tradesmen came next morning to install the window frames, complete with glass. By tomorrow evening, the space where the old garage doors had once been would be filled with a multi-paned, old-fashioned shop window she had bought from a salvage yard. The result would be pretty.

It would look a whole lot prettier, Felicity conceded, if she could afford to put a bull-nosed veranda on the front and clad the cement brick walls with weatherboard. And it would take a whole lot more work to make it livable inside. Whilst the roof space had been converted into a generous living area lit by loft windows, there was still a great deal to be done. Not even the second fixings were completed. Her house was nothing more, she decided, than a middle-aged tart with half her makeup on. There was no money left to finish it. Her ex had delivered a last parting gift of venom: he had maxed out the credit card they'd had in shared names. A letter from the bank demanding that she pay half of the outstanding amount lay crumpled in her pocket. It would take all that she had left. The implications were appalling. Moyne Shire Council were very specific regarding the deadline for completion of her rebuilding project. She would have to sell if she couldn't meet that condition. Her dream—everything—would be lost.

The frame of the old shop window, due to be installed the next day, leaned against the inside wall. Felicity's reflection stared back from it. The frames made her look as if she'd been crossed out—discarded, canceled. Was she really that insignificant? She examined her reflected image. She'd been told too often by her city friends that she was beautiful to hold to any false humility that she was not. But her good looks were definitely under siege by a dark smudge of building dust across her cheek, her gray pallor, and the grim set of her mouth. She had high cheekbones and dark brown eyes, the corners of which hinted at something oriental.

Felicity's black hair was tied back into a long ponytail, its volume at odds with her petite frame.

She moved her image to the next pane of glass. No improvement. There were four rows of five panes; she'd counted them. She resisted the urge to check herself in all of them. Instead, she leaned forward, rested her forehead on the old painted wood, and began to cry.

Felicity never cried for long. There was a little voice inside her that made a habit of mocking her weakness. It was the tyrant that urged control. *Always be in control. Always be precise. Always be right.* Her father had insisted on it when she was a child. He'd died five years ago of a heart attack. Her Italian mother had died earlier in childbirth—at Felicity's birth. She'd been born in the Solomon Islands where her father was a doctor. He'd worked with *Médecins Sans Frontières* and, at that time, still believed he could save the world.

"It looks as if you could use a coffee."

Felicity was appalled to be caught crying. She wiped a hand over her face and turned around. A woman with untidy red hair piled on top of her head stood beside the tailgate of the trailer. She was dressed in a tie-dyed skirt, a gypsy-style waistcoat, and wore a necklace of gum-nuts, seashells and beads.

"How about I shout you a brew from the café around the corner?"

Felicity sniffed and forced a smile. "That's very kind, but I want to get this lot ready for the rubbish tip."

"Hmm. Would it help morale if I gave you a hand to load it?"

"That's very kind of you but there's…" Felicity was interrupted.

"It would be payment for my asking if I could have some of the metal off-cuts on your trailer. I'd like to try and use them in some of my sculptures."

"Oh, of course. Take what you want." She held out her hand in a stiff, formal way. "I'm Flick, by the way. I'm trying to renovate this place but running out of money. Under a bit of pressure…as you can see."

"Yeah. Life's a bitch. I'm Gabrielle. Call me Gabs. I'm an artist. I live in a converted milking shed on my parents' property just out of town. It doesn't make a very good shop front, so I'm broke as well."

Despite her fragile state, Felicity laughed. Gabs grinned and also began to chuckle. It was enough to cause the last vestiges of propriety to crumble. They both convulsed with laughter and hung on to each other for support while wiping tears of mirth from their eyes.

"I agree, life's a bitch," said Felicity, catching her breath, "but I'm crazy enough to dream anyway."

"That's my girl." Gabs put her hands on Felicity's shoulders and studied her face. "Feeling better?"

Felicity sniffed and nodded. "Thanks."

Gabrielle glanced at her watch. "Hmm. I've got to run. I do some part-time waitressing at the café on the main street. But let's do that coffee as soon as we can."

"When are you next in town?" asked Felicity.

"I'm flexible."

"In two days, then. Here. Same time." Felicity leaned forward and kissed Gabs on the cheek. "Take what you like from the trailer. I'm off to chase…" She nearly said 'a dream.' "…an idea."

Felicity shivered. It was early spring, and the water was very cold. She lifted the inflator tube above her head and depressed the air dump valve. Slowly, she began to sink through the shafts of light slanting through the water. It was always a magical moment. She pinched her nose and blew to equalize the pressure as she descended. Her rate of descent began to increase as the water pressure squeezed air from her wetsuit. She bled air into her buoyancy control vest to slow it down.

Felicity looked around, orientating herself as the marine fairyland unfolded around her. A tiny glass cuttlefish with a frill of beating fins edged away from her…and a school of magpie perch parted to allow her to drift down through them. Normally, she would have dawdled in their midst to photograph them but today she wanted to go to depth, at least twenty meters, and search among the silt and kelp at the edge of the reef. Her air supply would be used three times more quickly than at the surface, so time was of the essence.

She had studied the local weather, the winds and the currents…and pored over the results for days and days, checking and recalculating. What if the ship had first hit Thunder Point and then been swept around into the bay where it was deliberately beached because of the damage? Surely there would be evidence of it. The sailors would have thrown everything they could spare overboard to lighten the ship. Perhaps people had been looking for evidence of the ship in the wrong place for all these years—if she was right.

Down she went.

The water was clear enough to allow the dappled sunlight to play on the waving fronds of kelp below her. Kelp never seemed to be still. Its long leathery fronds swayed to and fro in the slightest of currents in a hypnotic dance. Felicity knew it to be a dangerous dance. The straps of kelp were stronger than a man's arm and could easily entangle.

She worked her way down the tumbling rock face, which was covered with a fantastic array of sponges and seaweeds. Fish darted into crevices and under rock ledges as she brushed by. She'd searched the shallower regions of the reef in three earlier dives. Today was her deepest search yet...and possibly her last. The kelp forest was as deep as she could go.

Felicity tried not to disturb the silt as she finned her way slowly along the bottom of the rocky cliff. She was looking for anything out of place. But everything was disturbingly normal. Time passed and she looked at the dive computer poking out from under her waist-band. It showed that she had six minutes before she would need to ascend to the decompression stop five meters from the surface. She had tagged the depth on the Shark Cat's mooring line.

Beady eyes stared at her from a rock crevice. She turned away and looked down. *What's that?* It was a stick of something protruding from the silt by the kelp bed. The small stick was encrusted with marine life, but she could see a collar of verdigris where it protruded from the silt. Verdigris could mean only one thing—copper. She tugged at it. After a brief moment, it pulled free. There wasn't much length to it but what excited Felicity was that the section under the silt was bent into a perfect right angle. Nature usually avoided straight lines and right angles. The action of pulling the bent piece of copper free dislodged a piece of flat stone, pulling it half clear of the silt. She picked it up. As the cloud of silt floated away, she saw what seemed to be carving...

Ouch! Felicity felt a punch on her left forearm and a stinging pain. She jerked around to see a large moray eel thrashing its snakelike form in the water as it savaged her arm. Felicity twirled in the water, trying to shake off the writhing monster. She spun and flailed in panic, desperate and sick with revulsion.

Suddenly, the eel was gone. However, the entangling embrace of the kelp fronds now presented a far more deadly danger. She twisted and turned but only succeeded in entangling herself more. Felicity fought down rising panic and looked carefully at why she was so trapped. It didn't take long for her to see the reason: shark line. Long lengths of the tough fishing line were threaded through the kelp binding her tightly.

She tore at the fishing line, causing bloodied welts to appear on her hands. She was going to die. She knew it. *So stupid*. Not much air left. She thrashed and twirled. No way to get free. Getting tired. Losing strength.

What? She was dreaming now.

A figure in a black wetsuit was in front of her. It couldn't be true —the figure had no scuba tanks. No one swam at twenty meters without scuba tanks! She was hallucinating.

The figure held Felicity's shoulders to stop her twisting, gave her the okay signal, and began slicing at the kelp with a knife. Seconds later, he put his hand to his mouth and tapped her regulator.

It took a moment for her to understand that he needed to share her regulator so that he could breathe. She nodded.

He eased the regulator from her mouth and breathed on it hungrily. After taking five breaths, he returned it to Felicity's mouth. This maneuver was repeated a number of times as he cut away the fronds and fishing line. Eventually, Felicity was free enough to pull the emergency alternate regulator from its housing on her vest and thrust it toward her rescuer. He grabbed it, put it in his mouth, and breathed deeply before continuing to cut away at the kelp.

It wasn't long before she was free. Her rescuer wrapped an arm around her and began to kick for the surface. However, she fought herself free of him. The stranger let go immediately, holding up his hands to show acquiescence. She reached down, scooped up the carved stone that she had dislodged from the silt, and tucked it behind her vest cummerbund. Only then did she allow herself to be guided toward the surface.

Felicity looked down at the kelp forest that had so nearly killed her and noticed the very long fins of her companion. They were the fins of a free-diver. But he certainly wasn't free any more. Both of them were breathing from the same tank, each connected to it by an umbilical cord—forced close together. She felt his arm around her shoulder.

As they swam upward, it was she who needed to take control, pulling him back so that she didn't ascend too fast. The diving technique that worked for a free-diver definitely didn't work for a scuba diver who had spent time at depth. Felicity needed to decompress. She patted her hand down, signaling for him to slow down.

He nodded.

They drifted up toward the mooring line of the Shark Cat, keeping pace with the bubbles they exhaled. When they got to the tag on the mooring line five meters below the surface, Felicity held up a hand. She tapped her watch and splayed out her fingers. *We need to wait five minutes. Please understand me. Please.*

He pointed to her and made a ring with his forefinger and thumb.

He's asking if I'm okay. She nodded. *I'm fine.*

He gave her the thumbs up, grasped the mooring line, and bent around to examine Felicity's wounded forearm. A cloud of rust-red blood had been drifting out from the rip in her wetsuit. She watched as he unfastened the knife scabbard from his leg and strapped it around her forearm to staunch the flow.

It was an act of kindness that provoked an extraordinary emotion in her.

Minutes later, they broke the surface at the stern of the Shark Cat. Felicity pulled out the piece of flat stone from behind her cummerbund, reached up, and placed it in the outboard engine well.

Her companion helped her remove her fins; easing them free and throwing them into the boat. However, she then discovered she didn't have the strength to climb the ladder, hampered as she was with a wounded arm and her dive gear on. She fell back into the water.

Her rescuer reached around her from behind, undid the straps, and pulled the air tank and vest from her. He looped the assemblage over an arm and then undid her weight belt. Felicity had the disconcerting impression of being stripped by competent hands. She reached for the ladder and found that she was now able to climb it with ease. Once on board, she turned and hauled the dive gear into the boat as the stranger held it out to her. Felicity ignored the stabbing pain in her forearm, unfastened the regulator from the tank and lifted the cylinder into one of the storage slots along the side of the boat. It was an act designed to give the appearance of a normalcy she did not feel.

She turned to find that her companion had climbed aboard and was watching her. He pulled off his hood. Water hung from his dark, curling hair like jewels. He was slim and swarthy. Felicity had the impression of dark eyes, darker than her own, seeing rather more than she would have wished. His features were strong and pleasing. So was his body. His long limbs looked strong, even though his frame looked spare.

"First aid?" he asked. His voice was a soft purr—loud enough to be heard and nothing more.

Felicity pointed to a green box tied down with shock chords under the gunwale.

She reached around to locate the tape attached to the zip so she could undo the back of her wetsuit. *Where is the wretched thing?*

The stranger turned her around and unzipped the back of her wetsuit. Then he moved around to her front and pulled the wet suit carefully from her arms.

Her forearm was a mess. Blood was flowing freely from the macerated flesh. The man held a pad against it before pouring antiseptic fluid over the wound. He took her other hand and placed it over the pad to apply pressure while he unpeeled some antiseptic gauze from a foil pack and strapped it onto the wound with a roll of bandage. He didn't say a word.

Felicity felt it was important that he should know her name. "My name's Felicity. They call me Flick."

The stranger nodded. "They call me…" He paused, "Benjamin."

"Where do you live?"

"Port Fairy. I've a small woodworking business there."

"Oh! I live there too." *What an inane thing to say.*

Silence.

Felicity hid from her sense of awkwardness by walking to the back of the boat. She retrieved the flat piece of stone from the engine bay.

As she returned, Benjamin asked, "Will you be able to get this boat back by yourself?"

Felicity nodded. "It's moored to a pontoon. Simple."

Benjamin reached over, put a hand on hers, and turned the piece of stone over so he could see the carving etched on it. Looking up, he smiled, "Then I'll leave you with your Atlantis stone." With that, he donned his dive gear, sketched a wave, and slid into the sea.

Chapter 3

M arjorie Eddington never intended to be a spy—and didn't consider herself to be one. Her passion was anthropology, not national security. She sighed. Occasionally, life conspired to take her down paths she would never have chosen.

She sat alone at the old wooden table she had requisitioned as a desk. Her secretary and friend, Phoebe, was preparing a night-time drink for them both in the kitchen. Beside her, a standard lamp threw shadows against the wall of the Victorian room. It reeked of history, and she was glad she had booked the beautiful old holiday house.

Only three objects sat on the table. The first was a communiqué from Thames House, London, which gave details of a murder. The second was a letter from her doctor, confirming that her cancer was inoperable. The third was a laptop computer.

Marjorie scrolled down the computer's screen. Despite being in her mid-seventies, she loved computers and had embraced their technology with enthusiasm. Computers were a godsend for her area of research—genetic anthropology. She twitched her blue silk dressing gown across her lap and retied the chord around her slim frame as she gazed at the screen. She'd seen the data many times.

Thousands of genetic codes—row upon row of them—were summarized before her. They detailed the genetic history of indigenous Australians. The legal situation surrounding land rights and deals struck between mining companies and local aboriginal people now required genetic proof of heritage and ties to the land. Just occasionally, the data threw up some surprises.

She was looking at one of those surprises now. In among a long stream of coded letters was a single name: "Benjamin Bidjara." By itself, the name meant nothing but when coupled with the recent murder in London of a senior archivist, it claimed Marjorie's attention. Her interest had also been sharpened by a phone call she'd received earlier in the day.

Marjorie put an elbow on the table and massaged her temple. The pain wasn't too bad tonight. It did, however, remind her that time was at a premium. She reached into a drawer of the desk, took out a pocket Bible, and turned to Lamentations, chapter three:

But this I call to mind, and therefore I have hope: The steadfast love of the LORD never ceases…

She tucked the letter from her doctor into the page and closed the book.

Phoebe came in clutching two mugs of hot chocolate. Her stocky, buxom figure was squeezed into a pink flannel dressing gown. Marjorie smiled. To look at Phoebe, few would guess that she had a fearsome intellect and an extraordinary memory. That, and her instinct for caring, made her an ideal companion.

"How long have you been fetching me hot drinks, Phoebe?"

"Thirty-six years and three months."

"You know, of course, that you should be doing it for a husband, not a dried-up intellectual who is well past her use-by date."

"We should probably have made plans for that fifty years ago." Phoebe shrugged. "It never seemed to work out for me…and your fella was thoughtless enough to get himself killed somewhere up north—just a month before your wedding, wasn't it?" She placed a mug in front of her. "So, how are you feeling tonight?"

"Not too bad."

"Hmm." Unbidden, Phoebe reached across and picked up the communiqué from London. "Is this all you have from MI5?"

Marjorie nodded.

"And you can't get ASIO interested?"

"No. I've been trying for a month."

"But you think it could be important?"

Marjorie shrugged her thin shoulders. "That's why we're here."

"It makes a change for you to be trying to rev up ASIO. You're normally trying to cool them down." Phoebe smiled. "It was how we first met, if I remember. I was asked to contact you, tell you enough to alarm you, then 'afford you all the assistance you needed' to help us investigate." She laughed. "It didn't work. You were never alarmed. But it still took you five years and 250,000 dollars of the department's money to convince ASIO that there wasn't a problem."

"That was…um…"

"The threatened radicalization of the Aboriginal communities in northern Australia. ASIO wanted your singular skills…and your links with the church."

"Aah, yes. The World Council of Churches were providing funds for the *Gwalwa Daraniki* movement's 1973 conference. The government was worried."

"To be fair, they had some justification. The stuff in their *Bunji* newspaper could be pretty inflammatory."

Marjorie shook her head. "It was only ever going to lead to justice for indigenous Australians. Land rights had to happen." She folded her hands together and closed her eyes. The issues impinging on the well-being of indigenous Australians were horrendously complex, and it was becoming increasingly difficult to disentangle truth from greed. One thing she was sure of: it would take more than compensation claims and political correctness to build the dignity and autonomy of Australia's first inhabitants. They desperately needed meaningful jobs.

Phoebe tapped the communiqué from MI5 with a finger. "This is nasty."

"Throat cut. He was murdered in the small grove of trees between the National Archive and the railway bridge over the Thames." Marjorie leaned back. "What do we know about the National Archive at Kew?"

"It's the latest repository for the UK's public records. I think England's earliest records were stored in the Great Treasury off the cloisters at Westminster Abbey. They became the responsibility of the Public Records Office that relocated to the National Archive at Kew in 2003. They've got some pretty important documents there, including the Doomsday Book."

"Hmm."

"Why does this murder concern you?"

"A fifteenth century treaty was stolen."

"Yes, so I read. Is it significant for us?"

"To be honest, I'm not sure. It was a secret treaty signed between Henry VII of England and John II of Portugal. John was hedging his bets. He was signing treaties with both Spain and England at the time." Marjorie furrowed her brow as she tried to recall the details. "There was a flurry of treaties in the fourteenth and fifteenth centuries, mainly concerning who had rights to which lands in a world that was rapidly being discovered. Most were not worth the paper they were written on."

"What was the subject of this treaty?"

"Jave la Grande."

"Isn't that…?"

"Australia? Yes."

Benjamin waited in the interview room while Detective Richard Anderson went to check that Crime Scene had finished in his workshop. The door was open, allowing him to hear most of the conversation that was taking place.

"What the hell do you think you're doing crashing through the doorway of the deli?"

(Indistinct)

"Speak up."

"There was a jackhammer."

"So?"

"It sounded like gunfire."

"Is that a problem?"

(Indistinct)

"Speak up, man."

"It was a bit of a problem in Afghanistan."

"You were serving there?"

(Indistinct)

"Where?"

"Lots of places. The Tora Bora ridges, Shah Wali Kot in Kandahar."

"What did you do?"

"Long distance observation sorties, mostly."

There was a lengthy pause. "You would have been with the SAS, then."

There was no reply.

The interviewing officer's voice was kinder now. "Did you lose some mates?"

"A few. A Black Hawk went down in the north of the province." A pause.

"You've got post traumatic stress, haven't you?"

Silence. Then, barely audible…"Yes. A bit. Getting better. Noises can cause me to react."

"Well, your reaction caused two hundred dollars' worth of damage and succeeded in terrifying the occupants of Jamison's deli." There was a pause. "I'm afraid I can't allow you to sleep rough around here. Either go to the Salvos or move on. Where are you headed?"

"West, I suppose—anywhere I can get a bit of work."

The rest of the conversation was lost as Detective Anderson bustled back into the room. "Crime Scene has finished, Mr. Bidjara. You're free to go back to your shed. But I'd advise you to keep a low profile. The local council might have a dim view of you living in your workshop."

"Thank you."

"And I'd be grateful if you continued to keep O'Lauchlan at bay, at least for the moment. I'll draft something for him in a bit. He's waiting for you outside, incidentally."

Benjamin nodded. "Thanks for the warning."

As Benjamin left the room, a bearded man dressed in a camouflage jacket stepped out of the room next door and joined him in the corridor. Long blonde hair spilled out from under a black knitted cap. Although the man was the same height as Benjamin, he was bulkier. None of it looked like fat. His blue eyes appraised Benjamin briefly before he stepped aside to let him move ahead.

Marcus O'Lauchlan managed to look both slovenly and indolent as he leaned against the wall of the waiting room. He pushed himself off and came over to Ben, bobbing with excitement. "What can you tell me?"

"I can tell you that you are a good bloke who has done an old mate a good turn. I can tell you that you push too hard and would get on better with a bit more grace. I can tell you that you're welcome to come to my place and have a feed of fish…if you give me a few days' notice so that I can catch them. But I can't tell you anything more…largely because I don't know anything more."

"But Ben, surely…"

Benjamin held out his hand. "Thanks for helping me out, mate. If you want to yarn over old times, come over to my workshop next Thursday. It's pretty basic, but the fish will be great. Six-thirty. Bring a plate and some cutlery."

The comment succeeded in taking at least some of the wind from Marcus's sails. He puffed out his cheeks and shook Ben's hand. "You're crazy, d'you know that?"

Benjamin shrugged and turned around.

Marcus shouted behind him, "But I'll come."

Benjamin walked outside, grateful for the warm sunshine on his back. He'd left his ute parked under a Morton Bay fig. He glanced at the tree. Its wood was too soft for woodturning and its milky latex made it impossible to work with when it was green.

A low, white wall ran along the front of the police station. The stranger he'd seen inside the police station had hefted his rucksack onto it and was in the process of strapping it on. Benjamin paused to consult his instincts, but there was nothing. Nothing good; nothing bad. Unusual.

He called out to the stranger. "Throw your gear into the back of the ute. I can give you a lift as far as Port Fairy."

Benjamin drove the ute out of town. "I couldn't help overhearing some of your conversation with the police."

There was a pause before the stranger answered. "Yeah. Not real good."

"Happen often?"

"It's the first time I've ever dived through a door into a newspaper stand. It sort of upset the two old blokes buying their daily."

"Any of the bullets hit ya?"

"Not this time." The stranger gave a tired smile and scratched his chin.

There was a long pause. The passing trees caused the sunlight to flicker on Benjamin's face. Light, dark, light, dark. Benjamin surprised himself by saying, "It's not real easy, is it?" He bit his lip. *Too late now.*

The stranger raised a questioning eyebrow. "You know a bit about it?"

"PTSD? Yeah—had to see a counselor at school. There was a bit of trouble in my uncle's house where I lived as a kid."

"Violence?"

"A bit. But most of it was directed at my sister. Had to listen."

"Sorry, mate." There was a pause. "She okay now?"

Benjamin sighed. "She committed suicide when she was thirteen. A rope and a tree in the back garden. She was pregnant."

There was silence.

"Geez, what a happy pair we are." The stranger flexed his shoulders. "My psychologist says I need to talk about it to get a true perspective on the dramas in my life."

"Yeah. But sometimes I don't like perspective."

"And sometimes there are just too many dramas." The stranger breathed in deeply before asking, "Do you blame yourself?"

Benjamin didn't answer.

"How old were you at the time?"

Benjamin wished he hadn't started the conversation. He compressed his lips and said, "It started when I was nine. She died when I was eleven."

"Just a kid, then."

It was time to change the subject. "Where will you stay tonight?"

"Dunno. I'm not real good at sleeping indoors. All I need is a roof."

Benjamin nodded and pondered this information. Two minutes later, he cleared his throat and said, "I live in my workshop. There's a shed out the back where I rack some of my timber. It's dry and pretty clean…and there's an outside toilet. If you don't have anywhere else, you can use that. There's a shower inside you can use but its only got cold water."

"Thanks. Might check it out." The stranger leaned his head back. "What do I call you?"

"Benjamin."

"My name's Archie. Archie Hammond." He paused before adding, "Would you let me do a few jobs for you in payment?"

"Before you decide to stay, I think I'd better tell you that a bloke fell through the skylight, broke his neck and died two nights ago. No idea who he was. The police have been investigating the scene. They're only just letting me go back. I may have to tidy things up a bit."

Archie Hammond said nothing, so Benjamin continued. "I've organized some guys to put some safety glass in my skylight this afternoon. They might appreciate a hand—if you still want to stay."

"My, my, Benjamin. You do live an interesting life."

When they arrived at the workshop, Archie set to work with a broom, sweeping up the glass and vacuuming the floor. Benjamin made a pretense at normality by fastening a piece of black bean into his wood lathe and turning it into a bud vase.

Archie leaned on the broom and watched him.

Benjamin saw his interest and gave a commentary on what he was doing. "Good woodturning involves cutting the wood to shape rather than scraping it. The technique for cutting is harder to do but it's quicker. It gives a better finish, and it doesn't blunt the chisel as quickly."

A long ribbon of shaving spiraled off the wood as Benjamin carved. Archie picked it up from the floor and inspected it. "You make it look easy. How long does it take to learn?"

"I could teach you the basics in a few hours."

Archie nodded. "I reckon I'd like that."

Benjamin removed the wood and then re-chucked it in the lathe so that it spun off center in a noisy, blurring whirr. Archie stepped back in alarm.

"Don't worry, it's safe. I want to carve a pattern into the top of the spinning wood. If you look over my shoulder, you'll see the shape begin to appear."

Archie stepped closer and watched as Benjamin began to carve. "Impressive," he said, nodding.

"Spinning the wood off center lets you carve all sorts of interesting shapes."

A bell tinkled behind them as the workshop door opened. Benjamin had bought the spring-mounted bell from a second-hand shop that morning and installed it first thing after they had arrived. He turned around with the chisel in his hand. He saw, with relief, that his visitor was an elderly woman—quite harmless. She was wearing a navy twin set, blouse and skirt. A brooch was pinned in front of the frilly mandarin collar of her white blouse. She looked neat and totally out of place in his workshop.

Benjamin punched the 'off' switch on the lathe and turned back to face the woman. "Can I help you?"

The woman's eyes danced over the workshop, then looked Benjamin up and down. "I hope so. I bought this from the craft shop in town. They told me you made it. Is that true?"

Benjamin saw that she was holding a wooden candlestick. He recognized it immediately. He had made it from blackheart sassafras

—a good wood to work with, full of dark streaks and character. "Yes."

"Can you make me a pair of these but much larger, perhaps about half a meter long, for a dinner table?"

"Oh…umm, I think so. Let me check if I've got the wood."

Benjamin rummaged around his wood rack as the woman walked across to the lathe and inspected the half-finished bud vase. She nodded to Archie, "Hello."

"G'day, ma'am." Archie nodded toward the lathe. "I'm being given a wood-turning lesson."

"How intriguing. I would like to have watched."

Benjamin joined them. "I've got the wood, so, yes, I can make your candlesticks." He guided her to a stool by the workbench. "I can show you some options for shapes…even find you a cup of tea, if you like."

Bright eyes fixed themselves on him from under her bob of gray hair. "Thank you. I would appreciate that. Black, no sugar."

Archie volunteered, "I'll get it for you. Then you two can talk."

Benjamin nodded his thanks and pointed to the kettle. He sat his visitor on a stool, slid into the other, and pulled out a piece of paper.

"How do you begin to design a piece of work like this?" the woman asked.

Benjamin furrowed his brow. He was unused to explaining things that had become instinct for him over the years. "Oh…ahh… it's got to feel balanced. There are, um…only about six basic shapes, and you mix and match."

"How do you know what works?"

"Gut feeling, really. The shapes need to be ordered so that each sits on the next in a balanced way. Each shape should introduce the next." Benjamin picked up a pencil. "The classical shapes that have stood the test of time work well…or you can do the sweeping, long curves of modernism. Both can be beautiful. Which do you want?"

"Classical please."

"Okay." Benjamin began to sketch. "Good classical carving has long quiet shapes that lead into busy sections. The proportions have to be right. It's all about dignity."

She looked at his drawing. "That's good. I like it." She smiled, and then surprised him by asking, "What is it, do you think, that makes beauty?"

Benjamin shrugged. "One person's beauty is another person's disdain."

"And yet there is some sort of consensus…as the existence of art galleries attests."

Benjamin screwed his face up. "Some of their art is brutal, ugly, shocking."

"That art celebrates brokenness. It is making a statement rather than trying to be beautiful."

"Some see it as beautiful."

"Then they're broken."

"Isn't that…" Benjamin wanted to say "arrogant," but he didn't have the courage. He glanced at the visitor, noting the high carriage of her chin—the determined self-control—and said nothing.

She sniffed. "I think, Benjamin, that there is truth in beauty. We have an indication this truth exists because we have a general consensus about what beauty is, even in our brokenness." She caught his eyes. "I dare suggest that this points to a fundamental rightness. Exploring the origin of that rightness is a worthy life quest."

Ideas began tumbling around in Benjamin's heart until his head cried, "Enough!" And that delicate new thing—the brilliant, incandescent beginnings of things profound and important in his life—died. He picked up his pencil and continued to draw.

Something, however, piqued his curiosity. "How did you know my name?"

"The craft shop."

"Ahh." Benjamin tapped his pencil on the bench. "And may I ask your name?"

"My name is Marjorie; Marjorie Eddington."

Chapter 4

The kettle was whistling as the bell above the workshop door tinkled again. Benjamin looked around, both puzzled and surprised. He hadn't had any visitors to his workshop in eight months. Now he was having two in the same day…and some glaziers were coming later in the afternoon.

Benjamin recognized Felicity immediately. Her petite frame and feminine curves were squeezed into jeans, a white tee-shirt and a short black jacket. He had been wondering what her hair would look like when it wasn't wet. It now tumbled down her shoulders in luxurious waves almost to her waist. He had a mental image of a waterfall, photographed with long exposure…soft and blurred.

Felicity began diffidently. "Er…the sign on the door said you were open."

Benjamin nodded. "How's the arm?"

"Sore."

Silence.

"Why do you dive alone? It's dangerous."

"I don't usually."

"But you did."

"I wanted to test out a hunch without people knowing."

"The um…" *What delicate, beautiful eyes.*

"The Atlantis stone, I think you called it." Felicity smiled. "It's soaking in a cleaning solution at the moment. I'll start work on it tonight."

A polite cough reminded Benjamin that Marjorie Eddington was behind him. He turned as she stepped down from the stool. The elderly lady smiled at him. "I think it's time I left," she said. "When should I come back?"

"Can you give me five days?"

She nodded and looked up at him. "Beauty is found in all sorts of surprising places, isn't it?"

Archie walked over, holding a tin mug of black tea. He had taken off his camouflage jacket and was in his shirt sleeves. It hadn't diminished his bulk very much. "No tea, then?" he inquired.

Marjorie smiled at him. "I think you'll find a good use for it."

Archie turned to Felicity. "How do you have your tea?"

Felicity's somewhat bewildered expression broke into a smile. "Milk, no sugar."

Benjamin consigned the information to memory. *Milk, no sugar.* "Archie, you'll find milk in the bar fridge beside the timber rack."

Archie nodded.

Benjamin escorted Marjorie to the door and opened it for her. She held out a delicate hand. He took hold of her fingertips in what passed for a handshake.

"I'm glad to have found you, Benjamin," she said, and made her way down the steps.

Benjamin closed the door with a puzzled frown. He had an odd sensation that he'd missed something. Turning around, he discovered Felicity watching him from across the workshop. She was holding one hand over her heart…and the other was holding a familiar object.

"You forgot your dive knife," she said.

Benjamin walked over, took the sheathed knife from Felicity, and placed it on the bench. He was unsure why he'd left it with her—but he knew it wasn't forgetfulness.

"Thanks."

Silence.

She drew a breath and said, "When you said you were a wood-worker, I thought you were a builder, not a...a craftsman, an artist."

"I do lots of things. Why do you ask?"

"I wanted to ask if I could employ you to help finish my house." Felicity avoided his eyes and looked away. "I need a couple of builders for a few months to clad the outside and put a bull-nosed veranda up along the front."

"When would you want to start?"

"As soon as possible." She lowered her eyes. "Well, as soon as I've sold my car, actually."

Benjamin nodded. "You're selling your car so that you can pay for your house to be finished?"

Felicity avoided his eyes. "It's important that the outside of it gets finished."

Archie placed the mug of tea in front of Felicity.

"Thanks Archie," said Benjamin. "Can you grab that thin board over there and cut Felicity a drink coaster—eleven centimeters by eleven? You'll find a handsaw on the rack."

Archie nodded and turned away.

Benjamin watched Archie covertly as he set to work but reserved most of his attention for Felicity. "What does the doctor say about your arm?"

"The doctor—my brother, actually—tells me that the mouth of a moray eel can house all sorts of interesting bacteria." She shrugged. "He's filled me with antibiotics. I'll be fine."

"Money's tight?"

"Divorce. Didn't come out of it very well." Benjamin allowed his silence to invite Felicity to say more. She cleared her throat and continued. "I trained as an historian and worked for the Melbourne museum in Carlton Gardens for two years." She gave a shy smile. "Now trying my hand at being a writer. Disastrous financially."

Benjamin didn't know what to say. His feelings were in some turmoil...but he trusted his instincts to give him counsel. He waited. They were silent...and then there was the stirring of something.

"Where are you?" asked Felicity with a frown.

"Oh…" Benjamin nearly caught himself saying "at home," but he knew she wouldn't understand. He smiled. "Sorry, just thinking."

Felicity put her hand out, reaching for his. She steered it away at the last moment and took hold of the edge of the bench. "Thank you for saving my life, by the way."

"You're welcome."

Archie walked over to join them. "Here you are, mate." He held out the drink coaster that he had made.

Benjamin inspected his handiwork, noting the accuracy of the cut, the symmetry, and the care taken with sanding the edges. "Archie, would you be interested in helping me with a building job for a couple of months?"

Archie frowned and rubbed the back of his neck. "How do you see that working?"

"You could sleep where you like, out the back…or in here. Certainly, you could eat in here with me."

Archie regarded Benjamin with his pale blue eyes. "Mate, I wouldn't want to cramp your style. I'd better tell you that I'm on the road because I choose to be. I'm not broke. An investment banker is renting my flat in Hawthorn East, and I draw a government pension. I eat pretty well at cafés."

"Then only eat with me when you want."

"How about I buy the groceries, you teach me a bit of wood-work—and we both do the building job?"

"Sounds good." Benjamin turned to Felicity. "When do you want us to begin?"

Felicity dropped her head. "As soon as I sell the car. I've adver-tised it, but I don't know how long it will take to sell."

Benjamin watched Felicity closely. She was wringing her hands together in her lap. Her face was lowered, hidden by a mass of tumbling hair. He asked her at length, "What's the matter, Felicity?"

Felicity sniffed and tossed her head back. "Oh, nothing." She tried a smile, but it didn't work very well.

"Felicity?" Benjamin insisted.

"Oh, just stupid divorce things."

He waited for more.

She sighed. "It's just horribly ironic. My ex bought a car the day before I closed our shared bank account. It was an either-to-sign account."

"And…"

"He bought a luxury sports car, a Corvette Chevrolet. Now he's selling it…and will take the proceeds. He…he's a lawyer. He knows how to…"

"That's unjust. Did you confront him?"

Felicity's eyes began to well with tears. She looked away and bit at her knuckles.

"Felicity."

There was no response.

"Felicity," Benjamin said again.

"He hit me," she cried. "There…are you satisfied? He hit me." She hid her face in her hands.

"He hit you?"

Silence…then she nodded.

"Didn't you report it?"

"What was the point?" she said with exasperation. "I didn't need to take out a restraining order against him because I was never going to see him again."

Archie took out a box of matches, selected one, and put it in his mouth. He chewed on the end of it for a moment before saying, "So this geezer nicks half the cost of a Corvette from you…and you've got to sell your car?"

Felicity dropped her head.

Benjamin was conscious of something dangerous coming to life inside him. It was something he knew had always been there, something he'd always been a little bit afraid of; something he wasn't sure he could control. It was anger. It was bitterness at having to stand by helplessly while his sister was defiled and destroyed. It was a hatred of all things evil. *Bloody, bloody, bloody evil.* It was…he ran out of words.

Benjamin pushed his hands into the pockets of his canvas fisherman's smock. Inside his head, a mocking voice jeered at him. *Who do you to think you are, Throwback? You can't do anything about it. It's what*

37

happens…and it doesn't concern you.

No! he screamed back. *Listening to you killed my sister.*
You're nothing, Throwback!

Benjamin glanced at Felicity's bowed head. She held one hand to her chest and was sobbing.

*I am…*he paused. What was the truth that he could throw at his tormentor? *I am…angry…and I choose to ignore you.*

He eased himself upright…and discovered Archie watching him. Archie's face was implacable. He simply chewed on his matchstick.

"Has your ex sold the car, yet?" asked Benjamin.

"No," she whispered. "He's advertised it again in *The Age*. He's asking a lot of money for it."

Archie moved the matchstick to the corner of his mouth. "So we've got a job, then."

He was reputed to be the best forger of antiquities in the world… and he was Swiss. Doran Khayef approved. The Swiss were careful. They'd also had a lot of experience in handling and dating antiquities. The strongrooms and deposit boxes in their banks were filled with items of historical importance that had no right to be there. This particular man was also one of the best in the world at radio carbon dating antiques.

Khayef glanced at him. The forger didn't look the best in the world at anything. He was stick-thin, stooped and balding. The crisp white lab-coat could not hide his physical shortcomings or the unhealthy blue-gray pallor of his face. He was slumped forward at the stainless steel bench rubbing his eyes.

But the job was done.

Khayef looked around at the man's laboratory. It had cost him a lot of money to hire the antiquarian and his lab. The Swiss man had insisted on using his own laboratory. It contained an accelerator mass spectrometry unit, a micro laser cutter, humidifier, and various microscopes.

Khayef had been equally insistent that the antiquarian work alone.

The antiquarian had, non-stop, for the last forty hours.

Khayef's assistant, Eddie, stood behind his right elbow, ready to hear any instructions. He looked uncomfortable in his disposable coveralls and blue shoe coverings. They'd both had to wear them. Eddie would not enjoy being unable to get his hand inside his jacket —where the particular tools of his trade were kept. His swarthy face and fashionable three-day stubble seemed at odds with the sterile white room around him.

Khayef caught sight of his reflection off the glass of a laminar flow unit. He was shorter than he wanted to be and slightly more 'full-fleshed' than his doctor was happy with. But his hair still looked good. It was slightly blacker than nature had intended, and it swept back over his head in a slick wave. That, and his gold-rimmed spectacles, made him present well…plus the fact that his annual income was measured in the tens of millions.

He glanced down at the piece of vellum that was sandwiched between two pieces of glass. It looked very old. One corner had been cut off so that the various carbon isotopes it contained could be measured. The test would destroy the tiny piece that had been removed, but that didn't trouble Khayef. The only thing he wanted to know was whether the vellum—the ancient calf-skin with the treaty written on it—was what it purported to be.

"It is real?" he asked the antiquarian.

The Swiss man lifted his head from his hands. "Yes. No one can doubt it. The carbon dating is accurate to within thirty to fifty years." He pointed to a box file on his desk. "All the evidence any jury will need to be convinced of is in there. The information is also backed up on three memory sticks. They are inside the box as well."

"There are no more copies?"

"No."

Khayef turned his head to Eddie and pointed to the box file. "Get it."

Eddie nodded. As he stepped forward, he pointed to the Swiss man and raised an eyebrow.

"Kill him."

"You don't have to do this, Archie."

Archie sat back and regarded Benjamin without comment.

"You shouldn't. I'm not even sure how to pull it off…or if I'm breaking the law…or whether I can do it."

"I reckon that's a pretty good list of reasons for why I should get involved, then." He grinned. "This is the sort of thing I do."

"It might get difficult—maybe even physical."

Archie looked at Benjamin with his bleak eyes. It was an eloquent reply. *You idiot. I was trained for violence. I chose it as a profession…and I'm very good at it.* Benjamin raised a hand to acknowledge the folly of his remark and dropped his head. "What now, then?"

Archie pushed himself back from the bench. "I think it's time for a bit of sword drill."

"Sword drill?"

Archie nodded.

S - strengths of a course of action

W - weaknesses of a course of action

O - option chosen

R - resources allocated

D - delegate responsibilities

D - do the task

R - review its effectiveness

I - improvements—any needed?

L - lock in your achievement

L - look for new opportunities.

He slapped the table. "Get a piece of paper."

An hour later, Benjamin reached for the newspaper and pulled it toward him. He read the number under the advert and punched it into his phone. Archie was standing at the end of the bench. He'd crossed his legs and was looking at the ceiling, giving every appearance of being at ease.

After the fourth ring, Benjamin's call was answered.

"Nick Mercurio speaking."

Bastard. You hit her. "Good evening, Mr. Mercurio. I believe you have a Chevrolet Corvette for sale—almost new, I understand."

"Three months old: only twelve hundred on the clock. It's a good deal—virtually a new car…without the on-road costs. It'll save you ten thousand on a new car." Mr. Mercurio paused. "When would you like to see it?"

Presumptuous…a salesman…how useful. "Well…what's the time? Four-thirty. I'm running out of time today…and I'll be looking at another car this evening. So, how about I come around first thing in the morning, say eight o'clock? Would you be able to take me for a decent test-drive then? I can tell you that if I like it, I'll be buying it on the spot."

Come on, come on, Benjamin pleaded. *Let your greed trump your diary.*

"Oh! Right. Hang on a moment." There was a pause. "Yes, yes, I'll move an appointment and see you tomorrow morning." He gave his address.

Gotcha! "Thank you, Mr. Mercurio."

"Please call me Nick."

I want to call you a wife-beating, dishonest thug. "Right…Nick, if you could have the Notice of Disposal with you ready to sign, that would be good." He paused. "My name, by the way, is…Mr. Benjamin."

"See you tomorrow, Mr. Benjamin."

But Benjamin had hung up. He put the phone down on the top of the workbench and stared at it.

Archie pushed himself off the bench. "You did well."

Benjamin breathed in deeply. "Now what?"

"You've got half an hour to nip down to the op-shop and get some passable clothes."

"And then?"

"A meal and some sleep. We'll need to be on the road by three in the morning."

Chapter 5

A westerly change was pushing away the lingering evidence of a fine day. Shafts of light now fell from a turbulent sky onto the leaden sea, patterning its bleakness with pools of molten silver. Felicity turned her face into the wind and sought out its freshness.

She had gone for a walk to seek out better company than her thoughts. It had been an emotionally demanding day. Felicity was now standing at the end of Griffiths Island, looking out to sea. She had passed no one else, only a nankeen heron standing in the shallows of the lagoon, fishing for shrimp. Higher up the shore, a flock of seagulls had hunkered down for the evening, their feathers occasionally lifting in the wind.

She loved it here. The wild beauty of the coast and the purity of the sea rarely failed to invigorate. Sometimes they even entertained. It was not uncommon to find fur seals playing in the shallows. They often saluted her with their rubbery flippers as they rolled onto their sides to inspect her with bright eyes and bristly noses.

None today. She felt a little bereft.

Being bereft was rather too uncomfortably similar to being lonely—and she refused to let herself explore that. Everything was still too raw. And yet…what an extraordinary man! The strength of his arms pulling her free; his tanned skin and curling dark hair. Above all, his tenderness…and a sense of something that she couldn't define, a sense of being…understood. *Yes, that was it.*

She let her mind play among her recent memories. They felt… safe. What had Benjamin called the mysterious carved stone that had so nearly killed her? *The Atlantis stone.* She smiled. *Nice.* Even though the flat stone was encrusted with all sorts of marine organisms, there was clear evidence that it had been deliberately carved. She had pulled it from the deep, and although obviously not from the fabled city of Atlantis, it would nonetheless have a story to tell. In all probability, it would include real drama, quite possibly a wrecked ship. She shivered. The southern coast on which she lived wasn't called 'the ships' graveyard' for nothing. She just hoped that the stone had come from *her* ship, the one she'd been researching for so long: the mysterious mahogany ship.

Felicity looked at her watch. She had left the Atlantis stone soaking in a dilute ammonia solution for twenty-four hours to loosen the marine deposits that were growing on it. Enough time had elapsed now for her to wash it off, together with the organic material that had been loosened. The painstaking work of swabbing the stone with hydrogen peroxide and picking off the remaining marine growth would then follow—and she was anxious to make a start.

A large silver Audi was parked in front of her brother's home. It wasn't quite parallel to the curb; she wished she could straighten it. A tall, balding man in a gray suit unfolded himself from the front of the car as she walked up the driveway. She paused to let him catch up with her.

"Ms. Anderson?"

"Yes."

"My name is Andrew Carter. I'm a lawyer with the Khayef Group of companies. We occasionally offer funding to people researching topics that are in the national interest." He smiled. "It's our way of contributing back to society. We've heard that you're doing research into the mahogany ship." The man's eyes never left Felicity's face. "It may be mutually beneficial for us to speak."

"Oh." Felicity was in shock, and wondered how the man knew

of her work. She'd been careful to keep her investigation confidential. Almost as quickly, her mind then turned to the parlous state of her finances. Anything that might help her right now would be welcome.

"Please come inside, Mr. Carter." She led the way down the hallway, pausing occasionally to push the children's toys against the wall with her toe. The sound of children squabbling came from one of the bedrooms.

"Please excuse the mess. Three children live here." She led him through to the back of the house. Her bedroom and office were located in a room that had been created by enclosing a section of the back veranda. "Take a seat," she said, pointing to the only armchair. She sat herself in her office chair and waited for him to speak.

Mr. Carter cleared his throat and began. "The mahogany ship is one of the great unsolved mysteries of early Australian colonial history. We would look very seriously at funding anyone who was researching it."

"Plenty of people have researched it," Felicity said carefully. "No one has found definite evidence of it—yet."

"But you believe it exists, or at least once existed?"

Felicity nodded.

"Why?"

"There's a lot of cumulative evidence for it, Mr. Carter."

"I would appreciate a summary of that evidence, if you wouldn't mind."

Felicity guessed that the man was testing her. Their conversation was, in a very real sense, an examination. She drew a deep breath and began to speak.

"The town of Port Fairy was originally called Belfast. It began as a whaling station owned by the firm of Hewett and Company, which employed about one hundred people. Three men from the station were once in a whaleboat that was swamped by a wave and sunk. One of them drowned. His companions buried him and then walked back to Belfast. On the way, they reported seeing a ship up in the sand hills opposite Tower Hill."

"Was the sighting investigated?"

"There is the account of John Mills, who, along with his brother Charles and a sixteen-year-old whaler named Hugh Donnelly, visited the site to check it out. Evidently, they found the ship. John reported that its wood was as hard as iron." Felicity shrugged. "John's evidence has a fair deal of credibility because he went on to become the harbor master at Port Fairy."

"Would you say that this was enough evidence to prove the existence of the ship in a court of law?"

"Probably not, although there is other evidence to suggest its existence."

Carter pursed his lips. "And what other evidence is that?"

"A Captain John Mason visited the location in 1846 and reported seeing a vessel of about one hundred tons' displacement in the Hummocks. Only the hull remained, and the timbers were old and bleached." Felicity pushed her hair away from her face. "Eight years later, Alexander Rollo from the village of Panmure also reported seeing the vessel in the Hummocks. He said it was eighty meters inland behind the sand dunes."

"Do you know the nationality of the ship?"

"It was probably Portuguese. A local woman reported seeing a wrecked ship made of wooden panels rather than the usual long planks. It was a method the Portuguese used to build their caravels in the fourteenth and fifteenth centuries."

"But how certain can we be?"

"Nothing is certain, Mr. Carter. There is real discrepancy about where the ship actually was." She shrugged. "There's also a possibility that more than one ship was wrecked. The only thing we are certain of is that a good number of people have recorded seeing a wrecked ship west of Warrnambool."

Felicity swiveled her chair around, tapped on her computer keyboard, and uploaded a file. She referred to it as she spoke. "A fellow called James Jellie reported seeing a wreck in 1848. He was out riding and saw it by a large sand hill near the Merri Creek. And then there was Mrs. Manifold, wife of a Warrnambool magistrate. She saw the remains in 1860 when she was out riding."

Felicity scrolled down the computer screen. "We have a report from a Mr. Furnell who reported seeing a ship buried in sand when he was standing on Tower Hill. He was the local Inspector of Police, so his word should have some credence." She swung back around on her chair and faced her visitor. "The evidence for at least one ship up in the sand dunes is overwhelming."

"Ms. Anderson, this is important: What concrete evidence is there that the ship is Portuguese?"

"The evidence is only circumstantial at this stage. The most widely accepted theory suggests that the vessel is a missing ship from a Portuguese flotilla of three ships led by Cristóvão de Mendonça. The expedition sailed from Lisbon in 1519 for Goa, India, under the captaincy of Pedro Eanes. Once Mendonça arrived, the Portuguese Governor of India appointed him to lead the ships to the Moluccan Islands and beyond…to look for the Isles of Gold."

Felicity rested an elbow on the desk and arranged three pens into a straight line. "Secrecy was vital because they were sailing in waters deemed to be Spanish under the Treaty of Tordesillas."

The grandfather clock in the hallway chimed six o'clock. The children were fractious, wanting their tea. Felicity could hear her sister-in-law calling out from the kitchen for them to be quiet.

She wondered how much she should reveal to her visitor. The Atlantis stone was soaking in the very next room which her brother used as an office. It was sitting in a medical specimen tin on a workbench. She decided it was too early to tell anyone about it. The stone may have no significance at all.

Felicity did, however, want to present herself as a worthy candidate for a research grant, and so she pressed on. "There's some evidence that Mendonça may have lost a second ship from his flotilla. A ship similar to the one seen here was uncovered in a violent storm at Raupuke Beach, New Zealand, in 1877. The possibility that it is linked with Mendonça was indicated by the fact that local Maoris found a bell on the west coast of the North Island in 1836. It was inscribed with Tamil script, suggesting it came from the region of Goa in India, where Mendonça began his voyage."

"I didn't know that." Carter nodded slowly. "This information might be important."

"Really? I'm glad." Felicity wondered why it would be important to him, but she let it pass. She continued. "The link with New Zealand was made more likely when the Kiwis dredged up a Portuguese helmet from the top end of Wellington Harbour. It's on display in the Dominion Museum."

Felicity could hear the children being called for tea. There was a clatter, a banging, and the patter of tiny feet. Felicity arranged the three pens into a triangle. "Why did you come to see me, Mr. Carter?"

The man looked at her steadily before replying. "I'm aware that plenty of people have searched for the mahogany ship, including Monash university, but to my knowledge, no one is currently searching for it—except you. Would I be correct in thinking that?"

"Um, I think so. But how did you know about me?"

"We contacted the local newspaper. They thought you were probably researching it. They usually know what's going on."

Felicity was surprised. She couldn't think how the local newspaper could possibly have known.

"Ms. Anderson, if you find any evidence that this mahogany ship is Portuguese, will you contact me as soon as possible? I'm instructed to say that the Khayef Group will pay handsomely for the information." He smiled. "There would be a bonus if you told us about it before anyone else. We'd love to be the ones to make your research findings known publicly." He pulled an embossed card from his top pocket, scribbled on it, and gave it to her. "This is my personal number. Please let me know of any progress you make... and I'll be in touch in the next few weeks with a funding proposition."

After a typically chaotic tea with her brother's burgeoning family, Felicity returned to the back room and began using medical tweezers to pick away the marine growth on the Atlantis stone. It came off with great reluctance. She brushed on the hydrogen peroxide, let it fizz on the grubby surface, and continued the tedious task of picking the growth off with fine tweezers.

By midnight, she knew that she had uncovered something very special indeed.

The flat stone had indeed been carved, but the carving was incomplete. It had been a work-in-progress just before it sank off the rocky cliffs of Warrnambool. Half of the engraved letters were in deep relief, the others were not. They had only been chiseled roughly in readiness for carving. What was in no doubt at all was the meaning of the carving. The words *Ilhas do ouro*—land of gold—had been etched under the carving of a two-masted, lateen-rigged sailing ship.

Felicity could barely contain her excitement. She wanted to wake everyone in the house and tell them…what? What could the significance of her discovery be? Would it, she wondered, earn her a generous grant from the Khayef Group and provide her the material she needed to write a book? *Wow! That would be wonderful.* She wanted to run across town and tell Benjamin about the Atlantis stone…that all the drama it had caused off Thunder Point had been worth it.

She stared at the stone. Its color and shape began to niggle at a memory, something she had seen during her honors research into the mahogany ship. *What is it?*

Felicity leaned back and rubbed her eyes. They craved sleep, but she was high on adrenaline. This stone could, in all probability, have come all the way from Portugal, around the bottom of Africa…

That's it! She remembered.

Africa.

Felicity picked up the specimen tray containing the Atlantis stone and walked through to her private living area. She placed the tray on the desk, booted up her computer, and began to search through the data she had collected for her thesis three years earlier.

Eventually, she found it. It was an account written by a science journalist who had discovered a fragment of stone engraved with

Mendonça's name in South Africa. The stone had been clearly dated 1524.

Felicity searched through her file of stored images until she found a picture of Mendonça's stone. It was very similar to the Atlantis stone—too much alike to be a coincidence.

She reached for her phone and photographed the Atlantis stone in its steel tray. After uploading the image to her computer, she put the images of the two stones side by side. She reduced the size of the Atlantis stone image and moved it alongside the African stone. The ragged edges of the two stones matched perfectly!

Felicity sat back in her seat and ran a hand through her hair. Both stones had once been part of the same stone! How could that be? Mendonça's stone was dated 1524, a good two years after one of his caravels had foundered on Warrnambool's beach.

Something was wrong.

Felicity didn't know whether she should laugh with delight at what she had discovered, or cry in frustration that her theory about what had happened was blown to pieces.

In the end, she went to bed.

Chapter 6

Benjamin tried not to feel too self-conscious in his linen jacket, open shirt, and brown slacks. It wasn't easy as it was all quite alien to him. He sighed and pushed the button on the intercom of the double-story unit rising above him.

"Yes?" came a tinny response through the grill.

"Mr. Mercurio, Mr. Benjamin here to look at the Corvette."

"Ah, right on time. Good. I'll come down."

The car was sitting in the driveway. The metallic gray monster looked poised to strike. Benjamin had never driven anything like it. Archie had researched the car on his phone and schooled Benjamin on what to expect during their drive through the early hours of the morning.

Nick Mercurio was a large man with long sideburns and fashionably untidy hair. His gray suit didn't quite hide a small paunch. He shook Benjamin's hand and waved toward the car. "There she is: six point two liters of grunt, delivering three hundred and twenty-one kilowatts of power."

Benjamin broke in, "But with a drag coefficient of point two eight, it's moderately economical." He smiled. "Let's take her for a run. I want to see how she handles slow rush hour traffic and then do a fairly long run on the open road."

"Sounds good to me. I've got all morning." He handed Benjamin the keys.

Affecting a bravado he did not feel, Benjamin got into the car and listened as Mercurio took him through the features he needed to know to drive the car.

It was a relief to discover that the car was kinder to drive than it looked. It was an automatic which helped greatly.

Benjamin was nosing his way through the morning traffic, past the docklands and on toward the M1, when Mercurio's phone rang. Benjamin listened to the one-sided conversation.

"The Corvette? Sure, it's still for sale although I'm actually with another potential buyer at the moment. Sure, sure…I've got your number, and I'll get back to you shortly. No worries. Cheers." He turned to Ben. "Mr. Benjamin…by the way, what is your first name?"

"Mr. Benjamin is fine."

"Mr. Benjamin, the price has just gone up by five thousand dollars." Mercurio had a self-satisfied smirk on his face.

"Well, we'll just have to see if she's worth it, won't we?"

Benjamin threaded his way onto the M1 and began driving toward Werribee.

"Well, what do you think?" asked Mercurio.

"I'd want to tighten the suspension a fraction."

"What!"

"Please be quiet and let me listen to the engine."

Benjamin flew along the M1 as far as Seabrook, where he took the exit and began driving toward the coast. "I've always wanted to see what was down this road." He smiled. "And I think I can say, Nick, that we have a sale."

"That's great. Let's stop and we'll do the paperwork. I've brought the Notice of Disposal."

"Yes, let's do it." Benjamin pointed ahead of him. "I'll head down to the park at the end." Benjamin drove past bleak, salty marshland until he arrived at a small parking area. It was a desolate place.

Archie was there. He got up from the park bench and lounged against the back of it, ostensibly staring at Benjamin's white ute parked nearby.

Benjamin lowered both windows with the electric switch and turned off the engine. He faced his passenger and said evenly, "Mr. Mercurio, this car is being repossessed. You will be receiving a check for half the value of the car…less the costs we have incurred in repossessing it. You can expect the money to be in the mail within two days. Any prevarication on your part will add to the cost and will be deducted from the amount you receive. I am to instruct you that you are not to contact your ex-wife, or you will lose a good deal more. I understand she is considering placing a restraining order on you because of a violent attack. The actual amount of money you receive will be entirely at her discretion. Currently, she is willing to give you half the sale price."

Mercurio's mouth dropped open in surprise, then he bellowed in rage. "What the hell! Don't tell me the bitch has got you to steal this car? You can't do that! I'm a lawyer…and I'll take you to court for…"

"Shut up, Mercurio, and listen."

Mercurio twisted in his seat. "I'll knock the crap out of you, you little shit." He began to undo his seat belt.

"May I advise against violence, Mr. Mercurio. Do you see that man over there?" He pointed out the window. Archie was now facing them. He was chewing a matchstick and had his hands pushed into the pockets of a camouflage jacket. He looked down-right intimidating. "That man is one of the most violent men I know. That's why he's here. Now, please give me your phone."

"You're not bloody well going to steal my phone as well, you bastard!"

Benjamin put his hand out of the window and beckoned.

Archie heaved himself off the back of the park bench and began striding forward.

"No, no," screamed Mercurio.

Benjamin held up his hand.

Archie stopped, paused briefly, then continued to head toward them at an amble. He sat on the Corvette's bonnet—directly in front of Mercurio.

The car sagged pleasingly.

Mercurio gulped.

"Your phone, Mr. Mercurio."

Mercurio fumbled in his jacket pocket and handed across his phone.

Benjamin took it, opened it up, and scrolled through until he saw the number of the last person who had rung. He reached into his jacket pocket for a pen and wrote the number down on his hand.

Then he reached behind his back and pulled from his waistband a new washing-up cloth and a plastic bag containing a padded envelope. He showed the envelope to his bewildered passenger. "This envelope has your home address on it. I'm going to post your phone back to you via the nearest letterbox. You should receive it in a day or so."

Benjamin wiped the phone with the cloth and dropped it in the envelope.

"There. All done. Now…please sign the Notice of Disposal and get out of the car."

Mercurio did so with ill grace. He signed with an untidy flourish, threw the form down on Benjamin's lap, and hissed, "You haven't heard the last of this."

"Be very careful, Mr. Mercurio—very, very careful. The wrath of hell will descend on you if you cause your ex-wife or me any anxiety. If you act foolishly, I promise you, your life will never be the same again." Benjamin forced a smile and pointed up the road. "Laverton is about three kilometers away. You'll be able to catch a bus from there back to the city."

Archie opened the car door to expedite Mercurio's departure.

As Mercurio stood up, Archie faced him from a distance of a few inches and murmured, "I'd like the chance to meet you one day, Nick, so you can show me just how you hit your wife." His pale eyes bored into Mercurio's terrified face.

Benjamin shivered. It was chilling.

Archie walked back toward the ute. He got in and drove it past Mercurio, in the direction of the highway. Benjamin followed in the Corvette.

Two kilometers up the road, Benjamin flashed his lights, causing Archie to pull off into a lay-by and get out of the car. Archie strode back to Benjamin and sat himself in the front passenger seat. "We should be heading home, young Benjamin."

"I know, Archie. I just thought we might have a chance of tying things up a bit tighter."

"Didn't you say you wanted to go fishing this afternoon?"

"It shouldn't take too long."

"So, what's on your mind?"

Benjamin told him.

When he had finished, Archie stroked his beard. "I can't see much risk in that." He looked up and grinned. "I think it's worth a go. Make the call."

Benjamin took out Mercurio's phone and dialed the number he had written on his hand. After a long delay, it was answered.

"Pershore."

"Hello Mr. Pershore. You called earlier about the Corvette…Yes, yes…You're playing golf? Well, I'm sorry to interrupt your game, but I have two people interested in buying the car—you and someone else. I'm about to head out of town to see the other potential buyer but he quite a distance away. In fairness to you, being the first who called, I think you should have the first chance to buy it. If you pay the advertised price, it's yours. Would you be available?…Yes, yes…Well, if you can have a bank check ready for the amount specified in the ad that would be fine. Please make it payable to Felicity Mercurio…nee Anderson, as she goes by both names." Benjamin laughed. "It's more her car than mine. She's going to use the money for some building renovations. Oh, and Mr. Pershore, for your own peace of mind, may I suggest that you do a Vehicle Security Register investigation…Oh, right, you've already done it…Your address? Fine, I've got it. I'll see you in two hours. Eleven o'clock."

Benjamin rang off, leaned his head against the steering wheel, and began to let his adrenaline level subside. "Phew!" he said. "I'm not sure I'm cut out for this."

"I dunno. You seem pretty good at it to me." Archie scratched his stubble. "But the trouble is, young Benjamin, we've got a slightly hot car, and two hours to parade it under the noses of any passing policemen. Where are we going to meet this geezer?"

"Toorak." Benjamin told him the address.

Archie removed the matchstick and smiled. "Well, that's easy then. My home is just a few minutes north from there. We'll pop it in the garage and wait an hour or so."

"I thought you'd leased your house."

"I have—to my brother. Don't worry, I outrank him. Chances are, he and his wife will both be out at work. No one will know."

"Then…lead on, kindly light."

"What?"

"Never mind. Let's get going."

Two hours later, Benjamin parked outside a white, double-story house in Toorak. It had shuttered windows, a formal garden, and electronic gates. He revved the car unnecessarily loudly before he switched it off.

It had the intended effect. A florid man, still in his golfing garb, came down the driveway to meet him.

"Get in. I'll drive," he said without preamble. He was a man used to authority.

Twenty minutes later, Benjamin had a check for one hundred and ten thousand dollars.

Chapter 7

"You look terrible," said Gabrielle. She was wearing a long green dress with an embroidered bib. Her ginger hair was again piled up on her head and kept in place with what Felicity could only assume were chopsticks.

Felicity rubbed her eyes. They ached and felt gritty. "Thanks a lot."

"You're welcome. What have you been up to?"

"Late night."

"With whom?"

"On my own."

"Hmm…even worse."

The sunshine had made a late start in warming the day, but it was enough to persuade Felicity and Gabrielle to sit at a table on the pavement outside the café. Two cappuccinos and a dissected muffin sat in front of them.

"You must be pleased now that your windows have been put in. Replacing the garage door with that old shop window has transformed the front."

Felicity nodded. With all the excitement over the Atlantis stone, she hadn't really been able to think about her renovation project.

"The council insists that the place be in keeping with the old shops in the area. It's zoned both residential and commercial."

"Well, the old shop window looks great." She grinned. "Mind you, the rest of the building looks bloody awful."

"You're meant to be cheering me up."

Gabrielle cocked her head sideways. "No, I don't think I need to. Although you look knackered, you've got an energy about you today. What's cheered you up?"

Felicity was unsure how to answer. She bought herself some thinking time by reaching for her half of the muffin.

Two magpies strutted on the ground in front of her as she nibbled at it. She dropped a piece on the ground. The magpies ran toward it then paused, torn between fear and greed. One fixed her with a beady stare and darted forward to stab at the piece of muffin with its cruel beak. Its less brave companion lifted its head and warbled a song of entreaty.

How could Felicity explain the agony and ecstasy of the last forty-eight hours? What needed to be kept secret…and what could be shared to fuel a budding friendship?

"I have to sell my car…"

"That's bad."

"…to pay for some builders to clad my house in weatherboard and construct a bull-nosed veranda."

"That's good."

"…but they're not really builders."

"That's bad."

"…but one of them is…pretty special."

"Ooh, that's good!" Gabrielle leaned back and grinned.

"But he hasn't given any indication of…well…you know."

"No lingering looks?"

"Nope."

"No extra generous smiles?"

"Nope."

"No contrived meetings?"

"None."

Gabrielle put her hand on top of Felicity's. "Then, methinks you are scattering the seeds of your affection on stony ground." She squeezed her hand. "Guard your heart, Flick."

"Hmm."

"That doesn't convince me at all. Don't tell me you've already lost it."

"Certainly not," said Felicity, turning away.

Gabrielle reached out, turned Felicity's head back and tried to look into her eyes—but Felicity twisted away again. Gabrielle leaned back and sighed, "Ah, love...it is a madness, full of woes."

Felicity laughed despite herself. "Who said that?"

"I did. I often quote myself. It adds spice to the conversation."

"Well, nothing's happening. Seriously. He's just rather...unusual." Felicity threw her hair back and asked brightly, "How are your sculptures going?"

"Seriously?"

"Seriously."

"I'll show you if you like." Gabrielle took out her phone, dialed up her photo gallery, and passed the phone over.

Felicity scrolled slowly through the images. She was surprised by what she saw. Gabrielle's work was very good. Driftwood, rusted pieces of iron, fencing wire, and carved natural timber came together to suggest feelings, moods and possibilities. Her work in stone was particularly powerful and evocative. "How on earth do you get those fluid lines in the rock? It must take extraordinary patience to carve them."

"Do you like them?"

"I love them," said Felicity as she handed back the phone. "I really do. I didn't expect to see things so creative or so beautiful. How do you see the potential in such ordinary objects?"

"Well, that's it, darling. Everything's got potential."

"I hope I've been right in seeing potential in my old car garage. I'm beginning to wonder if it's all worth it."

"Hmm, the merry-go-round of capitalism does seem to invite you to walk a scary tightrope. It's probably the reason I opted out to become an artist. Certainly, I've been a disappointment to my parents. They sent me to a good school so I could learn the art of mindless consumerism." Gabrielle grinned. "I can't quite work this house-owning thing. The only benefit of owning your own home is that you get to choose which way around to hang the toilet roll."

Felicity moved her head slightly in order to line up two telephone poles down the street. Her mind was a long way away, teasing out the beginnings of an idea.

"Gabs, would it be possible to turn my shop front into an art gallery—a place to sell your work? It's in a fabulous location... plenty of foot traffic."

"Really?"

"Is it worth exploring?"

"You'd need to exhibit plenty of stuff other than mine."

"Hmm, I know. I've got some ideas about that."

"What ideas?"

"Well, as it happens, I know this wood-turner..."

That afternoon, Felicity took herself off for a walk. She needed to clear her head and do some serious thinking. Her arm ached but luckily there was no sign of infection. It did, however, give her an excuse not to do any physical work at the building site.

She walked along the Moyne River, pausing briefly to watch a fishing boat growl its way upstream. Its wash caused the water to slurp and gurgle on the rocks beside her. Turning south, she strolled beside the lagoon along a path that wound its way through the low-lying vegetation. She made her way to the southernmost point of Griffiths Island and sat down on a tussock of grass. Waves crashed and surged around the rocks in a confusion of swirls.

It was a fair representation of her mental state.

Feeling the need for calmer waters, Felicity got up and headed over to the beach behind the headland. When she got there, she took off her shoes and walked along the sand, allowing the last of the waves to run up the beach and cover her feet. The foam-streaked water sucked at her ankles as it swept back into the sea.

She walked the length of the beach, then turned and began

retracing her steps. Seagulls skittered across the sand in front of her, some lifting their wings in readiness to fly—undecided, like her.

The idea of making the bottom of her house into a gallery would certainly fit in with the local council regulations, but she wasn't so sure of her motives for doing it. Gabrielle had been enthusiastic, but what about Benjamin? How would he feel? Would he want to be linked with her in a commercial venture?

Felicity reached the end of the beach and stood in the shallows, watching the turquoise patterns of light shimmy and dance around her feet. Everything was so uncertain.

The noise of barking dogs told her that she was no longer alone. She looked over her shoulder and saw two Labradors, each holding the ends of the same stick. They were prancing around their owner, a gray-haired woman. However, Felicity's attention quickly turned to the man walking past them who was dressed in a wetsuit. Despite the cool wind, he had unzipped the front of his top. She recognized him immediately. Benjamin had looped his snorkel and fins over an arm and was carrying a bucket. In his other hand, he held an aluminum fishing spear. She watched his easy, languid gait.

When he came closer, she saw that his eyes were looking tired. They were no less dangerous for that; their dark depths interrogated her. She lowered her gaze. Beads of water were hanging between the muscles of his chest. *Safer to look at the bucket.* She pointed to it. "Hello. Any luck?"

"Two flathead, two strongfish, and a magpie perch. How's your arm?"

"Fine. No infection."

The silence shouted between them.

He smiled. "That's good."

The sight of his smile warmed her more than she wanted him to know. She fought for normal conversation. "The flatties should taste terrific. But I've never eaten a strongfish…or a magpie perch, for that matter."

"Felicity…"

She liked how he said her name. He said it slowly. Odd. Her friends usually called her Flick.

"I've got a school friend who is a cadet reporter with the local newspaper. He talks too much and is way too inquisitive—but fairly harmless. We're sharing a fish supper tonight in my workshop. If you want to find out what strongfish and magpie perch taste like, you're welcome to join us…about six-thirty."

"I'd like that," she said, a little too quickly. *Damn!* "What can I bring?"

She was surprised when he said, "A plate and a knife and fork. I'm afraid it's all pretty basic."

"Can I bring dessert?" she said, tossing back her hair—showing it off, just a little.

Benjamin didn't answer immediately. It was as if he was debating whether or not to tell her something. Eventually, he said, "That would be nice. It'll just be the three of us. Archie's looking after himself."

Felicity nodded. "Six-thirty then." Thinking that she'd said enough, she gave what she hoped was a carefree wave and trudged up the soft sand to the coastal path.

As she reached the low vegetation, she realized that she had been so dumbstruck that she hadn't thought of telling him about the Atlantis stone. She looked back over her shoulder to search for him on the beach. Benjamin was sitting on a rock, cleaning the fish. A throng of gulls was screeching and squabbling around him. He, in contrast, looked very much at peace. She wished she could share it. What on earth would she cook? Was there time to wash her hair?

Why is it always so much harder for a woman?

Chapter 8

Felicity hung a bag over one arm, cradled the Pavlova in the other, and climbed the wooden steps. Somewhat hampered by the bag, she tapped on the door.

Benjamin opened it almost straight away. She noticed that he had showered and taken a bit of care with his grooming. His long hair, still wet, was swept back. He wore jeans—clean, and a cream linen jacket. It was a good look. She felt slightly better about the time she had spent on her own grooming. Felicity held out the Pavlova. "Didn't have much time, so I bought a Pav base and loaded it up."

"It's good to see you."

Such a simple comment—but devastating to her mental composure.

"Thanks." He took the Pavlova and ushered her inside.

The workshop would always be a workshop, she conceded, but Benjamin had made an effort. He had placed a jar of wildflowers on the workbench and hung a kerosene hurricane lamp from a beam above it. Shadows from the eaves played over the ceiling. The kitchen area was a cabinet under a window. An electric fry pan and a plastic washing-up bowl sat on top of it.

The floor was clean, even under the various machines that sat patiently, waiting for work. Not much else was. Wood dust highlighted the cobwebs hanging from the roof beams. The fine film of wood dust on the walls was patterned with criss-crossed wiggly lines. It took a moment for Felicity to work out why. *Millipedes.* The wet winter meant that the town was experiencing something of a plague of them. They had obviously crawled through the dust on the walls and left their tracks. Their presence certainly didn't seem to trouble Benjamin. It troubled her though; their lines weren't straight!

"I've just planned a simple salad to go with the fish."

"Sounds fine. How are you cooking the fish?" She wasn't hugely interested, but the subject was safe.

"In flour...with slivers of lemon myrtle. It'll be garnished with samphire. I collected a bit from the marsh behind the foreshore."

Felicity wondered if she should confess to being a hopeless cook. *Never bothered to learn*, she corrected herself. She decided not to. "Sounds great." She searched for something else to say, and settled for pointing questioningly to a bowl of bright orange flowers.

"Nasturtium flowers from outside. Peppery...to add to the salad."

"Oh."

Felicity was rescued from airing any more of her ignorance by a sharp rap on the door.

The rising wind outside caused the potbelly stove to puff out some smoke as Benjamin opened the door.

An untidy figure in a three-quarter length coat came in clutching a bottle of wine and a shopping bag. "What sort of person tells his guests to bring cutlery and plates? Honestly, Ben..." He noticed Felicity. "Oh, hello."

"Felicity, allow me to present the usually unpresentable Marcus O'Lauchlan, scourge of the Rostrevor debating team and master of the split infinitive."

"Hello," she said. "I understand you two were at school together."

"Hmph. I went to school...he went rarely. His body may have been there, but his mind was usually elsewhere."

Marcus thrust the bottle at Benjamin. "A Clare Valley Riesling. Good with fish. Three glasses, my man."

"Oh…um." Benjamin glanced over to the washing-up bowl. "Would you settle for an enamel mug, a coffee cup, and a drinking glass?"

Marcus rolled his eyes.

Benjamin grinned. "Sit down. I'll see to it."

Marcus put his hands in his pockets, swished the open coat around him, and folded his angular frame into one of the two beautiful stools beside the workbench. Felicity took the other. She wondered what to say. A drill press stood nearby. Three books sat on its platform, each with library stickers on their spines. She twisted her head in an attempt to read their titles but was forestalled by Marcus asking a question.

"How do you know Benjamin?" He seemed to muse on his own question. "How does anyone know Benjamin, for that matter?" He smiled and raised an eyebrow.

"Oh…um…" Felicity went on to explain that they had met whilst diving. She didn't give the details, and explained that she was hoping to employ Benjamin to help her renovate the old car garage near the river.

"I've seen it. Ugly thing. Glad someone's renovating it." He jerked his head up. "You would be Felicity Anderson then, the doctor's sister?"

"Yes, that's right." She searched for something else to say. "And you're a journalist, I understand?"

"Yeah."

"Hmm. I planned to be a journalist at school—even learned shorthand…but history won. Went to uni and worked at Melbourne museum for two years." She shrugged. "Now I want to write. Crazy, huh?"

Marcus grinned. "I'm being careful not to say it's a woman's prerogative."

Benjamin came across with their wine. He handed Felicity the drinking glass. Marcus got the enamel mug. "Food will be ten minutes," he announced, and returned to his work.

When he left, Felicity leaned forward and whispered, "I know next to nothing about Benjamin. Can you please fill me in?"

Marcus looked into his mug and picked out a vinegar fly that had flown into it. Felicity continued to press him. "He's eloquent but reserved; distant but aware." She shrugged. "And there's an Aboriginal connection that I don't get."

Marcus took an experimental sip, seemed to enjoy it, and leaned back. "Relax. He's a nice guy." He looked up at her. "Are you two an item?"

"No!"

"Hmm." He regarded her from under his pale eyebrows. "Benjamin is part Aboriginal—not that you'd know it. Our school had an indigenous education program that collected students from remote locations all around Australia. It was a good program. They had some special classes and each student was allocated a mentor. I think Ben even lodged with his during the school holidays. He was a cabinet-maker."

"But he sounds so…cultured."

"Oh, that." Marcus smiled. "Blame Beanie for that."

"Beanie?"

"Yeah. He was our English teacher…and he was, in fact, English. He used to read us fabulous stories. Ben, in particular, loved them. They certainly motivated him. He became a voracious reader—Dickens, P.G. Wodehouse, John Buchan, Anthony Trollope—anything English. Over the years, his style of speech changed." Marcus leaned forward and whispered, "I think he worked pretty hard on it. Anyway, much as it pains me to admit it, by the time he left school, he had a bigger vocabulary than me, was top in English, and had the cultured Adelaide accent down pat."

"Then why didn't he go to university?"

"…and make something of himself?" Marcus wagged a finger at her. "You and your bourgeois ideas."

"Seriously."

Marcus sighed. "Nah. I don't think he would have coped with the strictures of university. He would have written them ten treaties when they wanted one, and one when they wanted ten. He's rest-less…and, I think, a little bit haunted."

"What do you mean?"

Benjamin forestalled further conversation by bringing over their dinner. He had presented it well. After explaining what each piece of fish was, he invited them to begin eating.

"What's this?" said Marcus, picking suspiciously at the samphire. "It's not what's normally on fish."

"You pusillanimous pedant. Try it. It's salty…and perfectly edible."

Marcus grinned at Felicity. "See what I mean?"

"What?" inquired Ben.

"Nothing," chorused Marcus and Felicity together.

By the time the Pavlova was served, conversation was flowing freely. As Felicity pushed a generous slice onto Marcus's plate, she felt emboldened to ask, "Marcus, how could Andrew Carter, a lawyer with the Khayef Group of companies, learn that I was doing research on the mahogany ship?"

"Are you?" he said, sitting himself up immediately.

"I was hoping for an answer."

"No idea."

"He said he got his information from the offices of the local paper—your paper."

"Ah."

"Ah, indeed."

"Well, come to think of it, I might have been responsible."

"What!"

Marcus held up his hands. "It was purely a mistake…a slip of the tongue. Honest." He sighed. "I'd done a little article on your brother towing in that boat with a busted engine. Remember? He'd been returning from diving. He let slip that he often dived, some-times with you, and that you were diving to see if you could find any clues to the mahogany ship." Marcus dropped his head. "Your brother actually asked me not to print that…but when I got this phone call, I sort of…forgot."

Felicity looked at him with exasperation. "Well, I don't know whether to thump you or thank you. As it's turned out, Khayef might offer me a research grant...and a large bonus if I find anything."

She was aware of Benjamin watching her.

"But something is troubling you. You're not sure." Benjamin said it as a statement, not a question.

Felicity was silent for a while.

The wood coals rattled as they settled inside the potbelly stove.

"Oh...um. I'm not..." She tried again. "Something's niggling. That's all." She thought back to her conversation with Mr. Carter. What was it? He had spoken of the grant as if it were a magnanimous gift, a contribution to Australian heritage...yet he had been unusually keen to get information on whether there was a Portuguese connection. She held on to the edge of the bench top to steady her thoughts. That's what didn't add up. Carter's line of questioning wasn't consistent with a philanthropic act. It belied an agenda—but she didn't know what it was.

"What is it?" asked Benjamin.

"Um, not sure. Too early to say. I need to think about it a bit more."

Benjamin nodded.

"Is there any substance to this mahogany ship business?" asked Marcus. "Were ships buzzing around this part of the world before Captain Cook did his thing?"

"I believe so—but up to now, there's been no knockout proof." *I've got that proof,* she thought to herself, trying not to let her elation show. *I'm just not ready to share it yet. Not to a journalist, anyway.* But she did want to share it with Benjamin. The Atlantis stone was a massive breakthrough in understanding Australia's earliest European history. She lowered her head in case her excitement showed. Steering the conversation to a safer subject, she hurried on. "Some believe that Jave la Grande, the Great Island of Java, was a reference to Australia." She shrugged. "The name appears on the French Dieppe School of Maps. Some sections of these maps are highly speculative, so you have to be careful. But one does show a coastline that could correspond to the southeast coast of Australia."

"Arrrr," parodied Marcus in his best pirate voice. "Beware. There be dragons in those parts."

"Seriously," Felicity protested, "a lot of nations were sending ships out to find gold. The mahogany ship was probably one of a fleet of three sent out by Portugal. Well before that fleet was sent out, ships were looking for Jave la Grande...or the Isle of Gold, as it was known. Over a decade earlier, the Portuguese explorer, Diogo Pacheco, lost a ship in Sumatra while he was looking for it." She smiled. "And there was plenty to motivate an explorer. A land of gold was spoken of in the Hindu legend of Suvarnadvipa, not to mention The Great Chronicle of Sri Lankan history."

"But nothing's been found to confirm that Portuguese gold fever reached as far as Warrnambool?" asked Benjamin.

Yes there has. You and I found it together. "No." She lowered her head again. "At least, not yet. The State Government of Victoria offered a reward of a quarter of a million dollars in 1992 to anyone who could locate the fabled vessel but withdrew the offer a year later."

"Curious. I wonder why?"

Felicity grinned. "It certainly helped fuel the odd conspiracy theory. A Canberra mathematician claimed to have stumbled across an 1849 document in the National Library that said that the British government had paid men to bury the ship in case its existence complicated British sovereignty rights over Australia. The story was even reported in the Age newspaper in 2005." She sighed. "A Sydney archaeologist investigated the claim but couldn't find the document and doubts its existence—so, I think it's all highly unlikely."

Benjamin got up and collected the plates.

Felicity turned in her seat and picked up one of the books sitting on the drill press. She looked at the cover—it was a Bryce Courtenay novel. She looked briefly at the other two books. "I see you use the library."

Benjamin spoke over his shoulder. "I like books, so I use libraries." He paused. "It took me a little while to get comfortable using them. In fact, I still find libraries and government agencies intimidating. All that political correctness gathered in one place can be terrifying."

Marcus looked around the workshop. "You don't have much by way of creature comforts. Where's your television?"

"I don't have one."

"Why?"

"I'm too easily frustrated by its banality. Books are better."

"Have you been into a bookshop recently?" he asked, querulously. "Books can be just as bad. Newspapers too, I'm ashamed to say. Sensationalism has replaced substance, and notoriety has replaced talent. It's all very depressing."

"Books give me more choice."

"You're a luddite."

"No, I'm selective." He pointed to a black case leaning against the end of the workbench. "I have a mobile and a laptop—even a website."

"Yeah, like living in a shed surrounded by woodwork machines is normal." Marcus yawned. "Anyway, I'd better get going—I've got an early start tomorrow." He turned to Felicity. "Promise me you'll tell me if you find anything interesting. I've got little enough to write about around here."

Felicity swallowed. "Sure. Of course."

Marcus eased himself off the stool and pulled his coat tight around him. "And you," he said, pointing to Benjamin. "You owe me a story."

"As I doubt you'd let me forget," said Benjamin. "But it's Sergeant Anderson you should be badgering, not me."

Marcus grunted and headed for the door. "Thanks, Ben. Enjoyed it—surprisingly. I'll call you tomorrow."

After Marcus left, Felicity asked, "What's all that about?"

"Aah, nothing. Um…a little incident that happened here the other night." He smiled weakly. "No felony on my part, I'm glad to say, but it's something the police are looking into. They've asked me to say nothing until they've made their inquiries."

"Oh." Felicity experienced a stab of disappointment. *Please trust me, Benjamin. I want to know…Let me in.* She drew in a breath and looked up to the ceiling. The two of them were alone…there were shadows…there was soft light from a kerosene lamp…everything was so right. "You weren't hurt or in any form of danger?"

"I'll tell you later."

Damn! She wanted to be angry, and she rounded on Benjamin in frustration. But all she saw was his eyes. They seemed tired…and strangely quiet. He was apparently content with his decision to not involve her. She turned her face from him to hide her emotions. "I'd better go too," she said.

Benjamin collected the plastic bag that contained her plates and cutlery, and led her down the steps to her car. As he opened the car door, he turned to face her. "Felicity, I had the impression that there was something going on—something that mattered to you—from what you said earlier." He drew a deep breath. "Would it help you to talk about it?"

Benjamin, you've not let me in. "No…no…at least, not yet. There are a few things I want to check out first."

"Fine. Just know that…you can, whenever you want."

Felicity nearly cracked. She put a hand on Benjamin's arm. "I've had a great night. Thank you."

Benjamin smiled. "Just one small thing." He took an envelope from his jacket pocket. "Archie and I weren't happy that you were having to sell your car when your ex had bought one with your money." He shrugged. "So we went to Melbourne last night and persuaded him to give us his car…and we've sold it." He handed the envelope to her. "Here's a check made out to you for one hundred and ten thousand dollars." He smiled. "Can I suggest that you send your ex-husband a check for half the cost of the car first thing tomorrow morning? Then you'll be safe, legally."

She was stunned. "What?" she said, not comprehending.

Benjamin explained again.

When the reality of what had happened began to register, Felicity put her hand over her stomach, tried to catch a sob…and failed. She began reaching out to Benjamin, then turned away and began to cry.

He reached out and drew her to himself, steadying her with his arms.

She sobbed because he'd cared; she sobbed for the joy of hope; she sobbed in relief; she sobbed because she'd sabotaged a romantic opportunity inside—simply because she was piqued. She wanted to go back inside and start over. *I want the shadows, the hurrican lamp, us… alone. I have something wonderful to share. I want this night to end differently.*

Benjamin let her go, and again held the car door open.

"Goodnight, Felicity. Sleep well."

Chapter 9

"Archie, listen to the wood. It'll tell you if your blade is sharp enough." Benjamin pushed the smoothing plane along the piece of Oregon. *Wheeee-hishssssss-zip.* "That's the sound of a happy plane." A curling piece of wood shaving fell to the floor. Benjamin picked it up and placed it on the kitchen cabinet.

Archie raised a quizzical eyebrow.

Benjamin continued to smooth the piece of wood. "If I'm away from the workshop, I take a chunk of fruit and nut slice for morning tea and wrap it in a piece of wood-shaving." He stood up and brushed the wood with his hand. "It's more friendly than a plastic bag." Benjamin handed the plane to Archie. "If I pick up one of your wood-shavings, it means you've made the grade."

He paused as he heard footsteps coming up the steps outside. Two loud raps on the door and the tinkling doorbell announced the arrival of Sergeant Anderson. Benjamin left Archie at his work and took the policeman across to the stools by the workbench.

Anderson nodded toward Archie. "Not your standard apprentice."

"He's handy."

"Hmph." The detective swung around on the stool and looked up at the new skylight.

"Any more disturbances?"

"No."

He swung back. "We've managed to find out who your intruder was." He mentioned a name. "Mean anything to you?"

"Never heard of him. Who is he?"

"He's a thug from Sydney. He's got form…and has links with an outlaw motorbike gang. The detective fixed Benjamin with an aggressive stare. "These gangs are linked with drugs and extortion… so tell me why such a person would be interested in you."

Benjamin shook his head. "Complete mystery."

The detective tapped a finger on the bench top. "And there's something else. We found two minor cuts on the man's back that were inconsistent with the rest of his injuries."

"He did fall through a glass skylight."

The detective shook his head. "The two cuts were surrounded with slight burning."

Benjamin frowned, not understanding.

"The wounds are consistent with the use of a wire-projecting stun gun—in other words, a taser."

"Oh."

"I don't suppose…"

"No…and I have no idea." Benjamin passed a hand over his head, trying to come to terms with what he'd learned. "I…I thought the police were the only ones allowed to use tasers."

"So did I," said Anderson dryly.

Benjamin was bewildered. He was journeying down a rabbit hole in which nothing made sense. A hired thug had tried to kill him…and someone else had stopped him doing so. The intervention was probably intended to be non-lethal—although the welfare of the victim had obviously not been seen as a high priority. He closed his eyes and pinched the top of his nose. "Who on earth…?"

"Have you seen this morning's paper?"

"Um, no," confessed Benjamin.

"Young O'Lauchlan has not done a great job in restraining himself. I gave him a press release two days ago. Your story reads like a bungled burglary—which it almost certainly wasn't. I didn't tell him about the gun."

"Probably wise."

The detective grunted as he got down from the stool. "Don't leave the area without telling me first."

After Anderson left, Benjamin sat back on his stool and tried to think. So many thoughts…swirling…making no sense, not to mention a disturbing email he'd received via his website that morning. He put his head in his hands. Then, of course, there was Felicity. It had been three days since he had entertained her and Marcus in the workshop. That evening had gone better than he had dared to hope, so he was bewildered as to why there had been no communication from her since. He was a little…what? He didn't know. It was simply that it mattered to him.

The previous afternoon, he was so restless thinking about her that he took himself out into the countryside, ostensibly to get permission from a farmer he knew to cut some wood from fallen trees. He threw the chainsaw in the back of the ute and headed inland.

As he drove through the farm gate, he saw a gaggle of utes and twin cabs outside the corrugated iron shearing shed. The shed's sliding door was open to let in some fresh air for the shearers. Someone had put a few folding chairs and a half bale of wool near the entrance so that they could relax in the cool air while enjoying a well-earned "smoko."

Benjamin could hear the flat chattering sound of the electric sheers, and the bump and clump of sheep moving in their pens on the wooden floor. The earthy, ammonia smell of their dung was hanging the air. He located the farmer, who nodded his permission and dismissed him with a wave. Benjamin drove along the track until he came to some picturesque grazing land, heavily dotted by large gum trees. He got out and leaned against the ute.

What was troubling Felicity the other night? he wondered. *Why didn't she want talk to me about it?* He kicked absently at a tuft of sedge and gazed around him. Shadows cast by clouds were marching across the hills. They'd brought a light shower that had left jewels glistening in the grass. He sighed and picked up the chainsaw.

Three hours later, the ute had a healthy load of wood, and the gum trees were beginning to cast long shadows over the emerald green grass. He closed the tailgate and tried to marshal his thoughts. It was a gentle time of day, magical. He was conscious of an ache, something unfulfilled…missing. Midges danced around him in the late sunshine. He brushed his way through them and climbed into the cab.

That was yesterday—but today, the feeling of emptiness was still with him. *Felicity.* It was all to do with Felicity, he admitted.

A draft under the door scattered some shavings across the floorboards. The wind was rising. Benjamin looked at the floor. A thug with a gun had died on that very spot…yet here he was, thinking about Felicity. He sighed. One way or another, he knew that nothing in his life was going to remain the same. He'd come to a point where his need for someone had grown stronger than his fear of relationships. But what should he do? What could he do?

Make something. He glanced across at Archie. His new apprentice was busy squaring up the ends of the posts that Benjamin would later turn to make stanchions for Felicity's bull-nosed veranda. *So, what can I make?*

After a moment's thought, he rummaged through his wood collection and pulled out a piece of Murray Valley pine—strong and warm. He took it across to the wood lathe.

"They're magnificent." Marjorie ran her hands down the curving flanks of one of the candlesticks. "This blackheart sassafras really is a beautiful wood. Smoky, like a candlestick should be." She turned around to him. "Why are things beautiful, Benjamin? Have you thought about it any more?"

Benjamin shrugged, unsure if he was going to keep up with the mercurial mind of Ms. Eddington.

Her bright eyes danced over him. "Shrugs should be used sparingly," she remonstrated, "and never as shields to hide behind."

Benjamin smiled at Marjorie's audacity…and began fighting for words. "Um, ah, beauty is…" He thought furiously. He dare not be careless with this formidable mind. "I think beauty has to do with order…an order that reflects the patterns and ratios seen in nature. Ratios that…er, work."

Marjorie cocked her head sideways. "Like the ratios of the golden rectangle that feature in the Parthenon and the Mona Lisa… hmm…" She seemed to retreat into some sort of internal reverie. Benjamin wasn't sure if she had asked a question or was making a statement. After a moment, she continued. "Certainly, the Fibonacci series of numbers describes ratios that we see in lots of places—in the spirals of seashells, in DNA, in tropical storms and in galaxies." She ran a finger lightly down one of the candlesticks. "It would be interesting to discover whether you've used those ratios here."

"I, er…don't measure things very much."

"You go by instinct?"

"Yes."

"And what does that tell you?"

Benjamin fought down the temptation to shrug. "Um…order is everywhere?"

She smiled at him. "Precisely. And if order is everywhere, then there is design…and if there is design, there is meaning." She smiled. "Didn't Paul Dirac say, 'God is a mathematician of a very high order, and he used very advanced mathematics in constructing the universe'?"

Benjamin forbore from asking who Paul Dirac was. "Hmm," he said.

Marjorie waved a finger. "Design bespeaks meaning. So, Benjamin, have you found your meaning?"

Benjamin laughed with slightly more bitterness than he had intended. "I don't even know who I am, far less what my meaning is."

"Oh, how sad." Marjorie looked him up and down. Eventually, she said. "My work in anthropology, particularly among indigenous Australians, suggests to me that your name is a local one, quite possibly from around here."

Her remark landed among his sensibilities like a bombshell. Benjamin managed to splutter, "Er...someone told me when I was young that my dad came from around here but I've no idea where."

"Is that the reason you choose to live here? Deep calls to deep, perhaps?"

Don't shrug. He didn't.

"So, what do you know about the people who lived here?" she asked.

"Nothing."

"Why?"

"Never bothered to ask."

"Well, Benjamin, let me tell you that the original inhabitants of the Moyne area were the Gunditjmara...and they were an extraordinary people."

Despite his apprehension, Benjamin's interest was piqued. Could it be that after all these years, something might emerge from the fog of unknowing that surrounded his identity?

Marjorie continued. "They were a river and lake people with a sophisticated culture. Their dwellings were built of stone, and, intriguingly, they engaged in aquaculture."

"I didn't know any blackfellas built with stone!"

"Yes. And they also built stone dams to create ponds in which they farmed eels." She smiled and wagged a finger at him. "But they were a feisty lot. They warred against the European colonialists in the mid-nineteenth century in what came to be called the Eumerella Wars. The fighting lasted about twenty years."

Benjamin's mind was reeling. "Um...are there any...um...left?"

"Certainly are. They've been very active in fighting for their land rights. They got them too. The Federal Court of Australia granted them native title to one hundred and forty-five thousand hectares of crown land near Portland and Yambuk. They also have title over Lady Julia Percy Island."

"But haven't the local mob had all their Aboriginality bred out of them by intermarrying?"

"There's certainly been a lot of that but heritage is still there." Marjorie smiled. "There's evidence that interbreeding has been happening for some time, even before settlement. The Henty family —early settlers near Portland—reported that a local tribe included people with fair skin and high cheekbones."

Benjamin rubbed the back of his neck as he pondered what he had learned. He glanced at Marjorie. She was sitting upright in her stool as if posing for a portrait.

"What's troubling you?" she demanded.

"Um, I had an email this morning."

Marjorie waited for him to elaborate.

"It came from a minister in the Uniting Church. He's a pilot, a bush padre who flies around the East Kimberley offering pastoral care to remote communities."

"And?"

"He tells me that my uncle, the one I lived with as a kid, has been missing for months and is presumed dead. Evidently, the elders want to speak to me about his 'sorry business'." He dropped his head. "My mother was Kija, one of their mob."

"I'm sad to hear about the death of your uncle. Were you close?"

Benjamin breathed in between his teeth. "No, I hated him."

"Oh."

"And vowed never to return."

"Yet the elders want to talk you."

"Yes." He stared at the floor. Sunlight through the workshop window had laid a golden trapezium on the rough planks.

"I think you should go…and, what's more, you should go as soon as possible."

Benjamin jerked his head up. "Why?"

Marjorie lifted up her chin. "Because it is your story. Because you need to fix things." She sniffed delicately. "We've been talking about beauty and meaning…and meaning gives identity. I think you are struggling to know who you are."

Benjamin stayed silent, appalled at being understood and having his pathology voiced.

She leaned forward and placed a hand on his arm. Benjamin looked down at it. Her skin was thin and papery, like last winter's leaves, half rotten and lying on the ground. "Benjamin, if you are to live your purpose, you must belong…at three levels."

Benjamin grunted, hoping that his mutinous state was not too obvious.

"First, you need to belong to at least one other person in a close relationship of love. Second, you need to belong to a community within which you have meaning…" She paused.

"And?" he asked, hoping to end things quickly.

"Third, you need to belong to God, to discover your purpose in living…and why it is that you are sacred."

Marjorie stepped down from her stool. "Take courage, Benjamin," she said, patting him on the shoulder. She reached down for her handbag. "Now, let me pay you for my beautiful candlesticks."

Benjamin wrapped Marjorie's purchases and carried them to her car, walking slowly to keep pace with Marjorie as she descended the steps. She gripped the handrail and negotiated them gingerly.

"Are you well?" he asked.

"No, but I don't talk about it."

Benjamin held the car door open and located the seat belt buckle for her.

Marjorie nodded her thanks and leaned back with a sigh. He was about to close the door when she said, "Benjamin, may I commission you for another job? There's no rush for it but seeing the quality of your work, I feel compelled to at least ask."

"Certainly. What is it?"

"I'd like a toolbox—a beautiful one to hold all the paraphernalia associated with my tapestry work. About this size." She indicated the dimensions with her hands. "I'd love it to be made of a local wood, if possible." She smiled through her fatigue. "Perhaps you might suggest one?"

"Oh." Benjamin pictured the wooded flatlands and swamps of

the local area in his mind's eye. "Um…I think Australian blackwood would work well. It's great for cabinet making, musical instruments —even boat-building. The wood is chocolate-colored and has dark honey streaks." He pointed inland. "The tree is pretty common around here because it grows well in creeks and wetlands."

"Perfect," she smiled.

Chapter 10

Felicity stamped on the brakes. She had been reversing out of the driveway, her mind a million miles away, and she hadn't been thinking.

The ancient white ute she had nearly driven into skidded to a halt and then reversed back into the curb.

Felicity held on to the steering wheel, mentally rehearsing an apology.

The bangings and whine of buzz saws behind her were a sign that the builders were in full swing, putting in place her second fixings. It was a good sound. She had called in to her renovation project to check on progress before making the visit that was so preoccupying her mind. *Damn. Silly. Nearly caused an accident.* She thumped the wheel.

"Hello."

And there he was. The very man she was going to visit…to apologize to. Benjamin.

"Are you alright?" he asked.

She closed her eyes and put her head back. "Um…distracted. So sorry. I…er, was just coming to visit…you actually. To apologize." She smiled weakly. "Now I have to apologize twice. Once for running away and not thanking you for a wonderful evening…and now for nearly crashing into you."

Benjamin said nothing for a long time…and simply looked at her.

Apprehension boiled around Felicity's heart.

"It's…good to see you. As it happens, I was coming to see you, to check that you were okay," he said.

"Oh." Relief…delight…flooded through her.

Silence.

"I'm…I'm fine." Her voice had a catch in it. She rushed on. "I got a call from a colleague at the museum where I used to work. She had some information that I needed to check out." *And I wanted space to examine what I feel about you, Benjamin Bidjara.* "I got back last night."

He nodded.

More silence.

"Would you like a coffee?" she said. "There's a great café around the corner. I've…er, got lots of things to tell you."

"I'd like that very much." He opened the car door for her.

Felicity felt absurdly happy walking beside Benjamin to the café. She didn't say anything; she didn't want to break the spell.

As they approached the café, Gabrielle came outside to wipe down the tables. Today, she was dressed in a floaty black dress with black lace everywhere. A trailing black ribbon tied up her hair. She spotted them coming toward her and stood with a hand on her hip, arms akimbo. She appraised Benjamin from head to tail—without much subtlety, before glancing at Felicity. Her lips were pressed together…but a small smile peeked around the edges.

Felicity gave the smallest of nods.

Gabrielle smiled. "The Melting Moments are crap, the apple muffin is the best, and the coffee is excellent. I make it."

Felicity laughed. "Hi Gabs." She leaned forward and gave Gabrielle a kiss. Then she stepped back and said, "This, is Benjamin…Benjamin, meet Gabrielle. She's a friend in need and a very talented artist. She does modern sculptures."

"And you're a wood-turner, I understand?" Gabrielle stepped forward to kiss Benjamin on the cheek.

Gabs, No! He'll know we've been talking about him! Felicity was about to say something crass to change the subject but Benjamin got in first.

"Thanks for being Felicity's friend-in-need." If he was unused to being kissed on the cheek by a stranger, he did well to conceal it. Benjamin smiled. "May we have two apple muffins, one long black, and a white coffee…" He turned to Felicity with a questioning eye. "Cappuccino?" On seeing her nod, he continued. "Cappuccino. And neither of us take sugar."

Felicity found that she was hanging on to Benjamin's arm. She had taken it whilst making the introduction and forgotten to let it go. *No sugar. He remembered!* She gave his arm a squeeze.

Once they were seated at an outside table, Felicity wondered where on earth she should begin. There was so much to share.

Benjamin was watching her under his long eyelashes. He looked calm. She felt far from calm. Taking a deep breath, she began. "I had a wonderful time the other night…and I was busting to share something with you but Marcus was there and, well…"

"He's a nosy journalist who can be a little careless with other people's sensibilities and confidences," prompted Benjamin.

Felicity nodded and leaned forward. "The thing I really wanted to share with you is that we've had a fabulously significant historical breakthrough."

"We?"

She looked down shyly. "We. It's your Atlantis stone…which I wouldn't have if it weren't for you."

He nodded. "What about it?"

"It's Portuguese. It's part of a carved stone, the other half of which is in South Africa. It categorically proves that the Portuguese were here well before white settlement." She looked up at him. "Don't you see? It all ties in with the mahogany ship."

"I've heard of the ship." Benjamin smiled. "Well, everyone around here has. How does your discovery tie in with it?"

"The best theory is that the ship was one of three in a flotilla led by Cristóvão de Mendonça to look for new lands in which they might find gold. It had to be a secret expedition because they were technically infringing the Treaty of Tordesillas, which Portugal had signed. It reserved discoveries in this part of the world for Spain." She pulled her chair closer to the table. Most people believe it likely that the mahogany ship was one of Mendonça's ships that was wrecked here."

Benjamin nodded. "But where does our stone fit in?"

"I can't be sure of the exact scenario, but it must have been something like this." She cleared her throat. "A sailor had been carving a picture of his own ship, and another picture of the whole flotilla, on a flat stone. Under his own ship, he'd etched the words *Ilhas do ouro*—land of gold; and under the flotilla, he'd etched Mendonça's name. But the trouble was, the carving was proof that Portugal was infringing the treaty. My guess is that someone in authority ordered the stone to be broken in two so that the connection couldn't be made. The sailor kept one half and gave the other to a friend on another ship. When one ship struck the rocks off Warrnambool, some sailors must have made it into a rowing boat. Our luckless sailor managed to take his ditty bag with him, but the boat foundered and everything sank, including his stone." She paused to make sure Benjamin had taken it all in.

"Go on."

"The other sailor, with his piece of rock, took two years to get to South Africa on his way back to Portugal. While he was there, he finished carving the rock. He etched the date, 1524, under the picture of Mendonça's flotilla." Felicity reached her hand half way across the table. "That piece of rock is still in South Africa. I learned about it from a book written by a science journalist when I was doing my thesis." She looked at Benjamin anxiously. "Do you think it's plausible?"

Benjamin took an eternity to answer. Eventually, he cleared his throat. "Felicity, the exact story of how the two pieces of stone came to be at opposite ends of the Indian Ocean will probably never be known but your hypothesis is certainly reasonable." He smiled. "What is not in doubt is that because of your tenacity and hard work, you have positive proof that Mendonça's Portuguese flotilla was here." He leaned back. "I think that's amazing. At the very least, it's got to be the subject of your first book."

Felicity laughed with relief. "You believe me?"

Benjamin nodded, but his face turned serious. "But may I ask a question that's been concerning me?"

Felicity frowned.

"You were undecided the other night about whether you should get involved with the Khayef Group. Why? What's troubling you?"

Felicity swallowed. "Yes, um…they said they wanted to be philanthropic and help research Australian heritage, but their line of questioning suggested they had an agenda." She shrugged. "I'm nervous of committing until I know what it is."

Benjamin nodded. "Instincts are powerful. Don't do anything you're not comfortable with." He leaned back and stretched his legs. "I…um, took the liberty of ringing Marcus yesterday and asked if he could dig around a bit and find some information about them." He gave a lopsided grin. "If anyone can, it'll be him. He's tenacious."

"Here you are ladies and gentlemen." Gabrielle placed a tray with coffee and muffins on the table. She turned to Benjamin. "You are a gentleman, I take it?"

"No, I am completely unused to civilized surroundings, and I eat with my mouth open."

Gabrielle straightened up and sighed. "You're a gentleman. Most of my customers wouldn't even know that eating with your mouth open is bad manners." She turned on her heels and went into the café, calling back to Felicity over her shoulder, "He'll do."

Felicity closed her eyes and wished the ground would open up and swallow her.

Benjamin appeared not to hear.

She watched him eat…and wondered how much to tell him… how much he would believe. Would he understand? Would he even want to know?

She was brought up with a start when he spoke. "Felicity, I'm part blackfella…and we…" Benjamin swallowed. "We blackfellas have all the time in the world." He looked up at her. "So, take your time."

"Oh! Um…" *How does he do that? How does he know?* She rubbed her forehead and tried to marshal her thoughts. With some diffidence, she began. "I've been away for the last two days…" She paused. "No, let me go back a bit." She put down her fork, put her hands together, and said, "How much do you know about Sardinia?"

Benjamin raised his eyebrows. "Sardinia! As in the island in the Mediterranean?"

"Yes."

"Assume complete ignorance. Tell me everything that it would be helpful for me to know."

"Er, right." Felicity swallowed.

"Sardinia's history has been politically messy for almost all of its history. Phoenicians, Carthaginians, Romans, Italians, and Spanish all controlled it at various times—when it wasn't being pillaged by Vandal raiders and Arab corsairs. It's now under the rule of Italy, although there's no great enthusiasm from either Italy or Sardinia regarding the arrangement."

Benjamin nodded. "I'm guessing that somehow Sardinia's politics were significant when Portugal was signing treaties with everyone to decide who would own what parts of the world?"

Felicity nodded. "Sardinia became a Spanish territory after the unification of the Spanish kingdoms in 1479, so they owned it —sort of."

"Sort of?"

"Yes. The 'sort of' is actually very important."

"Why?"

"Well, the locals were fairly resentful of the Spanish. So much so, that it was the perfect place for John II of Portugal and Henry VII of England to send their emissaries to sign a treaty." Felicity shrugged. "What better place to sign it? It was well away from spies in their royal courts…and right under the noses of the Spanish. It was the last place the Spanish would have been watching closely."

"Cheeky."

"Very."

"A local dignitary in the southern Sardinian city of Cagliari was chosen to be a witness to the treaty. He was considered ideal because his nationalistic pride had been hurt by being forced by the Spanish to conscript local labor to renovate Cagliari's city walls."

"Was that a problem?"

"His main project was to turn one of the towers in the wall into a prison...largely to hold dissenting Sards."

Benjamin pulled a face. "Yeah, I suppose that would do it."

"The next to invade Cagliari were the English. A naval fleet under Sir John Leake bombarded the city into submission in 1708 and ransacked the place. The thing is, a student researching for a PhD has recently been looking at the documents seized on that occasion which hadn't previously attracted much attention. I've just read his thesis." She caught herself jiggling up and down with excitement...and forced herself to sit still. "It makes mention of the treaty that Portugal and England signed concerning who would own what if countries east of Africa were discovered."

Felicity lowered her gaze. "I needed to get away for a bit to do some thinking, so when a colleague at Melbourne museum, who knew I'd done a thesis in this area, alerted me to this new research, I had to check it out." She returned her gaze to Benjamin. "That's why I went to Melbourne."

Benjamin said nothing and looked at her for a long while before nodding. "Find anything interesting?"

Yes, Benjamin. I found that I love you. Felicity sniffed. She forced her thoughts back to the subject in hand and continued. "Yes. Some very interesting stuff." Mercifully, she felt her excitement start to flood back. "It mentions a rough draft text of what was in the treaty." She reached down to her shoulder bag, pulled out a piece of paper, and smoothed it out on the table. "I've got a translation of it. Here, listen to this."

The bearer of this document has the right to collect and mine for gold in any great lands in the South Seas east of the lands of Africa.

To encourage development in new lands and earnest endeavor, no tax of any kind will be levied on gold that does not leave the lands in which it is found.

To encourage exploration, and notwithstanding who holds this document, the one who discovers any great land or isles east of Africa will have rightful claim on any gold found within sixty leagues of their point of landing. This right shall extend to the descendants of those who discover the land—if they can prove lineage.

This should prevent murder and war…and preserve good order.

"But no one's actually got the treaty?"

"There's one copy. It is potentially dangerous, legally, so it's kept safe in the British National Archive at Kew. Its existence has been kept quiet, but a little bit of information leaked out a few years back. One of their curators became too loquacious when giving a lecture on the National Archive." Felicity grinned. "Evidently, he was pulled off PR work pretty quickly."

"Just one copy?"

"Well…" She drew in a breath. "Three copies were made originally. One was kept in Lisbon but it was destroyed in the great fire of 1755. The other was kept in Cagliari somewhere but no one has managed to find it. Most people think it was lost…" She trailed off.

She glanced up and caught Benjamin watching her closely. He nodded and said slowly. "But you're not so sure."

Felicity dropped her head. "No…well…sort of." She began chewing her lips. "It's just that the PhD I've read mentions something that could be a clue as to where the mutinous Sard hid his witnessed copy of the treaty."

"What gives you that idea?"

"He talks about keeping it in a place 'which could never forget.'"

Benjamin looked at her quizzically.

Felicity lifted her chin and stared at him defiantly. "I think it's in an elephant."

"What!"

"Seriously." She grabbed his arm, willing him to believe her. "The Sard had been asked to keep the treaty safe, so he organized for it to be kept in a place which could never forget. At first, I thought this was a grammatical error—everyone did." She shook Benjamin's arm. "But then I learned about a tower in Cagliari."

"A tower."

"Yes." She leaned forward. "It's called the elephant tower. It was the prison tower the Sard nobleman was conscripting labor for."

"Aah." Benjamin nodded. "An elephant never forgets."

"Precisely."

"But where on earth would you begin to find something as small as a piece of parchment in something as massive as a medieval stone tower?"

Felicity searched his face, wanting him to understand her excitement. "Because the tower has a small elephant statue above its gate. It's the craziest thing, which no one has ever been able to make sense of." She banged a finger on the table. "If a copy of the treaty was hidden inside, it would make perfect sense of everything."

After a long pause, Benjamin smiled. "Felicity, you might be on to something."

She tilted her head back and closed her eyes, ostensibly to allow the sun to play fully on her face. In reality, she sought to hide tears of relief that Benjamin had understood her. After a moment, she opened her eyes and watched some gulls wheel through the air above her searching for abandoned food scraps.

Benjamin cleared his throat. "I've left something in my car that I'd like to give you." He rushed on, as if embarrassed. "And then I'd like to take the opportunity of making a few more measurements for the bull-nose. I want a firm picture of it in my mind before I start turning your veranda posts."

"Sure." Felicity forced her thoughts back to her building project, glad of the opportunity to share some of her recent ideas with Benjamin.

"Benjamin…"

"Yes."

"I've been thinking. Cladding the house is routine builder's work —which I can now pay a builder to do, thanks to you. Would it be a better use of your talents to ask you to turn matching posts for the bull-nose on the first floor balcony at the rear of the house? It's in the plans…but I wasn't going to build it because of costs." She smiled. "I can afford it now."

"I think you should build it."

"Oh, really?"

"Hmm. Have you noticed that the building behind yours has a SOLD sticker across its sale board—and has had for some time?"

"What…the old fish co-op shed?"

Benjamin nodded.

"No," Felicity admitted. "I've been pretty distracted recently."

"Unless you go down to the riverfront, you probably won't see it. I only saw it because I walk along there sometimes to look at the boats."

"Yes," she said, trying to remember the last time she'd done the same. She'd always appreciated that the banks of the river had been beautifully developed. Luxury houses ran down to a boardwalk running along the water's edge. Boats, including her brother's Shark Cat, were moored alongside it. However, she preferred to walk along the coast where it was wild and desolate.

"Why don't I show you?"

They walked together along the river foreshore until they came to a rusted, corrugated iron shed. There were no fences, so they walked around the back. Felicity could see the top of her new house behind the back fence. The gable under the new roof hadn't been filled in because the builders were awaiting her final decision on whether to put in French doors to a balcony. She could see inside to where the light from the new dormer windows shone against the raked ceiling. The prospect of looking from a balcony at an industrial shed wall scarred by drainpipes hadn't excited her. She looked at it glumly.

"Felicity, I think you should see the display board that's been put up in front of the property."

Benjamin walked Felicity around to the road in front of the shed to a display board that the developers had erected. It showed the plans of four luxury townhouses and an artist's impression of the finished development.

"Look," he said, pointing to the plans. "There's a gap between the second and third townhouses. You'll have a narrow but clear view of the river." He smiled his quiet smile. "A balcony with a picture window would add two hundred thousand dollars to the value of your property."

Felicity was in shock at the realization, and her head began to spin. Extraordinary. Her fortunes, which had recently been so desperate, had completely turned around. She glanced at Benjamin. And it had all happened since…then her phone rang. *Damn!*

She recognized her brother's voice immediately. "Flick, sorry to spoil your day. But we've been burgled—or, more particularly, you've been burgled. Can you come home? The police are around here." He paused. "It must have happened while we were shopping in Warrnambool. And Flick, I'd better warn you; things are pretty messy. Everything in the filing cabinet is on the floor and your computer's gone. I don't know what else."

Once the shock of hearing the news had subsided sufficiently for Felicity to think, she blurted, "What about the Atlantis stone? Is that gone?"

"What the hell are you talking about, Flick?"

Felicity pinched the top of her nose. "Sorry. Forget it. I'll come straight around."

Chapter 11

Archie leaned on the broom as Benjamin told him about the burglary of Felicity's room at the back of her brother's house. Archie had been sweeping the wood shavings to an open trapdoor in the floor, where they were allowed to fall into a bin four feet below.

Benjamin was fiddling with the parts of a dismembered three-jawed chuck on the bench in front of him. "The thing is, do you think there is any chance this could be a revenge thing organized by Felicity's ex? Have we stirred up a fight?"

"No, mate. By the sound of it, the thief made a bit of a mess and nicked a computer and a camera. There's not enough damage to signify anything vindictive." Archie closed the hatchway and secured it with the bolt. "It's just someone looking for money to feed a habit. How's Flick coping?"

Benjamin passed a hand across his mouth and wrestled with how much he should say.

"Hmm…There's, er…another possibility."

Benjamin's diffidence succeeded in getting Archie's attention. As Benjamin searched for the right words, Archie prompted him. "I think you should tell me what's going on, young Benji."

"Felicity has been digging around, researching the idea that the Portuguese first landed here in the early sixteenth century. She believes the mahogany ship spoken of by early settlers near Warrnambool was one of the Portuguese ships. Anyway, she's recently found a stone on the sea floor that proves they were here. The thing is, there are some people who seem fairly interested in this whole thing for some reason."

Archie nodded. "And who would these people be?"

"The Khayef Group."

"The mob that's been in and out of the news in the last year?"

"Have they?"

"Yeah. They're behind a massive development on Sydney Harbour."

"Well, I don't know about that, but they seem pretty interested in Felicity's research." Benjamin shrugged. "Felicity not only had her computer and external hard drives stolen but also a stone..." He paused as he remembered Felicity's tears of anguish at discovering that her Atlantis stone had been stolen. She had wept and remonstrated with herself until he had enfolded her in his arms and calmed her. "It was really important for her research because it proves a Portuguese connection with Australia." He pursed his lips. "And there were other more valuable things in the house that were untouched."

"Well mate, there are two options. It was either an amateurish jerk looking for a bit of extra money who didn't have the bottle to ransack the whole house..."

"Or?"

"Or a professional who wanted the information that Felicity had." Archie's bleak eyes regarded Benjamin. "Fingerprints?"

"Too early to say. The police had started dusting for prints when I left. Sergeant Anderson did let slip that the handles on the filing cabinet had been wiped clean."

Archie nodded slowly. "Then the signs are not good, Benji boy." He pulled out a matchstick and started to chew it. "Someone wants Flick's computer...and that could be a bit of a concern." The matchstick bobbled up and down. "You say that she'd made a connection with early Portuguese explorers?"

"Yes, but I'd be grateful if you kept that to yourself, at least until Felicity knows how she's going to handle it."

"Before I promise that, mate, I need to make a phone call."

Archie pushed himself off the bench and sauntered to the back door.

Benjamin watched him leave. *What on earth did he mean by that?* He chewed his lip. Too many disturbing things were happening…and his spirit was screaming at him to be careful.

Benjamin looked around for something to do and settled on the task of stepping up his security. He picked up an empty paint tin and went out through the back door. He could see Archie by the woodshed speaking into his mobile. Over by the bushes, a willy-wagtail was proclaiming its authority. *Chitta, chitta, chitta.* He stared at it briefly as it swung its tail from side to side…and shivered. The little bird had the teasing habit of flying just a few paces away when you came close to it and wagging its tail, almost daring you to follow it. It was said that its antics had enticed babies to crawl after it— beyond the edge of the camp, where dingoes could snatch them. Whether or not this was true, the story had earned the bird a terrible nickname, "the devil bird."

Benjamin turned away; watching the devil bird wasn't a good omen for the future. He walked over to the fence where most of the posts were encrusted with white Italian snails. The shells of dead snails lay scattered around the bottom of the posts. Benjamin went from post to post, scooping up the empty shells into the tin. Then he made his way to the path between the workshop and the fence, and scattered the shells on the ground. If anyone walked down the path, the tiny crushed shells would tell him that they had been there.

Next, he checked that the strong anchor strands spun by the orb web-spinner spider outside the kitchen window were in place. Each night, the spider would spin a beautiful net between these strands. Benjamin had encouraged it to do so by placing a light to attract insects by the window. A broken web could tell you a lot.

Archie ambled across to him. He nodded approval when he

understood what Benjamin was doing. "Mate," he said, "could you give Flick a call and see if it's okay for us to pick her up in half an hour? There's someone we need to visit."

"I'm afraid I haven't been entirely forthcoming about my reasons for first coming to see you, Benjamin." Marjorie lay back against the pillows on her bed and smiled weakly. The curtains were drawn and the resultant gloom highlighted the pale, waxy pallor of her face. Archie, Felicity, and Benjamin were seated around the high brass bed in chairs that had been borrowed from the dining room. Behind them, an indomitable-looking woman, who had been introduced to them as Phoebe, came and went with cups of tea, staying only to insert an extra pillow behind Marjorie. "It's not one of her good days," Phoebe had said to them.

Marjorie continued. "My exchanges with you, Benjamin, were entirely authentic and, I must say, very enjoyable." She pointed toward the dining room. "Your candlesticks look good, don't you think?"

Benjamin nodded.

"Aah...where to begin?" Marjorie closed her eyes. "You have probably heard that the Dutchman, Willen Janszoon, was the first European to discover Australia. He encountered it in his ship, *Duyfken*, because he failed to turn north quickly enough after rounding the Cape of Good Hope. He was heading to Batavia, modern-day Jakarta, the center of the spice trade." She pulled at her pillow. "His was the first of rather a lot of Dutch ships that bumped into Western Australia, most with disastrous consequences. We estimate that over two hundred Europeans made it ashore because we can pick up sequences of their genetic code in that of the local Aboriginals, sequences that could only have come from Europe.

A lot of indigenous Australians have had their genetics mapped. It became necessary in order to prove who had rights to royalties from mining companies working on indigenous land." She flopped a hand over toward Benjamin. "That includes you, Benjamin. You must have given a saliva swab when you were a child."

Marjorie turned her head back on the pillow. "I hope this doesn't come as too much of a shock…but you, Benjamin, have a sequence in your genetic code that could only have come from Portugal. It's come from your father's side. And as best as I can determine, you are the only one in Australia who has it." She smiled. "You are, in fact, living proof that the Portuguese visited Australia well before the Dutch discovered it in 1606."

Felicity leaned forward. "Miss Eddington…"

"Marjorie, please."

"…Benjamin and I have recently found something from the seafloor off Warrnambool that also proves that the Portuguese were here." Felicity bit her lip. "But it's just been stolen from me. Is there a connection?"

"You found a stone, I believe, dear."

Felicity nodded.

"I'm afraid there is a connection—and that's why I asked Archie to bring you here."

Benjamin looked at Archie as a faint suspicion started to form in his mind.

"Yes, Benjamin, I'm afraid that your first meeting with Archie was not as much of an accident as you might have thought. He's been minding your back for a while, now." Marjorie sighed. "Perhaps I should explain. Archie, Phoebe, and I have been employed from time to time by ASIO—although the official status of this particular exercise is a little uncertain. Technically, we are all retired. Archie, particularly, should be retired because of his post traumatic stress." She smiled at him. "But he keeps proving too useful. I brought him in when I began to see which way the wind was blowing."

Benjamin cleared his throat. "And what way is the wind blowing, Marjorie? Is Felicity in any danger?"

"I fear she may be. I heard of the burglary…and that was enough for me to show my hand." She began coughing. Phoebe immediately came to her side, gave her a drink of water, and settled her down.

"I apologize," said Marjorie. She closed her eyes and continued to speak. "A very secret treaty was stolen from Britain's National Archives at Kew. It was potentially dangerous legally, so it was never allowed to be copied. This means that if the document surfaces—as I very much fear it will—it will be impossible for the British to prove it is their stolen treaty." She paused and breathed deeply before continuing. "Two other copies once existed. One, we know, was destroyed. The other has never been found. The thieves will simply claim it is the other."

Benjamin glanced at Felicity. A furrow was forming on her brow. He turned back to Marjorie. "Marjorie, I think Felicity knows a bit about this treaty. She may have something to add."

Felicity did not reply as he expected. She put a hand to her forehead. "Oh no! It can't be." She turned to Benjamin. "The treaty, of course! Benjamin…is a proven descendant of the original discoverers. That would mean…he has rights over any gold." She turned a questioning look to Marjorie. "Is that right?"

"That's it exactly, my dear." She smiled. "You've made the connection."

"Oh," Felicity exclaimed weakly. She leaned forward with a hand over her heart. "Then…then that means…Benjamin could be in danger."

"I'm afraid so. Which is why you are all here."

"But…what gold? What gold am I meant…" Benjamin shook his head in bewilderment. "…to have rights over?"

Marjorie tilted her head back on the pillow. She was obviously running out of energy. Felicity leaned forward and took her hand. Marjorie smiled. "Can you tell him, dear?"

"I…I think so." Felicity moistened her lips. "The rough draft of the treaty's content has been made known in a PhD that's recently been submitted." She reached back and picked up her shoulder bag. "I've still got the text of it in my bag." Felicity pulled out the piece of paper and unfolded it. "It says that anyone finding gold will be exempt from paying taxes on any of the gold that stays in the country in which it's found." She looked up. "This was presumably to ensure that there were plenty of funds available locally to pay for the mining venture." She ran her finger along the writing and then read out loud: "...*have rightful claim on any gold found within sixty leagues of their point of landing. This right shall extend to the descendants of those who discover the land—if they can prove lineage.*" She looked up at Benjamin. "And you can prove lineage."

Benjamin rubbed his forehead. "Who else knows about this?"

Phoebe, who had been standing in the background, said brusquely, "A computer storing a summary of the results of the genetic testing of indigenous Australians was hacked into six months ago. We have to assume that information about Mr. Bidjara is known."

Archie flexed his shoulders. His hands were deep in the pockets of his camouflage jacket, as if to restrain himself from bursting out like a coiled spring. "The fact that someone has tried to kill you, Benjy boy, is a fair indication of that."

"What!" exclaimed Felicity. She turned to Benjamin and stared at him. "When? You didn't tell me that!"

Benjamin shrugged apologetically. "It was the...um, little fracas, the break-in that the police were investigating at my place."

"I thought it was just a burglary."

"No. A gun was involved...but the police didn't want that widely known."

"Oh," she said weakly.

Benjamin turned back to Marjorie. "How far is sixty leagues?"

Phoebe answered in Marjorie's stead. "A league could be a Portuguese maritime league, but it is more likely to be a geometric league—the equivalent of 2.67 nautical miles. So we're talking about three hundred kilometers, roughly."

Marjorie nodded her thanks to Phoebe. "You now know why Phoebe is so indispensable to me." She smiled. "Do go on, dear."

Phoebe blew out her cheeks. "A distance of that radius from Warrnambool would include all of Victoria's main gold mining areas—certainly the golden triangle of Stawell, Ballarat and Bendigo."

"Is gold still mined there today?" asked Benjamin.

"Yes, both alluvial and quartz body mining is still being carried out. One mine aims to produce three million tonnes of ore in the next ten years. With ten grams per tonne of high grade gold, that's roughly one million ounces. And with gold at 1,232 US dollars per ounce, that's about 1.3 billion dollars."

"That's just one mine?"

"Yes but a good one."

"How many are there?"

"One company owns most of the tenements. It has five mines and two processing sites."

"And which company is that?"

Felicity broke in and said tiredly, "The Khayef Group."

Phoebe nodded. "And if they can avoid paying corporate tax, minerals resources tax, and state royalties, they gain an extra forty-two percent profit."

Archie whistled.

Marjorie broke in. "So, my dears, we need to take care until I can scare ASIO into a little more action." She patted Felicity's hand. "And we need to keep both you and Benjamin free from harm." She smiled at her. "The very last thing Khayef want is for you to prove there is a Portuguese connection with Victoria. If you proved that, and also presented Benjamin, you would destroy their ability to mine gold free of taxes. Technically, all the gold would belong to Benjamin."

Benjamin passed a hand over his head. "Good grief."

Felicity dabbed at her eyes with a handkerchief. "But what can we do? They've taken the Atlantis stone…"

"What's that, dear?"

"That's the name Benjamin gave to the stone, the one we found that proves the Portuguese came to Warrnambool." Felicity sniffed. "It was such a fabulous find…an amazing historical breakthrough. It's heart-breaking to have lost it…" Felicity lowered her head. "It's wretched to think…they've stolen my computer, my camera, my backup hard drives, my files…everything…and Benjamin is in as much danger as ever."

"And so are you, dear," said Marjorie. "Whilst Benjamin remains alive, they will be concerned that you don't find anything else proving a Portuguese connection."

Benjamin looked up to the ceiling. A faint breeze caused the dried remains of a fly to shiver in a spider's web on the lampshade. He watched it. Was he a fly or was he a spider? What did his instincts tell him? Could he see through his anger and the emotion he felt for Felicity? He sat with his head bowed, waiting.

The fly was dead. The spider was not.

He sat up, squared his shoulders, and said, "There is a chance that Felicity can put a spanner in Khayef's plans."

"What?" said Felicity, spinning around.

Benjamin faced her. "Didn't you tell me that you had a fair idea where the other copy of the treaty is, the one Khayef claims to have —the one in Sardinia?"

Silence hung in the room as the beginnings of hope began to stir.

Marjorie turned her head. "Do tell me about it, dear."

Felicity recounted how she had become convinced that the real Sardinian treaty was inside the statue of the elephant in Cagliari. She trailed off. "If we could get it, it would change everything. The police would have proof that Khayef's treaty was the stolen British copy."

Marjorie turned her head. "Archie?"

Archie rubbed his chin. "Could be doable. I'd probably need to take Felicity with me so I could navigate any historical issues."

"I'd like you to take Benjamin too, so you can keep him out of harm's way for a while." Marjorie looked at Felicity and smiled. "How would you and Benjamin like to spend some time in Sardinia? Phoebe and I will sort out the paperwork and organize the funding."

Benjamin raised a questioning eye to Felicity. Her lips were pressed together, and she was looking pale. She gave a single nod and lowered her head.

"We'll go," he said, "as long as we don't do anything that might put Felicity in danger."

"Good," said Marjorie. She turned to Archie. "Archie, it has to be you who leads the team. You understand risks and can assess danger."

Archie nodded, accepting it in much the same way as if he'd been asked to nip down to the corner store and buy a carton of milk.

"That's fine, then, dears." She turned to Benjamin. "Do you have a passport?"

"Er, no!"

"See Phoebe about it before you go. She'll take your photograph and, if you email your details later today, she will get your application fast-tracked. Expect to leave within a week." Marjorie lay back and folded her hands together. However she had not finished speaking. "Benjamin," she said, "when are you planning to travel up north?"

Benjamin blinked in surprise. He'd only finished making plans to head up to the Kimberley the previous day. "Um…I'll be going up the day after tomorrow but only for two days."

Marjorie nodded her approval. "I'm pleased to hear it. Come and see me when you get back." She closed her eyes. "Stay safe, all of you. I'll be praying for you."

Some minutes later, Benjamin, Archie, and Felicity took their leave. As they walked out to the ute, Benjamin murmured, "Archie, you wouldn't by any chance possess a taser?"

Archie said nothing.

Chapter 12

Benjamin watched the Cessna 210 taxi up to the end of the dirt runway in a plume of dust. Ken McLeod, the pilot, was a flying padre with the Uniting Church. He had promised to pick Benjamin up in two days' time when he would be flying from Halls Creek back to Kununurra.

As the plane hurtled down the runway, Benjamin threw his swag over his shoulders and began to walk across the sparse scrubland to the town he'd vowed never to set foot in again.

Small white houses with deep verandas were set out in a grid pattern reflecting the institutionalizing hand of the white man. Rusted car bodies and the glint of light on discarded glass bottles was evidence of the town's cultural torment. The comfort and convenience of Western ways had come at a terrible cost—the degrading of a people's identity, meaning and purpose. Smart phones rather than the wisdom of the elders were now defining the identity of the young, introducing them to concepts they were poorly equipped to manage. The result was a growing culture of resentment, passivity, and hopelessness.

He scuffed his way through the red dust to the town, in a sour mood. However, his grim thoughts were sabotaged by the sight of a group of children who were running and skipping their way toward him. They were accompanied, inevitably, by a motley pack of the town's dogs.

None of the children wore anything more than a pair of shorts. As they came closer, their curiosity gave way to shyness. Big eyes— dark, liquid pools—stared at Benjamin from beneath tousled hair. More than a few had snotty noses, but they nonetheless looked adorable…and, as Benjamin knew only too well, deceptively inno- cent. The sight of them began triggering memories of the past. Rather surprisingly, they were happy thoughts—memories of messing about at the waterhole with children just like those running toward him. He looked over to the hills in the northeast. That's where he'd gone with the women after the dry season to dig up nests of harvester ants and collect their store of grass seeds. He particu- larly remembered walking with the old men along the creek bed as they taught him the names of the bushes and trees…and what they were good for. He had loved that. To know about the land around him, the trees, the stories—that was what centered him and stilled him…before he'd had to return to…

Benjamin greeted the children in their own language. They responded with a barrage of questions that quickly established who he was. They danced around him as he walked into the town, demanding to know if he was carrying anything interesting. He led them back to the schoolhouse where the students were at morning recess—a fact that explained why so many of them were available to meet him. Benjamin was not at all sure they wouldn't have come even if they had been in class. Despite government incentives, chil- dren didn't need much of an excuse to absent themselves from school. Benjamin had been the exception; he'd loved school and seen it as a place of safety…of escape.

Ten minutes later, he was standing in front of his old home, the house of his uncle and an assortment of relatives who came and went week by week. It appeared to be deserted. His uncle's recent death would explain that: no one wanted to go near the place. Benjamin mounted the steps and opened the front door. The house had been cleaned out. There was no sign of his uncle ever having lived there. Even his uncle's sour, musky smell was gone. The house was completely bare. It was highly unusual.

Benjamin stepped from the front room, back into the hallway. He stood there, staring at the handle of the door on the left. Flakes of paint had worn off to reveal the metal underneath. It was the handle his uncle had turned to check that he was asleep—before opening the door on the right, to his sister's room.

He screwed his eyes shut to block out the memories of the whispered wheedling, her cry, the slap…and her muffled sobbing. The familiar voice shrieked at him: "You should have done something!" He wiped a hand across his eyes and walked down the cracked linoleum to the back door. Benjamin pushed his way through the flimsy fly-screen door and stepped out to the weedy, baked earth of the backyard. Very little had changed. The lemon tree in the rear corner had obviously not been watered for some time; it was barely alive. His uncle had loved it. He had routinely peed against the trunk. "It's good for it," he would say before using the hose to wash his pee into the soil, occasionally swishing the water over his feet to cool them.

The other tree was still there. The big one—the one on which he'd built a swing with some rope he'd found—the rope she had used.

Behind him, a gust of wind pushed the fly-screen door open. It creaked and groaned a little before banging shut again with a "klat." Someone had come in the front door. He listened to the footsteps. As he did, a swirl of hot wind raised a spiral of red dust. A williwilli. It swayed briefly like a live thing before it whisked into the air and dissipated. Benjamin shivered. He knew it to be the spirit of his sister—restless and crying for help. He put his head in his hands.

"Ay, Benji."

Benjamin looked around to see the flat, impassive face of a woman looking at him through the fly-screen. Which auntie was it? Aah, yes…red bandanna…same face…a lot older. Auntie Doola. He nodded, "Auntie." It wasn't much of a greeting after twelve years of absence…but then again, not much more was expected.

"You stayin'?"

"Nah, just visiting." Benjamin instinctively slipped into the patois of his childhood, adopting the unemotional monotones of his people. It was brutal, direct, and economical. No energy was ever wasted on such niceties as 'please' or 'thank you.'

Auntie Doola scowled. "This bad place." She paused. "Where's ya swag?"

"At the schoolhouse."

Silence followed. The woman continued to stare at him through the fly-screen. Eventually, she said, "Jabirrjabirr waitin' for you."

Benjamin knew better than to ask how it was that one of his people's elders already knew he was in town. He looked at her, asking with his silence for more information.

Auntie Doola turned her head and nodded over her shoulder. "Men's place." Taking understanding for granted, she turned and padded back down the hall on her bare feet.

Benjamin felt a prickle of unease. The men's place was not somewhere anyone went without invitation. It was on the other side of town from the airstrip, near the bank of the river. The men met there to talk their business under the shade of some big trees—pretty much as they had done for centuries. The earth under the trees had been worn flat over the years. A fire was sometimes lit in the middle of the clearing for special occasions. The fire used for communal cooking was closer to the town, and everyone gathered there. It was a popular place, particularly if anyone was cooking kangaroo tail. Incongruously, this delicacy could be bought frozen from the tiny supermarket in town, albeit at considerable expense. Hunting, he reflected sadly, was no longer seen to be a priority. The women would burn the hair off the tail in the fire and scrape it clean before wrapping it in foil and nesting it between rocks that had been heated in the fire.

Fire.

Fire was important here. It allowed hospitality and communality. As a child, he had always stood at the back, away from the fire, acutely conscious of his white skin—not wanting to be visible but desperately wanting to belong. Hiding in the background sometimes allowed him to hear things he shouldn't have heard. On one occasion, the men had talked about the local welfare officer. He was a half-caste like Benjamin but was generally considered to be a good bloke—at least when the men were sober. The officer had asked if he could receive the initiation rights that would make him a member of the community. Benjamin winced as he remembered the conversation.

"We took 'is blood and made a scar inside 'is arm by the elbow. We didn't tell 'im 'ee got the scar on the wrong arm. 'Ee not one of us."

This remark had struck Benjamin in the heart. He was at the age when boys were being tapped on the shoulder and went missing with the older men for five weeks. They returned, still sore from the initiation cuts on their flesh, but they returned as people who belonged—who had begun their journey to manhood. Their initiation process would continue over three months, a necessary concession to the white men who were insisting that the kids go to school. The old men spoke of days when the process had taken five years.

Initiation signaled a big change in a boy's life. Before it happened, kids could run pretty wild, larking about down by the river, playing string games…and annoying the girls. However, initiation quietened them down. The boys would be taken in hand. They would begin to hear the dreamtime stories, *their* story…and learn the responsibilities that attended being a man.

No one had tapped Benjamin on the shoulder.

A short time later, he'd found his sister hanging from the gum tree in the backyard.

When the Christian Brothers came to the remote school a month later, they had been impressed with Benjamin's school grades and offered him one of the scholarships to Rostrevor College reserved for remote indigenous people. The school was in Adelaide, on the other side of the continent.

He had accepted the scholarship immediately.

Benjamin swatted at the flies…or was it at the conflicting emotions that were assaulting him? He threaded his way through the low scrub and spinifex to the river. It was really little more than a creek which dried out to rock pools for some months of the year.

There was, however, a rich stand of trees along its banks—eucalypts mostly, including woollybutt and iron bark. The wood of the iron bark was highly resistant to fire, so lengths of it were often used in the cooking fire to turn and arrange the food.

Benjamin could smell wood-smoke as he approached the trees sheltering the men's place. The fire was alight. Unusual. It was warm…and it was early in the day.

Three men were sitting on the ground on the far side of the meeting place. Benjamin recognized them immediately.

Jabirrjabirr was sitting in the middle, with one leg cocked in front of him and the other straight out…pretty much how Benjamin remembered him sitting twelve years ago. He had scruffy work-boots on and a battered hat. His gray whiskery beard seemed to have grown a little in length over the years. A thin wisp of smoke drifted up from a small fire on the edge of the fire pit.

Benjamin stood respectfully, just back from the beaten earth of the meeting place, waiting. It was rude to come to a man's fire without permission. The men watched him in silence for some time, assessing him. Finally, Jabirrjabirr raised his head slightly. Benjamin came forward, not looking into their eyes, greeting each of them by name as he sat down.

More silence followed.

"Ay Benji, been longtime. You big now…a man," murmured Jabirrjabirr.

"I still have much to learn," said Ben politely.

"Why you come back?"

"Sky fella, bush padre, tell me to come here and talk." Benjamin knew that it was, in fact, Jabirrjabirr who had asked him to come. The question meant that he was still being assessed.

Silence.

"Your uncle…gone. Bad business."

"My uncle…gone. Good business."

Jabirrjabirr showed no expression, then nodded. "Bad man."

Jabirrjabirr's comment caused Benjamin to react. "Yes. Why you not help us…help my sister?"

"You angry, Benji?"

"Little bit. Mostly sad. Very sad."

"So you run away and become a whitefella?"

"You say I don't belong. Maybe you give me initiation scar on wrong arm. Maybe no initiation at all. I am 'Throwback,' remember."

A long silence followed.

"Some things we not allowed to do, Benji. Our ancestor spirits watch."

"But my mother was Kija."

"Your mother was half-caste…your father from mob down south. Maybe 'ee half-cast too. Look at your skin."

"I can't be blackfella…and can't be whitefella." Benjamin dropped his head.

Jabirrjabirr picked up a small stone and started tapping it on the ground rhythmically. *Tap, tap…tap, tap.* As he did, he looked up at Benjamin, eyes glittering in his weather-beaten face. "Benji, it's time you heard some stories. You got no one else to tell 'em, so I tell you."

Jabirrjabirr looked ahead, seeing into another time. "Your mother was a good woman. Good lookin'. Caused a few fights. She married your dad…a Gunditjmara man from long way. Jabirrjabirr inclined his chin to the south. "'Ee come up with a mob of blokes to work on the big water job."

Benjamin knew that Jabirrjabirr was referring to the huge Ord River irrigation scheme that had transformed agriculture in the Eastern Kimberleys.

Benjamin watched the smoke from the fire curl through the tree branches and caress the leaves before disappearing into the sky. Jabirrjabirr continued. "Your mum was another bloke's missus before, but she run away with her daughter. She became your father's missus and got pregnant…with you." Jabirrjabirr kept up the rhythmic tapping of the stone on the ground.

"But you didn't want to be born. Got stuck." *Tap, tap…tap, tap.*

Benjamin found the rhythm soothing, like a mother's heartbeat. It was quite at odds with the drama of the story he was hearing.

"Your father died trying to get her to hospital where you was born. 'Ee got the mission bloke to drive you to hospital but 'is truck got stuck in the creek in the floods. Your dad got your mum out and went back for the other fella but both died." Jabirrjabirr paused before adding, "Your dad was a good fella."

Tap, tap…tap, tap.

Benjamin was stunned. He had known nothing of this story, nor had he appreciated the drama surrounding his birth. His father hadn't run off as he'd always supposed; he had loved his wife enough to risk his life. His head swam as he sought to understand the significance of what he had learned. His dad was…good, even heroic. He had cared for his woman.

Jabirrjabirr continued. "You was born…but your mum never came good. Became a drinker and lost her looks." Jabirrjabirr put a hand on his chest. "Sick heart. She died when you was little." He looked at Benjamin. "You seen her grave?"

Benjamin nodded.

Silence. *Tap, tap…tap, tap.* Curling smoke. Swirling thoughts.

"Did you bury…my father?" asked Benjamin eventually. How strange it was to say those words, "my father." He couldn't remember having ever said them before. Tears began to well up in his eyes. He could now speak of him—and know him to be, as he was, Gunditjmara.

"We put 'im on a platform in a tree."

Benjamin knew that this was conventional practice. After several months, the bones would be collected, painted with red ocher, and laid to rest in a special place. He blurted, "Did anyone get his bones?"

Jabirrjabirr looked away and shrugged.

Benjamin closed his eyes. No one had got them. No one had laid them to rest. Over the years, the tree platform would have collapsed…and the dingoes would have got to the bones. Benjamin pinched the top of his nose to repress a surge of emotion and deep sadness. His father may have been a good fella, but he was not one of them.

Tap, tap…Tap, tap. The heartbeat continued.

Jabirrjabirr glanced at Benjamin. "Now you know your story.

Every man should know his story. This…your story." The tapping stopped abruptly. "Now I tell you another story. This…a story of what happens in Kija country…maybe long time ago, maybe not."

Benjamin was instantly aware that the mood of this story was different. The very air was scratchy and violent. There was a harsh edge to Jabirrjabirr's voice.

"For longtime, if a fella sneaks into our land from another blackfella mob wanting trouble, we catch him and kill him. But killing is bad. If the other tribe find the dead body, they have to start a war and kill for pay back. This bad. Many people can get killed, perhaps for longtime. So, we hide the body so 'ee can't be found." He looked at Benjamin with bleak eyes. "No body. No payback. It's good."

The smoke from the fire now twisted and turned, writhing as if in agony. Benjamin knew he was about to be told something that would be significant to him. He held his breath.

Jabirrjabirr continued. "You know them termite mounds? We got many sorts in our country. Big ones, small ones, fat ones, sharp ones. The critters always busy mending and building with mud. We put a hole in one and put the fella inside. Little time later, critters fix the hole…and 'ees gone. No one sees 'im."

Barely pausing for breath, Jabirrjabirr asked, "You know why your uncle had a limp?"

Benjamin blinked at the change in direction of the conversation. "Um, yeah. He told us he had an accident while fencing up at the homestead."

Jabirrjabirr fixed Benjamin with the same bleak look. "'Ee not tell truth. 'Ee limp 'cos we spear 'im in the thigh."

Benjamin was shocked. This was the most severe form of punishment a blackfella could receive short of death. "Why?"

"'Ee hurt a girl."

An awful possibility of the significance of this conversation was beginning to suggest itself. "He raped my sister," he said. "Often. Bashed me many times to keep me quiet."

Silence.

Jabirrjabirr continued as if he hadn't heard. "'Ees not here any more. No one knows where 'ee gone. Maybe longways." He pursed his lips. "No sorry business for 'im. Can't do it if there's no body."

Benjamin was appalled. He asked carefully, "Did he hurt another girl…recently?"

"Maybe." Jabirrjabirr looked directly at Benjamin. "Real black-fellas, we look after our women. We not shit."

Benjamin nodded slowly.

Jabirrjabirr continued savagely. "If you have blackfella heart, you will look after your women."

The challenge, more than the harshness of the language, kept Benjamin mute.

Jabirrjabirr got to his feet, picked up a machete lying beside him and said, "You, me…we go up the river and have a look at some old places, eh?"

Benjamin stood up, bewildered, trying to keep pace with what was happening.

Together, they made their way through the trees beside the creek. The mood had again changed completely. It was apparent that Jabirrjabirr remembered how much Benjamin had loved bush-walking with the men as a child. He was continuing to teach him as if the twelve years of absence had never happened.

"What's 'ee good for?" he asked, pointing to a small tree.

Benjamin replied immediately, "Crush his leaves and put 'em in a waterhole. Stuns the fish, and they float to the surface."

Jabirrjabirr laughed. "Bit like whitefella grog and sit-down money, eh. They put it in our waterhole…and we float on the surface an' do nothing. Forget that we are fish."

It was too appallingly true for Benjamin to laugh.

Benjamin caught site of a yellow-billed spoonbill swaying its beak back and forth in the shallows. He stopped to look around him. So much of this land lived within his very soul…and yet so much of it remained alien to him. The rock art of the ancient inhabitants was among the oldest in the world—but he hadn't been taken to the caves to see the special places. He hadn't seen the engraved images, the hand stencils of his ancestors, the animal motifs or the mysterious *gwion, gwion*. And yet the land, the country, spoke to him. He could feel it. It was full of life. It carried the song lines and trading paths of his people that stretched from the desert to the coast.

"What's 'ee good for?" demanded Jabirrjabirr again.

Benjamin looked to where he was pointing and laughed. "Don't start a fire with that one. He's stinkwood. Easy carving. Good for coolamon."

"Have you made a coolamon?"

"Nah."

"You make one. It's men's work. Men make the coolamon for the women."

Benjamin began to understand what Jabirrjabirr was doing. In his own way, he was inviting Benjamin to engage in tasks that the men in the community did—fully initiated men.

"Here, I'll cut you a piece." Jabirrjabirr set about cutting the tree trunk with deft, economical strokes.

Twenty minutes later, Benjamin was carrying a log of wood under an arm. Goodness knows what the airline flying him back to Melbourne would think of it.

Things became even more complicated when Jabirrjabirr stopped by a small tree and tapped it with the back of the machete, listening to the sound that indicated that the heart of the trunk had been hollowed out by termites. "What's him?"

"Bloodwood. Good for didgeridoo."

"You wanna make one?"

Benjamin grinned. He was loving the experience of being back in the bush, so strange and yet so familiar. It was magical, and he didn't want it to end. "Yes," he said.

Two hours later, as the heat began to shimmer on the distant horizon, Benjamin and Jabirrjabirr retraced their steps back to the men's place. When they arrived, the two elders were still seated in exactly the same position…and the fire was continuing to burn quietly.

As Benjamin placed his long piece of bloodwood and his stumpy log of stinkwood on the ground, Jabirrjabirr stood directly in front of him and challenged him. "You friend with us people now?"

The directness of the question was startling, but Benjamin answered truthfully. "Yes."

"You had a bad spirit."

Benjamin said nothing.

The two old men stood up as Jabirrjabirr picked up a piece of flat rock and went to the fire. He used a stick to scrape some burning coals onto the rock. Smoke drifted from the coals as he returned to stand in front of Benjamin. Then Jabirrjabirr began to chant in a flat nasal tone, making sounds that Benjamin didn't understand even though he knew their language. The two old men beside him began to stamp their thin legs on the ground in unison. As Jabirrjabirr chanted, he moved forward and waved the smoking coals around all sides of Benjamin. Then, he stopped in front of him…and spat a thin spray of spit into Benjamin's face.

Jabirrjabirr was seeking to exorcise the evil spirits afflicting Benjamin…and was declaring him to be a friend.

Chapter 13

Felicity woke early to the experimental chirps of the first birds heralding the dawn chorus. She ran her hand through her hair and reached for her dressing gown. Her thoughts immediately turned to Benjamin. He would have spent his first night in the Kimberley. How was he feeling? What was it like returning to his home after so many years? Even more alarmingly: would he want to return to the Kimberley to live?

She doubted it, but the thought still haunted her. It was curious how bereft she felt, even though he'd only been absent for a day. He was a very long way away.

Felicity pushed her feet into her slippers and went to her desk, where her brother's old computer was sitting. He'd kindly given it to her as a replacement for the one that had been stolen.

She sighed, summoned her resolve and began the tedious business of reconfiguring the computer for her own use. Fortunately, she had uploaded most of her documents to the cloud, so it was simply a question of downloading them. Her personal photographs, however, took more time, as she had stored them on some DVDs. These had been placed in a pile alongside her music CDs, and escaped the burglar's attention.

The big question was: how much of her data concerning the Atlantis stone had she remembered to put on the cloud? Had she uploaded the photographs she'd taken of it?

Three hours later, she was still in her dressing gown and hadn't yet had breakfast. The yells, bangs, and chatter of her brother's family had come and gone. She was now alone. With her heart in her mouth, she accessed the folder she'd downloaded from the cloud containing her files on the mahogany ship.

Oh no! No, no, no.

None of the pictures that she had taken of the Atlantis stone were there. She'd not uploaded any of them to the cloud.

A sickening wave of disappointment washed over her. She berated herself savagely. *Stupid, stupid, stupid. A once-in-a-lifetime discovery…and now no record of it. All gone. Lost.* There was no evidence of the extraordinary discovery she and Benjamin had made. She put her head in her hands in anguish, too heartbroken and sick of heart to cry.

Eventually, she did cry.

Half an hour later, she forced herself to get some breakfast. She slopped into the kitchen and put the kettle on. After straightening all the chairs, she pushed the fruit bowl until it was perfectly in the center of the table. Then she cried again.

She made herself a cup of coffee, returned to her computer, and downloaded her emails. One was from her old colleague at the museum. She rolled her eyes when she saw the subject line: 'Portuguese kangaroo.' It seemed there would be no respite from being tormented by riddles left by ancient Portuguese explorers.

The email recounted the discovery of an old Portuguese prayer book, dated between 1580 and 1620. The book was thought to have once belonged to a nun named Caterina de Carvalho, as her name had been written in it. One paragraph in the book began with a letter D. What made it extraordinary was that it had been decorated with a picture of a creature not unlike a kangaroo. As she continued reading, she was saddened to learn that the prayer book would not be coming to Australia or, indeed, Portugal. It was now in the New York gallery, 'Les Enluminures.'

Felicity leaned back in her chair, stretched her legs and looked down at her purple fluffy slippers. Maybe, just maybe, she could find the emotional energy to continue her historical investigations—despite the heartbreak and setbacks she'd suffered. What was far less certain was whether she had the intestinal fortitude to cope with the threat to Benjamin posed by Khayef. Did she have what it took to challenge the plans of a big corporation? She picked up a pencil and banged it on the desk. The lead broke.

She told herself that she would do whatever it took to keep Benjamin safe. But Sardinia! Could she really pull it off?

The front door bell rang.

Felicity went down the hall and looked through the spy hole. It was Archie, and he was holding a small parcel. She breathed a sigh of relief and opened the door.

Archie looked her up and down. "Sleep late?"

Damn. She'd been so preoccupied that she'd forgotten she was still in her slippers and dressing gown. "No. Got up too early. Coffee?"

"No, I won't, thanks. I just came to ask if you've got my number on speed dial…and to give you something."

She pulled out her phone. "What's your number?"

Archie told her. He went on to say, "If you're uncertain of anything, the very slightest thing, call me. Even if you don't leave a message, I'll be around here in three minutes. Second thing: Don't open the door to anyone you don't know. Call me instead." He ran his eyes over the front windows of the house, presumably assessing their security. "Got it?"

Felicity nodded. "Is it really that bad?"

Archie gave a laconic grin. "Plan for the worst…"

"…and hope for the best," Felicity finished. She looked at Archie's weather-beaten face and grizzled beard. "Are we going to be able to pull this Sardinia thing off?"

Archie looked at her steadily for a moment. "If the treaty is where you say it is, we've got a good chance of getting it." He trapped the small parcel under his arm as he fished around in his pocket for a matchstick. "I've already organized the gear we need. That's why I'm a bit late coming here this morning."

"But what about Benjamin? He's never been outside of Australia—or anywhere much for that matter."

Archie smiled. "Flick, your bloke has just heisted a one hundred and twenty thousand-dollar car from a Melbourne lawyer—and was calm as you like. He reads people and situations well. He'll be okay." He pulled the parcel from under his arm. "And he's asked me to give you this. Sorry it's taken so long to get it to you." He handed it to her. "See ya later. Remember, call me if you have even the faintest suspicion of trouble."

"Righty ho."

Felicity weighed the parcel in her hand as she took it through to the back room. *A parcel from Benjamin.* She ran a finger over the top of it. It felt good to have something tangible from him—whatever it was. She undid the brown wrapping paper slowly, prolonging the pleasure.

The object inside was made of a honey-colored wood with dark highlights running through it. She lifted it out. It was a wooden goblet. What made it extraordinary was the fact that two wooden rings encircled the thin stem. The wooden bangles were trapped between the base and the bowl of the cup. It had obviously all been cut from a single piece of wood. She held it up and jiggled the two rings with her finger. It was exquisitely made.

Within the brown paper, there was a note:

Dear Felicity,

   I meant to give this to you the other day but events conspired against it. It is a Celtic friendship cup—just a small token of my gratitude for your friendship. Its diagnostic feature is, of course, the two trapped rings.

   Your friend,

   Benjamin

Felicity sat down, placed the cup beside her computer, and stared at it. Occasionally, she reached out and stroked its curves.

After some minutes of this, she shook her head to pull herself out of her reverie and booted up the computer...but the thrall of Benjamin's gift continued. Idly, she typed 'Celtic friendship cup' into her search engine.

Nothing with that name was shown.

Google gave its nearest interpretation: 'Celtic lovers' cup'...and there was a picture of one with its two trapped rings.

Doran Khayef glared at the view from his window. Normally, he enjoyed it. He could look across the heart of Sydney toward Circular Quay where the ferries bustled in and out. They serviced the most beautiful harbor in the world. The iconic 'coat hanger,' Sydney Harbour Bridge, could be seen to the left. He glowered. Considering the price he had paid to secure two floors of this building, he damn well should enjoy the view. He was on the twenty-first floor. Going higher would have cost more. *One day...one day.*

Khayef balled his fist. Andrew Carter would be waiting for him in the reception area outside his office; he would leave him there a while longer, stewing. Khayef was a man who knew how to make apprehension and fear work for him. Carter would be feeling uncomfortable despite sitting in one of the deep-buttoned Chesterfield settees hired to decorate his suite of offices.

He wanted the office area to look like an elite gentleman's club. The floors had been covered with carefully renovated hardwood planks. Expensive rugs had been placed between leather armchairs; and discrete spotlights highlighted antique oil paintings on the paneled walls. Glass cases holding old maritime artifacts completed the illusion. By the time a visitor had been whisked up the building in a glass-sided lift and spent time in the large reception area, they were convinced of the respectability of the Khayef Group...and intimidated.

Personally, Khayef hated the décor. He preferred the modern, minimalist look.

He glanced to the left of the vista before him…but, as usual, he couldn't see as far west as he wanted…yet. Someday, his building project on the foreshore to the west would soar into the sky—high enough to rival anything else in Sydney. But he had a cash flow problem. He needed money now, not in two years' time. He would have to do something very quickly. *Damn!*

He turned around and punched the intercom button. "Send Carter in."

Khayef had his back to Carter when he entered. "What did you find and what does she know?" Khayef demanded.

"Ah-hem." Carter cleared his throat. "Ms. Anderson's computer only contained further details of what she'd already told me. But I think we were wise to be concerned; she's been very industrious. The case for the Portuguese being the first to discover South-East Australia is growing…but is, as yet, a long way from being compelling."

Khayef turned around and banged his fist on the desk. "It must be compelling. Use her to get anything that will prove it." He glared at Carter. "What we can't afford are any complications arising from this fellow, Bidjara." He thrust his head forward. "Are you sure he's the only one with the Portuguese genes?"

Carter shrugged. "As far as we know but nothing is certain. That's why we need to ensure that his link to the…er, Portuguese connection is never established."

Khayef pursed his lips as he reviewed what he'd heard. After a while, he waved at Carter dismissively. "You're off the case as of now. I'll organize others to take over the business that needs to be done. Just keep your ear to the ground for any historical complications."

"Yes sir." Carter paused. "There was something we found in Ms. Anderson's possession that I can't make sense of."

"Why not?" barked Khayef. "It's what I pay you for."

"Aah, because there are no notes explaining its significance." Carter drew breath. "She's taken rather a lot of pictures of a stone with engravings on it. It's not anything I know of or have seen written about. Fortunately, we have the stone. Our man took it with the rest of Ms. Anderson's things because it looked archaeological." Carter sniffed. "I think it was as well he did."

"So, we're clear to push ahead with our claim using the treaty?"

"Yes sir. Whoever did the authentication of the treaty has done an excellent job. And I've put together a plausible cover story to explain how the treaty came into our possession."

"What is it? I'd better know for when the bastards grill me."

"I'll send through a full briefing. But essentially, the story is that we have the Sardinian copy of the treaty. We bought it from a dealer in Argentina. He had access to it because it was taken there by the Germans who occupied Sardinia during the war." Carter shrugged. "The English will, of course, suspect it is the stolen document, but they won't be able to prove it."

Khayef nodded. "Right. Get on with it. Tell reception to find Eddie and send him here."

"Certainly, sir."

Before Carter had even left the room, Khayef was thinking about his next problem. It was one that would call for Eddie's particular skills…and those of an organization he despised, the Saracens. They were a particularly vicious motorbike gang. Khayef had aligned himself with them because their muscle proved invaluable in pushing his projects through. They exerted considerable influence among both building contractors and the unions.

He pursed his lips. *Power.* The country didn't understand power. It didn't understand the way things were done in the real world— certainly, the rest of the world. Power brought order. It got things done. And, he conceded, it also made you rich.

There was a knock on the door.

"Come."

Eddie came in and stood with his hands folded in front of him.

Khayef scowled. "The bloke you chose screwed up last time. I don't want any more mistakes. I want Bidjara dead within a fortnight."

"I'll see to it, sir."

Marjorie lay back in the cane deck chair that someone had pulled into the sun. Doing so made her straw hat tip onto her nose. She laughed, took it off, and placed it on the grass beside a jug of lemonade.

The garden around her was looking wonderful, if a little unkempt. Spring was knocking diffidently at the door, signaling its arrival with crocuses and daffodils. A profusion of growth was springing up from a warming earth impatient to bring life. She smiled as she watched two shield bugs crawl along one arm of her deck chair. They were co-joined at their rear agreeing to walk together whilst propagating their species. *Very sensible.*

Marjorie's thoughts turned to Benjamin and Felicity. She loved their youthful optimism, their naïveté, and the potential that they embodied. Life's griefs had wounded them both, but they hadn't yet been diminished by its excesses or by its cynicism. Much was still possible. She wondered whether they would walk through life together; hopefully they would.

A squeak from the garden gate returned Marjorie to the present. She turned and saw Benjamin walking over the grass toward her. As usual, he was wearing jeans and his artisan's canvas top.

Benjamin nodded. "Archie gave me your message. You wanted to see me?" He looked at her for a moment. "How are you feeling?"

"I'm having a good day," she smiled. "Thanks for coming, Benjamin. Phoebe's got your passport. Collect it from her before you go." She pointed to the chair beside her. "Now tell me, how was your trip?"

"Surprising…disturbing…and liberating," he said, sitting down. "I'm glad I went."

"It was time you did."

Benjamin nodded. "And is it time you told me what's wrong with you?"

"I have cancer. Terminal. I'll be in Melbourne having a canula put into me while you are in Sardina."

"I'm sorry to hear that."

A butterfly fluttered between them untidily as if it had forgotten where it was going.

After a moment's silence, Benjamin said, "You're a remarkable woman."

She acknowledged his compliment by inclining her head. "Death is a door we must all pass through at some stage. It holds no fears for me." She raised her chin. "Do you believe it is a door, Benjamin, or simply nothingness?"

Benjamin lowered his head. "No blackfella thinks his ancestors are ever truly gone. They watch."

"Hmm. But it's not just a question of cultural beliefs is it? It's a question of what is true."

Benjamin waited for Marjorie to elaborate.

She liked that about him—he gave time. She eased her head back. "Any spiritual claim concerning humanity needs to make sense of why we live and why we die. To be careless of these two great mysteries is a culpable folly."

She saw him smile and shake his head. Perhaps she was being too strong. *Better ease back.*

"It seems to me," Benjamin said slowly, "that we humans are either obsessed with death or we hide from it. We refer to it in hushed tones with euphemisms."

"Silly, isn't it?"

Benjamin nodded.

"Why is it, do you think, that we have this innate compulsion to avoid death and survive for as long as possible? Is it just a useful instinct we've developed to help us propagate our species?"

Benjamin said nothing. Marjorie glanced at him, trying to gauge how he was feeling.

He was fine. His silence was making space for thought, not disengagement.

She continued. "It's interesting, isn't it, that this instinct doesn't switch off once we've performed our biological duty and had children. We don't just surrender to death, calm in the knowledge that we have done our job. Instead, we become social burdens, clog up supermarket queues, and use up more than our fair share of medical resources."

Benjamin smiled, then lowered his head again. "Death is not nice. It ruptures bonds of love. I hate it."

"But surely death is a good thing. It clears the stage of old organisms and makes space for new ones to develop. Death drives the whole engine of biological evolution. It has resulted in you."

He looked at her. "But you don't believe that."

She smiled. "No. It's a cold, empirical answer that, whilst partly true, doesn't address the full mystery of why life exists."

"So, does the answer get warmer?"

Marjorie acknowledged Benjamin's question with a nod. "I think it has to do with a man who overcame death, whose love took him to a cross." She smiled. "That's a story that warms things up a lot—and finding your place in it will introduce you to an eternal cosmic adventure." She reached out and patted his arm. "Pop inside, dear, and see Phoebe."

Evening had fallen by the time Benjamin took his leave of Phoebe and Marjorie. His time with them had been surreal. Marjorie, in particular, had taken him places with her thinking that he'd never been before. She'd ripped apart the lazy, safe place he'd hidden himself away in.

He felt the passport in his top pocket. It was an odd sensation to own one. He had read the words inside it: '…*requests all those who it may concern to allow the bearer, an Australian Citizen, to pass freely without let or hindrance…*'

Belonging. The idea caused him to think again of Felicity. He had seen almost nothing of her since his return. Archie had encouraged her to spend as many daylight hours as possible with a friend to help ensure her safety. She had chosen to spend her days either with the workmen at the building site or with Gabrielle.

The moon moved behind a cloud. Benjamin looked up. Most of the Milky Way could still be seen. Centaurus, half-man and half-beast, was in mid-leap across the southern sky. Benjamin wondered which he was.

His phone rang. It was Marcus.

"Hello, oh destitute one," said Marcus brightly.

"I'll get cutlery and plates for your next visit."

"Hmph. I'll believe that when it happens. Now listen. I've been getting the goss on Khayef. I've gotta tell you, you wouldn't want to mess with these guys. They're big…and getting bigger. One of their blue ribbon projects is that huge Sydney harbor development. It's been in the news for most of this year. There's a bit of scandal regarding CFMEU union bosses getting backhanders for awarding contracts and ensuring industrial peace. It's even washing up on the shores of some government ministers."[1]

Marcus paused before demanding, "Ben, are you listening?"

"Yep."

"Seriously, Ben. You want to be careful around these guys. The word is, they've got the Saracens doing some of their stand over work. There are all sorts of sweetheart deals going on between them and Khayef. Just be careful, okay?"

"Thanks Marcus, I will. By the way, I'll be out of town for the best part of a week."

"You're heading off for some well-deserved truancy?"

"Sort of."

"Where are you off to?"

"To a place that's well away from nosy people."

Marcus ignored the rebuff. "Come on."

"I might send you a holiday snap."

"Hmph. Well you're probably due for some dull time after all the excitement of your break-in."

"Yeah, a break would be good." *I'm actually going overseas to find a treaty of massive historical significance that will stop me from being killed…and I'll be in the presence of a woman I can't stop thinking about…and I'll be accompanied by a trained killer who suffers PTSD.*

"I'll see you when I get back." Benjamin rang off.

He could smell wood smoke in the crisp night air. The delicious realization came to him that some of the wood smoke was probably coming from his own chimney. A warming fire would be waiting for him at the workshop. He wished, with all his heart that Felicity could be with him to share it. As it was, he was sharing it with Archie. It was his turn to cook tonight. "The food will be fairly light," Archie had warned, "Nothing spicy. You need to sleep and be ready for tomorrow."

Chapter 14

F elicity watched as Archie fiddled with a yellow, hand-held scanner. A cable led from it to the backpack strapped on his back.

"Is it working?" she asked.

Archie was chewing a matchstick. Felicity could see it nodding somewhere between his blonde mustache and beard. "Just checking it now." He placed the scanner on the floor and moved it from side to side while looking at the small screen above the handle. "Hmm. Cagliari's builders seem to have done a fair job putting the reinforcing rods into the concrete floor."

"You can see them?"

"Yeah. Pretty clearly, actually."

"Impressive. How does it work?"

"This little baby is a subsurface imaging radar. It uses unmodulated continuous-wave signals to find listening devices embedded in concrete walls." He grinned. "It's ASIO's best."

She chewed her lip. "But will it be able to find a cavity in a stone elephant?"

"Probably."

"Probably!"

Archie shrugged and returned his attention to the scanner.

Felicity spun around in exasperation.

They had booked a family suite in a hotel on the edge of the ancient city of Cagliari in Sardinia. Benjamin and Archie were sharing the main bedroom; Felicity had her own room to the side. The rooms were basic but comfortable enough. The best feature was the large balcony. Felicity walked outside to join Benjamin who was leaning on the balustrade.

Below her, in the tangle of narrow laneways, the café waiters were busy laying outdoor settings in readiness for the evening trade.

Benjamin was staring at the old city that rose up the hill in front of them. The evening light played on the orange terracotta tiles of the rooftops. Typically, he didn't say a word. His silence seemed to invite her to join in his stillness. She looked out at the ancient buildings and tried to see what he was seeing.

The domes of Cagliari's churches dotted the city. Felicity resisted a compulsion to count them. Everything in Sardinia was so different. Nearly all the buildings were adorned with ornate Romanesque corbels and had shuttered windows above tiny balconies. Geraniums could be seen spilling from pots behind the decorative, wrought iron rails. Some balconies still had the day's washing hanging out on clotheslines. It was enchanting.

Benjamin pointed to the sky just above the horizon. "Can you see them?"

Felicity searched the sky until she saw some tiny black dots where Benjamin was pointing. She watched as the dots resolved themselves into a flock of flamingos. The sun burnished their pink and black wings as they flew overhead, trailing their impossibly long legs behind them.

Benjamin smiled. "Mario, the porter, tells me they fly over almost every night. Evidently, they feed in the salt pans during the day and roost at night in the headwaters of the estuary."

"Why am I not surprised you know this?" Felicity had aimed at levity but was unable to hide a catch in her voice.

It was not lost on Benjamin. "What's the matter?" he asked.

Felicity lowered her head. "Oh…I suppose I'm a little apprehensive about what we are attempting."

Benjamin put a hand on top of hers on the balustrade. "You are resourceful, you speak the language, and you are very bright." He cocked a thumb. "And we've got Archie. I'd say that's a pretty good hand."

She wanted to say, "…and I've got you," but she didn't.

Benjamin turned around. "Archie, will it be okay if Felicity and I head into the old city this evening?"

Archie joined them on the balcony. "Yeah, you're safe enough here. No one knows you…and you're way overdue some time on your own. Enjoy the evening together." He rolled his shoulders. "I'll probably head down to Poetto Beach. They've got live music and beach cafés there." He grinned. "It doesn't really get going 'til late, so don't wait up for me."

Benjamin nodded and took Felicity's arm. It was such an innocent action but its significance for Felicity wasn't lost. "Let's take the map and wander up to the elephant tower. We've got time so see it before the light fades if we leave now. Then we'll have a better idea of what our options might be."

Felicity delighted in the simple pleasure of being with Benjamin as they walked through the narrow streets. Most had cobbled drainways running down the middle which, she thought, must present a fair hazard to the motorbikes and scooters that hurtled down the laneways. They also learned quickly to duck into a doorway whenever a car drove by—the wing mirrors passing dangerously close.

There seemed to be a church every one hundred meters along each road. Felicity pulled Benjamin inside one of them. He trailed behind her. They gazed around at the extravagantly ornate décor—the gold, the carvings, the paintings, the icons.

Benjamin didn't stay long. He edged toward the door.

"What's the matter?"

"Don't know. Wrong feeling. Need to leave."

Back in the laneway, Benjamin breathed deeply. He looked at Felicity apologetically and shrugged, "Don't ask. I don't understand either."

She took him by the arm. "You are a strange fellow, Benjamin Bidjara—but fortunately, fairly nice."

They continued deeper into the heart of the old city. Many of the stone houses lining the laneways had huge wooden doors, some of which had metal knockers cast in the shape of a hand holding a ball.

Benjamin paused to point out a small green lizard warming itself on an ancient wall in the last of the sunshine. Felicity smiled. Benjamin saw very different things from most other people. She stole a glance at him. *I'd love to understand your world, Benjamin. Please let me in.*

The city was busy. Everyone seemed to be getting ready for the festival of St Efisio. The streets were bedecked with flags, and police were everywhere. It seemed to Felicity that the Sard police were either dressed in extravagant finery as if about to go on parade, or wearing flack jackets and toting machine guns as if ready to storm a building. She gave a wry smile. Despite the heavy police presence, the worthy denizens of Cagliari continued to park their cars with a singular lack of regard for any road rules. It seemed the cramped streets of the old city bred a certain tolerance. Felicity approved.

She held on to Benjamin's arm as they made their way up Via Universita toward the Elephant Tower.

"What's the story with this elephant tower?" Benjamin asked.

"It was one of three towers built in 1307 to bolster the city walls surrounding Castello Hill." She pointed to the tower's parapet as it began to peer over the rooftops. "The Aragonese from Spain were occupying the island—and the Sards hated them. The tower had originally been built on three sides without a rear wall. But the Spanish organized for the northern wall to be enclosed when they decided to turn it into a prison." She began pulling at Benjamin's arm, unable to contain her excitement at being so close to the tower they had traveled so far to see. "As you might imagine, it didn't do much to endear them to the locals."

As they strode up the hill, the tower disentangled itself from the surrounding buildings and began to soar higher and higher above them. Soon, Felicity could see its grim portcullis. It seemed curiously at odds with the limestone walls that glowed pleasantly in the evening sun.

The stone elephant was immediately visible. It was about sixty centimeters long and sat on a plinth above one side of the gateway.

Benjamin shook his head. "That's bizarre. I can't imagine there were many elephants trotting around Sardinia in medieval times."

Felicity squeezed his arm. "That's precisely why it needs investigating. There are just too many coincidences for us not to investigate." She wrinkled her nose. "I just wish we could do it without making ourselves public to the authorities in the museum. It could all be a complete fizzer."

Benjamin pointed to the rooftop balcony of the house abutting the tower. "A medium-sized ladder would get Archie and his gizmo up to the elephant easily enough—if we had access to that balcony."

"I don't like your chances. It looks to be a private house."

Benjamin rubbed his chin. "Maybe…" He gazed around him. "Maybe there's a chance."

"What's going on in that head of yours?" demanded Felicity.

Benjamin smiled. "I think we should buy some ribbon."

"What?"

"I'll explain later. But first, let's get something to eat."

The light began to fade as they made their way back into the labyrinth of alleyways.

It seemed to Felicity that almost every building was in need of repair. She smiled to herself. The locals wore their rich historical heritage as casually as the jumpers they threw around their shoulders. The Carthaginians, Romans, Spanish, and Italians had all left their mark. The result was a delightful jumble of history. Certainly, none of the repairs done in the last two hundred years seemed to be more than temporary. Live and let live. Leave the repairs to another generation—another millennium.

The locals were beginning to spill into the streets and seat themselves at the pavement cafés. The old men had such interesting faces. They dressed badly, talked loudly, and gesticulated extravagantly.

The young men were in stark contrast. They were full of hubris, carefully coiffed, and expensively casual. A group of young women, most as small in stature as Felicity, were close by. They looked beautiful...and conspicuously ignored the young men. They were playing the oldest game on earth.

Felicity looked up at Benjamin. *What sort of game am I playing?*

Felicity and Benjamin stepped off the narrow pavement to make way for a young man escorting an elderly priest dressed in a black cassock and a wide-brimmed hat. As she did, she caught sight of a sign on the wall. It read, *Cucina Sarda tipica*—"typical Sard cuisine." "This'll do," she said, and towed Benjamin through the doorway. They walked down the steps into a room with a vaulted stone ceiling. Groups of people were sitting at long trestle tables. Felicity gazed around, intrigued. There was history here that she knew nothing about.

Once they were seated, a waiter poured some local red wine from an earthenware jug into glass tumblers.

Benjamin looked up at her from under his dark eyelashes and smiled. "This is very different from anything I've ever experienced, or expected to experience." He took a sip of the wine, coughed, and pulled a face. "I'm afraid there's a lot I've yet to get used to."

"Including me?" *Damn.* She'd said it before realizing.

Benjamin was silent for a while, then reached over and placed a hand over hers. "You, I never want to get used to you."

"Oh," she said weakly.

The wall lights threw dark shadows across the vaulted ceiling. *What now?*

She replayed what she had heard. There had been no hint of levity in Benjamin's voice. She studied his face. Composed. Soft... yes, soft eyes. "Umm, you do realize that a girl might take that to be a romantic overture, don't you?" she said carefully.

"It was fully intended to be one."

She put a hand to her breast, "What? You...me...?"

Benjamin nodded.

"Then..."

He lifted a finger to his lips. "Shh," he said, and paused. "Feel it. Feel what I'm saying…in your spirit."

Felicity furrowed her brow. *What on earth…?*

He looked at her calmly. Did she see a touch of fear, or was it hope in his eyes? Then she realized. It was entreaty. He was inviting her into his world, his Aboriginal world where things were different.

Felicity opened her mouth to protest, but said nothing. She just knew she would feel nothing. Her emotions were in turmoil. She wanted to feel Benjamin's lips on her own, feel his arms around her. She wanted to give him warmth and tenderness. She wanted release —and she wanted it right now.

"Shhh," Benjamin insisted. He breathed it out, almost like a sigh.

Your world. What…? Felicity reached out, took his hand, and closed her eyes. What was he inviting her into?

Over the next few seconds, her grip on his fingers relaxed. She felt him put his other hand over her entwined fingers, covering… owning…protecting. It was…delicious. Extraordinary. Something warm was rising up from within her. It was…

Thunk.

Felicity opened her eyes with a start as the waiter placed a plate of sizzling pecorino cheese in front of them. She looked down in an attempt to hide her embarrassment from the man serving them.

Benjamin removed his hands.

After the waiter left, he asked quietly, "Feel it?"

Felicity was silent for a while. "I…I think so," she smiled. "It was…" *How do I explain it?* "…very nice." She felt herself blushing. "You were very close."

He nodded. "I always will be."

Felicity wasn't sure she understood. If this was romance, it was the strangest she'd ever experienced—but oddly, the deepest. She leaned back to allow the waiter to reach over and deposit two large plates in the center of the table. One of them held a dizzying array of seafood, the other had strips of charcoal-cooked lamb.

Benjamin looked at her, almost shyly. "Felicity, this…may take a bit to work out." He paused. "I don't want to hurt you with my woundedness. Fear of that has stopped me kissing you quite a few times recently." He smiled, then became serious again. "I'm still not sure who I am. I'm part Aboriginal, but I don't belong. I'm part whitefella, but I don't…" He shook his head.

Felicity reached over and reclaimed his hand. "Benjamin, I am a divorced woman who's had her dreams shattered." She squeezed his hand. "I too am trying to find…" *You.* "…what I hope for." She took her hand away to wipe a tear from her eye. "And," she said with a sniff, "I still want a kiss. I'm a very western girl."

"Felicity, I've known for the last three hours exactly where in this city I will kiss you."

She gulped. "You have?"

"Yes," he said, reaching over to drop a piece of baby octopus into her mouth.

"Where?" she choked.

"Under the archway at Bastioni di Saint Remy. We walked up the steps through it, remember?"

She couldn't. There had been so many archways.

"When I knew I would kiss you tonight, I needed to find the right place." He smiled. "It has fabulous views over the entire city and the harbor from there…not that I expect to see them."

Benjamin watched Felicity and Archie covertly from across the road as he sought to play the role of a tourist. He lifted up his phone and took a photograph.

They looked totally convincing. Felicity was chatting to a stout Italian woman dressed in black. She was standing on the top step of the house that leaned against the elephant tower. Archie was standing well back, looking mildly bored. He was wearing an orange workman's vest and carrying a lightweight collapsible ladder. The haversack on his back had a few ribbons trailing from under the top flap. Benjamin thought it was a nice touch.

He saw Felicity point to the bunches of ribbons on the door-knockers of the nearby houses and then point up to the elephant.

The elderly woman standing on the top step peered up the street, shrugged, and beckoned for them to come in, pausing only to wag a finger at Archie.

Archie had the good sense to nod and hug the ladder to himself with both hands.

Soon, all three of them emerged on the rooftop balcony. Archie unfolded the ladder. A few seconds later, he was standing at the top of it, unhitching the scanner from his belt. With maddening slowness, he swept it back and forth over the side of the elephant.

The old woman pointed to Archie and spoke to Felicity.

Benjamin held his breath.

Felicity spoke briefly…and the woman nodded.

By the time the dialogue was over, Archie had hooked a bunch of ribbons around the neck of the elephant and was coming down the ladder.

Four minutes later, the ladder had been left at the site of a building renovation, the orange vest was in a rubbish bin, and the three of them were seated among a bunch of tourists at a pavement café.

Felicity was looking pale. She hugged herself and leaned forward as the demons of anxiety caught up with her. Benjamin took her by the shoulders and held her to himself until he judged that her anxiety was beginning to dissipate. The top of her hair brushed his chin as he held her. He felt warmth from the soft pressures of her body…and he felt her trust. It was a giddy feeling. Memories of the previous night—the gentleness, the hunger, the unspoken questions, the answers, the delight—flooded back to him. He kissed the top of her head, partly to assure himself it wasn't all a dream. He knew that reality and dreaming had untidy boundaries.

Felicity's breathing gradually slowed down, and she unfolded herself from Benjamin's arms.

He asked her, "What did you say to the woman when she pointed to Archie?"

Felicity, managed half a laugh. "I was going to so say, 'Run for your life, Archie,' but found myself saying to her, 'He's taking the opportunity to scan the elephant to ensure it hasn't developed any cracks.'"

Archie was holding the scanner on the table in front of him, shielding the screen from the sun as he played back the images. "You did well, Flick," he murmured. "Calm and resourceful."

"Calm...yeah." She leaned across to try and see the images. "But have we got anything? Let me see."

Archie tilted the screen toward her. "Sorry, mate, it looks like we've drawn a blank. I've run through the film twice, and there is not a dickybird—no hint of a secret cavity inside. Nothing. Just marble." He shrugged and gave a lopsided grin. "We've come a long way to get a decent cup of coffee, so we might as well have one."

Benjamin could feel the disbelief, angst, and heavy responsibility of being so expensively wrong—flood into Felicity. The grief of it caused her small frame to tighten and shudder.

He spoke quietly. "We all agreed it was worth a shot, Felicity. It was our choice to chase it down, not just yours." He took her by the shoulder and held her back against his chest. She twisted around, grabbed the lapel of his jacket, and began to sob against it. He continued. "We've discovered that the copy of the treaty is not in the elephant. That means, if it still exists, it has to be somewhere—probably in Cagliari." He looked at his watch. "We've got twenty-eight hours to find it before we have to leave for the airport. So, where do we begin?"

"What are the options?" asked Archie.

Benjamin ticked them off on his fingers. "One: the treaty no longer exists. Two: it no longer exists in Cagliari. Three: it exists somewhere else in Cagliari."

"Gee, mate, how many elephants can there be in Cagliari?" said Archie, taking off his knitted cap and rubbing his unruly hair.

Benjamin shrugged.

Felicity pushed herself up from his chest. "What did you say, Archie?"

"How many elephants..."

"Of course!" she said, slapping her forehead. She twisted

around. "Archie, I need to go back up the hill to the Cittdella dei Musei and ask the staff there a question."

Archie nodded. "How long do you think that will take?"

Felicity shrugged. "Thirty minutes. Maybe forty."

"Do you need anything to help you?"

"No."

"Risks?"

"None."

Archie scratched his beard. "Take Ben with you. He adds presence and gives good support." He smiled. "Three's a crowd, so I'll stay here." He pointed to a restaurant fifty meters up the road. "We rendezvous there in forty minutes. Call me if anything changes." Archie leaned back and closed his eyes, giving every appearance of enjoying the sunshine.

Benjamin looked at the map and guided Felicity past the Cathedral of Santa Maria, up the hill until they came to a small square. Another grim medieval tower stood at the far side. He checked the map again. "The museum has to be through the archway, under that tower." He turned to Felicity. "Are you sure you're up for this?"

She shrugged and looked very forlorn. "I have to try. We've come too far to stop now."

"What do you want to ask the staff?"

"There is a chance that the elephant has been replaced. The one we saw had a couple of broken tusks and the odd pock mark, probably caused by bullets...but I think it looked a bit too pristine to be the original one from the fourteenth century."

"You're going to ask if it's been replaced—preferably without arousing too much curiosity?"

Felicity nodded.

"Then hold my hand. It's what tourists do."

"Hmm. Then I suspect we're going to do a great deal of sightseeing."

They walked through the archway, across a square to a modern-looking building. Old stone artifacts could be seen on display through its glass windows. Felicity pushed through the door and began heading for the information desk. Benjamin steered her aside, where he made a pretense of studying an ancient Roman plinth. "Take your time, Felicity. You're a tourist." He let his gaze sweep over the two people behind the information desk. "Go to the older man on the left. He's kinder, knows more, and has time."

She jerked his arm and demanded, "How do you...?"

"I watch." He smiled. "Ready?"

She nodded.

He murmured in her ear. "Speak Italian but badly. Make it clear you're making an effort to speak their language but are Australian."

They ambled over to the desk. Felicity smiled at the older man and spoke to him.

Benjamin didn't understand the conversation but was impressed with Felicity. She was friendly but didn't overdo it. He watched her point to a photograph of the elephant in a collage of pictures behind the information desk.

More conversation. Felicity laughed easily. *Brilliant.* Her face showed incredulity, then doubt, then interest.

The old man smiled condescendingly, confident in his knowledge and pleased at having the chance to share it. He pulled a map out from under the counter, circled a section of it with a pen, and handed it to Felicity. She reached for her purse, but the old man held up a hand. It was a gift. He bowed when Felicity waved her thanks. She turned, smiled at Benjamin, and made for the door.

Once they had walked outside and around the corner, Felicity collapsed into Benjamin's arms. He held her until the tension in her body began to ease. She placed her fists against his chest. After a moment, she lifted up her head and began to beat her fists lightly against his chest. "I know where it is," she said. "There is an original elephant...and it's embedded in the end of a retaining wall where they are excavating the remains of that old church near our hotel."

She looked up at him with shining eyes. "It was replaced after Sards from the north occupied the city in 1795. They were revolting against feudalism. Evidently, they shot up the old elephant so badly that it was barely recognizable. It was pulled down and cemented into a retaining wall. Can you believe that?" She shook her head. "That's pretty much what happened to the Rosetta stone."

"What's that?"

"Oh, it was a piece of rock used as a building stone in Egypt. A French soldier found it during the Napoleonic wars. It was actually an ancient stele from 200 BC which had a royal inscription on it written in three languages. Archaeologists used it to decode Egyptian hieroglyphics."

"Wow!"

"Wow indeed." Felicity grabbed his hand. "Let's go find our stone."

Chapter 15

B enjamin, Felicity, and Archie looked through the cyclone fence cordoning off the renovation site. Two young men and a woman were on their knees with tiny trowels and brushes, scraping away the debris covering a stone floor.

"I can see it from here," said Felicity, bobbing up and down. "See, it's the big stone on the bottom of the buttress of the retaining wall—right where the curator said it would be."

Benjamin put out a hand to steady her. "Umm. It might be good if you could appear a little more chilled."

Felicity stopped bouncing, gripped the cyclone fence, and whispered, "But we won't be able to get in."

Benjamin could hear the desperation in her voice. He turned to Archie and raised a questioning eyebrow.

Archie murmured, "We probably can." He turned away and asked conversationally, "Ben, which of those guys on the floor is the boss?"

Benjamin flicked his eyes over them and turned casually back. "None of them. They're laughing occasionally and two are flirting —they're big kids out on an excursion."

"Then we need to act now, before the boss comes back."

Benjamin nodded. "Can we pretend we're sweeping the retaining wall to ensure that there are no old water pipes that may cause problems?"

Archie nodded. "Perfect. But we need props." He turned to Felicity. "Flick, there's a stationery shop around the corner which has printing facilities. Can you print off a sheet headed 'CAGLIARI WATER AUTHORITY' and put it on a clipboard? You'll be able to buy one there."

Felicity's mouth dropped open. Benjamin prompted her gently, "Time is probably of the essence."

Felicity nodded, squared her shoulders, and walked off.

"Archie, we need to talk." Benjamin pointed to a low stone parapet beside some steps. After they sat down on it, he said, "I'm not too sure of the right course of action if we discover there's a hidden cavity in that rock. Felicity intends to tell the local authorities about it…and hope they will extract the treaty from the old elephant and make it available for the public to see." He shrugged. "The trouble is, I don't have faith that bureaucrats will be that accommodating. It's too uncertain. We could do all this sleuthing and still not end up with a document that would stop Khayef pursuing their ambitions and their killing."

Archie swung the backpack off his shoulders and pulled out the scanner. "You aren't suggesting we should engage in anything scurrilous are you?" He grinned. "Because if you are, you're starting to take to this cloak and dagger stuff rather too well."

Benjamin didn't smile. "What are our options? I can tell you now, Felicity won't countenance anything dodgy."

Archie sniffed. "Yeah, I know. But the reality is, this isn't just an archaeological adventure. As you say, lives are at stake—yours in particular. If you're going to survive this business, you're going to have to use tactics that are appropriate against people who kill." He looked at Benjamin candidly with his pale blue eyes. "That can take you into some pretty gray areas."

Benjamin nodded. "Options?"

"Only one. If we find the treaty, we take it. We don't tell the authorities. We'll give it to the Italian government eventually when all this is over. The reality is, we need it now. They don't." Archie swung the backpack back over his shoulders and hooked the scanner onto his belt. "We just need to work out how to get in there."

Benjamin gazed up at the picturesque balconies under the shuttered windows along the laneway. "I don't want Felicity to get involved in…um…anything gray. She found the elephant, but now it's just you and me." He paused. "So, when do we get in there and investigate it?"

Archie rubbed his grizzled beard and was silent for a while. "Their siesta is between twelve and four o'clock. That's our window of opportunity." He turned to Ben. "You're the handyman. If I had to drill up the arse of a marble elephant, extract something, and put back a plug of stone so that no one would know, what would I need?"

Benjamin thought quickly. He had to get this right. Nothing must be allowed to reflect back on Felicity. He clenched his hand into a fist. As long as he lived, no one else he loved would ever be hurt again. "You would need a cordless drill, two battery packs, gray masonry adhesive, a concrete hole saw, and barbecue tongs."

"Barbecue tongs?"

"To pull it out with."

Archie nodded. "Presumably, the masonry adhesive is for gluing the stone plug back in place afterward."

"Yeah." He paused. "There's a hardware place on the main road by the docks."

They were silent for a while.

"Archie, I'm happy to do this. I'm used to operating drills."

"No, mate. This is where I pull rank. You need to take care of Felicity. Take her for a nice long walk this afternoon." He pointed to a pile of hessian bundled up in the corner of the excavation site. "I'll throw that hessian over that spare piece of cyclone fencing and pull it in front of the buttress. No one will see what I'm doing behind it."

"The locked gate?"

"No problem."

"If you're caught?"

He grinned. "They'd need to run bloody fast."

Benjamin looked up as Felicity came walking toward them clutching a clipboard. He watched the feminine sway of her hips and the movement of her hair. She looked fantastic. He smiled to himself, knowing that she was completely unaware of the impact she was making.

She showed him the headed page on the clipboard. "Well done," he said hugging her briefly around the shoulders. He turned and outlined his plan. "We go in and tell them we're scanning for old water pipes behind the retaining wall that might burst and ruin their renovation work."

Felicity bit her lip. "I...I suppose so." She looked up at him and prodded him on the shoulder. "If I do this, I demand a succession of excellent pizzas and irresponsible amounts of red wine tonight as compensation."

Benjamin kissed her on the cheek. "Anything else?"

"Yes but you'll have to work that out for yourself."

"Hmm."

Archie stood up. "Let's do it."

Felicity led them through the gate in the cyclone fence, spoke briefly to the young archaeologists, and walked over to the retaining wall. She beckoned Benjamin and Archie to follow her. The archaeologists sat back on their haunches and watched for a few seconds before continuing their work.

Benjamin pulled the spare panel of fencing across the buttress, ostensibly to gain access to the wall behind it. Then he strolled over to the corner of the site, where he pulled the pile of hessian away and looked around, apparently bewildered, before hefting it over the top of the fencing panel. He beckoned Archie across and pointing to the space where the hessian had been.

Archie whispered, "Thanks mate," and made a pretense of passing the scanner over the area.

Benjamin nodded. It would only take Archie a few seconds to spread the hessian out like a curtain and be invisible to the public. *Please God, let this work.*

Archie stood up and returned his attention to the retaining wall.

Benjamin watched him work his way along the stonework until

he came to the buttress, where he took particular care to scan the stones at its base. When he had finished, he stood up, stretched extravagantly, and pointed to the gate.

Felicity waved her thanks to the archaeologists and followed Archie through the gate. "Ciao."

They waved back.

The three of them had no chance to talk. Archie pointed up the laneway. "Back to the hotel."

Benjamin could feel Felicity's excitement as she hung onto his arm. She was trying not to skip.

Once they were alone in the lift and on their way up to the top floor, she demanded, "Well?"

Archie smiled. "It's there, Flick. I could see it on the display panel as soon as I started to scan it."

Felicity gave a squeal of delight and clapped her hands together. The lift bounced as she jumped up and down.

Archie laughed and tried to stop himself from being strangled as Felicity hugged him. "Well done, Flick. You were right."

When they got into their apartment, Benjamin pulled out a bottle of limoncello from the fridge. He'd bought it after the waiter suggested it as a digestivo the previous night. Unlike the wine, he had enjoyed it. "I think a celebration is in order."

"You bet, buddy," said Felicity as she pored over the images being played back on the scanner's display. "There it is!" she squealed. "Look."

Benjamin peered over her shoulder. A clear picture of a cavity could be seen inside the elephant, just in from where the tail would normally be. What was equally exciting was that a long cylinder was visible inside it.

Archie sat back. "Flick, I think we'd better chat about what happens now. Would you be okay with not going to the authorities with this information until we're back in Australia? It would simplify matters and avoid the risk of our being caught up in any investigations." He shrugged. "Whilst we may not have broken any rules, we've certainly bent a few."

Felicity twisted around and accepted a glass of limoncello from Benjamin. "If you think that's wise—okay."

———

Felicity was always grateful to finally be seated on a plane. It was the sense she had that all the waiting, the queues, and the worry were over. She grabbed Benjamin's arm and sighed contentedly.

Archie took his place in the third seat by the aisle. As he sat down, he poked a thin ivory canister into the seat pocket in front of him.

"What's that?" asked Felicity, only slightly interested.

"A souvenir. Got it yesterday afternoon. Quite old, I think."

A dreadful suspicion began to cross her mind. "You…you've not got the treaty, have you? Tell me you haven't. That's…" She struggled to find the words. "That's theft of national artifacts. There are all sorts of rules…"

"…and red tape," finished Archie. He rolled the matchstick in his mouth to one side and said, "Relax. There's no treaty in the cylinder."

Felicity leaned back against the seat. "That's good, then."

"It's rolled up in the newspaper in the seat pocket in front of Ben." Archie closed his eyes. "I couldn't do twelve across. What's a Latin fig?"

Chapter 16

B enjamin could see that Felicity was not in a good mental state as they collected the ute from the long stay car park. On the flight, she'd been terribly conflicted. One moment, she was holding his hand and resting her head on his shoulder, apparently very much at peace...and in the next, she was reaching out to touch the rolled up newspaper in front of Benjamin as if to confirm what was happening was real. Felicity had unrolled it just once to check that the precious document inside it was safe. It was—sort of. Safe, he conceded, was probably too ambitious a word. The treaty was brown, brittle, and fragile. Benjamin thought it would have about as much chance of being unwound as a waffle cone.

Felicity had grilled Archie about it repeatedly until he'd closed his eyes and refused to engage. He'd said that it was highly likely it would escape scrutiny at Melbourne's Tullamarine Airport, but if it were discovered, a phone call to Marjorie would sort things out. After all, the Australian government should be very pleased to have it.

Before they exited the airport terminal, Felicity insisted on going into the toilet, where she reinserted the treaty into its ivory canister for safekeeping. Once she was back in the ute, squeezed between

Benjamin and Archie, she brooked no argument. She slapped the console in front of her. "This document has got to go to a cold, dry place where we know it's going to be safe from physical damage… and safe from developing mold. It needs to go to a friend of mine at the Melbourne Museum. So, that's got to be our first port of call."

"Um…shouldn't we head over to Warringal Private Hospital first and chat with Marjorie? There are probably all sorts of protocols and permissions that will require her diplomacy." Benjamin shrugged. "And we haven't even confirmed that it actually is the treaty."

"Precisely my point," insisted Felicity. "I don't want a bunch of ignorant policemen storing it on a shelf under a brick used to break a jeweler's window."

Archie felt compelled to object. "I think ASIO can be relied on to take a little more care than that."

But Felicity remained adamant and pointed ahead. "The museum. Drop me there and pick me up when you've seen Marjorie."

It was the morning rush hour, and the traffic was horrendous. Benjamin drove into the city along the M2 as far as Flemington, where he took the slip road off the motorway. He wound his way around Melbourne University and joined the Eastern Freeway.

Felicity looked glumly at the traffic. "Look, just drop me off at Nicholson. I'll hop a tram down to the museum. It's just a kilometer straight down the road. You can keep going and head up Heidelberg to the hospital."

Archie pursed his lips and thought about it. "I suppose it's okay," he said eventually.

Benjamin incurred some indignant toots from drivers as he dropped Felicity off near the busy intersection. She grabbed her trolley bag containing the precious ivory cylinder from the back of the ute, waved goodbye, and headed off to the tram stop.

Benjamin loved watching her walk but not walking away. He experienced a sense of desolation watching her go…and a gnawing sense of anxiety.

Half an hour later, he was driving along the front of the Mercy

Hospital for Women. It was a massive white edifice with a sloping gray and orange-pillared portico. He felt as if a child had been playing with giant colored blocks and left them in a rather untidy pattern. The Warringal Private Hospital on the other side of the road was an altogether more humble affair.

They found Marjorie in a private room. Benjamin was shocked. She looked pale and jaundiced. Tubes filtered down to her from various machines.

She smiled weakly and raised a hand in welcome as Benjamin and Archie came in and drew up chairs beside the bed. Phoebe was seated in an armchair on the other side of the bed, knitting.

Archie took over the conversation and gave a summary of all that had occurred in Sardinia.

When he finished, Marjorie settled her head back on her pillow and said, "Bravo. You've all done exceptionally well." She turned to Phoebe, who had continued knitting throughout Archie's report. "What do you suggest, Phoebe? Things are little complicated diplomatically."

Phoebe kept her eyes on her knitting, "A few discreet inquiries are in order. If what you have is indeed the other copy of the treaty, the state and federal government will have all they need to forestall any legal claims by the Khayef Group to be exempt from paying mining tax. However, the document officially belongs to Italy."

Clickety-clack, clickety-clack...knit one, purl one.

Phoebe continued. "I suspect the document may well end up residing in some safe place in Australia and only be viewed by legal teams when occasion demands. I'll put a call through to the museum to ensure the document remains in safe hands until we know its status." She looked over her knitting at them. "Felicity is probably right to take it there. They will know how to care for it best."

The hospital machines blinked and beeped in the silence.

Benjamin reached out and took hold of Marjorie's hand. "And how are you feeling?"

"You have all made me feel much better."

"But how are you feeling physically."

"It is an irrelevance—although, I concede, I don't have as much time to fiddle about and be pathetic as I once thought."

Phoebe blew out her cheeks and snorted. "You've never just fiddled about or been pathetic in your life."

Benjamin glanced at both women. There was real love between them, one that he didn't understand. It may not be sexual, but it was certainly there. Life and love...both were bewildering things. He cleared his throat. "Er, do you still want me to make you a box for your tapestry paraphernalia?"

Marjorie squeezed his hand. "Of course, dear. It represents hope."

Benjamin nodded and allowed his thoughts to turn to Felicity. He excused himself, walked over to the corner of the room, and called her. He furrowed his brow as he heard the recorded refrain: *The mobile phone with the number you have called is currently switched off. Please call again later.* Benjamin was puzzled. He looked up the number of the museum and put a call through to the information desk.

"Oh, hi," he said when the phone was answered. "I'm calling to ask about Felicity Anderson, or Felicity Mercurio as she was once known. She used to work at the museum. She would have checked in at the information desk and is probably with you now. Can I please speak with her?"

"Hang on a moment, sir, and I'll check. May I ask who you are?"

"I'm Benjamin Bidjara, Felicity's boyfriend."

"Oh, right. Well, I can tell you that no Felicity Anderson or Mercurio has signed in, but I think we have a note for you. Hang on one moment." There was a brief pause. "Are you there, sir?"

"Yes." A wave of apprehension began to wash over him. "Still here."

"Yes sir, we have a note for you, left here by a young boy."

"What?" None of what he was hearing made any sense.

When no more information was forthcoming, Benjamin thanked the receptionist and rang off. He turned to Archie. "Mate, I've got a bad feeling about this. Felicity hasn't been seen at the information desk…and evidently she's organized for a note to be left for us. We'd better go."

Archie nodded and stood up.

Marjorie's brow furrowed with concern and held out a hand toward them. "Let me know what has happened the instant you learn anything."

Phoebe glanced up from her knitting. "Come back here if you are uncertain about anything and we'll talk options."

Archie nodded.

Benjamin gave Marjorie's hand a squeeze and followed Archie out the door.

Benjamin burrowed his way through the traffic on Nicholson Street toward Carlton Gardens, where the Melbourne Museum was located. Up ahead, he could see some giant signs—all angled, and white writing on a gray sloping wall saying: 'MELBOURNE MUSEUM.' It too was angled. The uncharitable thought flashed through his mind that Melbournians seemed incapable of building anything that wasn't crooked.

He swung into a museum service road and parked in a loading bay, trusting that the ute's grubby tray top would give the illusion he was there on business.

Both he and Archie strode along a walkway under a long, sloping plaza roof to the museum entrance. Benjamin saw that a twin plaza roof extended toward the entrance from the other direction. To the left was the stolid form of the Royal Exhibition building. It looked more like a cathedral with its Gothic Victorian architecture and domed central tower, and was in stark contrast to the modern glass façade of the museum.

They pushed through the museum doors and headed to the information booth directly in front of them. Benjamin leaned over the counter, and a woman smiled politely up at him.

"Hello. My name is Benjamin Bidjara." He flashed open his

wallet and showed his driving license. "I understand you have a message for me from Felicity Mercurio who used to work here."

"Ah, yes sir. You called half an hour ago." She fished under the counter and pulled out a white business envelope. "Here it is."

Benjamin murmured his thanks and took it from her. He turned away and ripped open the envelope.

Dear Ben,

I have decided to go away for a few months to try and sort things out in my head. I'm sorry to spring this surprise on you.

I'll see you probably, in a while.

Go carefully.

Felicity

Benjamin could feel the blood drain from his face.

"What's the matter, mate?" inquired Archie.

"Something's badly wrong." Benjamin shook his head, trying to shake off the nightmare that was beginning to unfold. *No, no. It's not possible. Something's very wrong.* He swung around to Archie. "Something's very wrong. This isn't true."

Archie came around to Benjamin's side and read the note. When he'd finished, he put a hand on Benjamin's shoulder and gave it a squeeze. "I agree, mate. Something's happened. I've seen you two together the last few days, and this doesn't fit at all. It's suss— particularly given the circumstances and everything else that's going down." He turned around and walked back to the information booth, leaving Benjamin to look dumbly at the letter. The shock of what he saw...of what it claimed...froze his mind into immobility.

Archie came back a minute later. "The receptionist hardly remembers the boy. She said it was just a kid, about sixteen years old, who was carrying a skateboard. He was probably given twenty bucks to deliver it by a bloke who was outside." He shook his head. "There's no lead there." He nodded to the entrance. "Let's go outside and sort this out."

They made their way outside and sat down on a long orange bench. Benjamin put his head in his hands.

Archie was all business. "Right, mate, what's wrong with this letter? It's been carefully crafted to persuade any policeman not to waste time looking for her but why do we know it's crap?"

Benjamin wanted to scream, *Because she loves me—that's why!* He drew a deep breath and flicked the edge of the paper with his finger, forcing himself to see it clearly. There were several things wrong with it. He knew that instinctively—but what were they?

Archie waited patiently as Benjamin analyzed the letter.

After a few minutes, Benjamin sighed, "The letter is addressed to Ben." He looked up. "She never calls me Ben."

"Keep going."

"And there is nothing to 'sort out'. We had just…discovered…" He gave a shuddering sigh. "We've just discovered each other. It's new and magical. There's nothing old, jaded or complicated."

"And?"

"And there's no mention of the treaty. She hasn't signed in as she would have to do if she arrived here with it, so the treaty is still with her." He shook his head. "She'd never go without first making sure the treaty is safe. It's like it doesn't even exist."

"Anything else?"

"The signature is wrong. It may look like a badly scrawled *Felicity* but it's not her handwriting." Benjamin shook his head. "I don't know what to make of it." He threw the letter down onto the bench in disgust. "About the only thing I believe is her comment to go carefully."

Archie nodded and got to his feet. "Come on, mate. Let's show it to the boss and to Phoebe. If anyone can make sense of it, those two can."

Phoebe handed Benjamin a red ballpoint pen. "Draw over Felicity's signature but only on the part of it that you know is consistent with her normal signature."

Benjamin took the pen and nodded, forcing himself to be still and quiet…to be with Felicity. He was now over the shock of the suggestion that she'd run away from him. Deep down, he knew beyond all doubt it was untrue—which meant only one thing: Felicity had been abducted and forced to write a note aimed at satisfying the police. He glanced again at the message. She was trying to reach out to him, to say that what she was writing was not true…and to warn him to be careful. But what else was she trying to say?

He closed his eyes and called her to mind. Would she come? He waited. Then, in the midst of knowing, she came…faint but there. Their connection still existed. Benjamin nodded. Felicity was okay.

He blinked and rubbed his forehead, drawing out from his memory the two or three times he'd seen Felicity's signature. He didn't have much to remember it by…but then he didn't need much. He was able to recall detail, to describe things that mattered to him, to recall shapes and ratios he'd seen years before in order to replicate them on his wood lathe. All he needed was quiet.

After five minutes, he bent over the letter that lay on the hospital bed table and traced over Felicity's signature. He drew a line under the *F* and then traced the *e-l-i-c*.

He handed the paper over to Phoebe. "The F is more printed than Felicity normally writes it. Only the *e-l-i-c* is consistent with her normal signature."

Phoebe took the letter and stared at it. Almost immediately, she glance up and asked, "Does Felicity know Pitman shorthand?"

Benjamin nodded. "She said she once wanted to be a journalist, so yes. Why?"

Phoebe bent the letter between her fingers. "Because I think she's incorporated shorthand very cleverly into her signature." She leaned forward, put the letter on the table and stabbed at it with her stubby finger. "See the dash just before her name—that's *K*. Then there's the odd-looking *F*…" She looked up. "That's *KF*."

"Khayef," murmured Marjorie. She was lying on her bed with her eyes closed, as if in prayer. "Anything else?"

"Yes. See here? This long *S* shape that slides off to the bottom right is *4*."

"And the squiggles after it?" asked Benjamin.

"The little subtext that looks like a *20* means *weeks*." She tapped the final mark. "And that supertext *l* means *die*."

"Four weeks...die," said Marjorie quietly.

Benjamin sat in silence as he tried to digest the significance of what he had heard and its dreadful possibilities.

Phoebe resumed her knitting. Clickety-clack, clickety-clack.

"Gentlemen," said Marjorie, "The gloves are now off regarding Khayef. If we take this letter to the police, they will trouble Khayef with a search or two and some uncomfortable questioning but nothing will be found." She sighed. "I'm afraid it's up to us." She breathed deeply as if to draw in energy. "This means we will be operating in a gray area legally." She turned to Phoebe. "What are the options?"

Phoebe answered immediately. "Khayef needs Felicity's expertise as an historical archivist to unravel and authenticate the Sardinian treaty. After which, she will be killed. They must have hinted as much for her to put it into the letter." She sniffed. "So, the first objective is to locate and rescue Felicity. I estimate our window of opportunity to be about four weeks."

Marjorie continued on from Phoebe as if taking for granted that they thought and spoke with one voice. "The second objective is the complete destruction of the Khayef Group. It is evil."

Benjamin would have thought it absurd to hear such a statement from a frail old woman dying of cancer, had it not been for the disturbing conviction in her voice. He glanced at Archie. He wasn't smiling. Benjamin shook his head. It was surreal.

Marjorie breathed heavily to catch her breath, then turned to Archie and asked, "Priorities and possibilities?"

Archie looked at her with his bleak eyes. "Any rescue of Flick will be a big blow to Khayef. It may even cause some people to be arrested, but it is unlikely to kill the company. We have to do something that will cause the Khayef Group to implode...as well as expose the abduction of Felicity and attempted murder of Ben."

Phoebe nodded as she pulled a length of wool from the ball.

Benjamin put his head in his hands. "But they've got everything. They've got Felicity. They've got the real treaty from Sardinia. And they've got the Atlantis stone, which prevents any Portuguese connection being made." He shook his head. "They've got everything."

"That's not quite true, mate," said Archie. "They haven't got you." He nodded to Benjamin. "You'll have to expect a note pretty soon requiring you to present yourself somewhere, probably in exchange for Felicity. They want you, mate, every bit as much as the treaty."

"What are our options?" asked Marjorie.

Archie put his hands behind his head and chewed at a lip. "We get in first and call for a meeting with Khayef. That'll mean we regain some initiative and put them off balance."

Phoebe shook her head. "Too dangerous. Benjamin will be killed."

"We call the meeting but it's up to us whether Ben attends it."

"What concrete benefit could we obtain from such a meeting?"

"Use it as a way of getting a visual on the enemy—to gain intel."

"How do we do it?" asked Phoebe.

"I'm working on it," smiled Archie.

They were silent for a while.

"Let that stew for a while," said Marjorie. "Meanwhile, Phoebe and I will call in every favor we can in order to obtain information through ASIO and the police about anything connected with the Khayef Group." She reached out toward Phoebe. "Will you apply some pressure and dig around, dear?"

Phoebe nodded.

"The next issue," announced Marjorie, "is the safety and security of Felicity. May I suggest we work to a three-week time frame, just to be safe."

A knife turned in Benjamin's heart. He screwed up his eyes and lifted his head in anguish.

Marjorie patted his hand. "I know this is difficult but right now we need your input."

Benjamin forced the storm within him to quieten slightly. He breathed a deep breath. "What do you need from me?"

Marjorie nodded approvingly and glanced at Archie.

Archie leaned back and stretched his legs out. "What connection did Felicity have with Khayef?"

"It was through a lawyer, a bloke called Carter. He gave Felicity his business card."

"Can we get that card?"

"It shouldn't be too hard. I imagine it's in Felicity's office somewhere." Benjamin shrugged. "It's in her brother's house. I've never been inside it, but I'll call in and get it when I get back."

Archie nodded. "Didn't you say that this joker from Khayef was a bit of a history buff?"

"I think so."

"Then there is some chance that he'll be somewhere close to Felicity when she does her history thing for them."

Marjorie nodded and closed her eyes. She looked exhausted.

Phoebe glanced at her. "I think, gentlemen, that is all we can do for now." Her face was expressionless as she looked at both men over her knitting. "I'll be in touch."

Two hours later, Archie and Benjamin were well down the Princes Highway, on their way back to Port Fairy. There was very little conversation between them. Benjamin was grateful. His mind was trying to comb out the facts of what he'd just experienced from his screaming emotions. He wondered at Marjorie's extraordinary calm. She'd gone into hospital ostensibly to have a shunt fitted but hadn't left as expected—or at least, not yet. He wondered if she was lying on her deathbed. *What would it be like to have her serenity? Does knowing God change things?* Benjamin began to marshal together the words of what he hoped was a prayer…but his thinking was side-tracked by a niggling question and a disturbing conviction.

By the time they reached the town of Colac, he was able to articulate it. How did the Khayef Group know that Felicity had gone to Sardinia and been ready to abduct her on her return?

He thought he knew the answer…and he didn't like it.

Chapter 17

"Where is she?" Doran Khayef demanded.

Eddie pointed to a white van parked outside the work-site's cyclone fence. "In there."

"And the treaty?"

Eddie lifted up a white plastic shopping bag.

Khayef permitted himself a single nod. "Come inside." He turned, pushed his way through the door of the demountable site office, and took off his hard hat. All around him, he could hear the sound of engines revving and whirring…and scaffolding poles clanking as they were repositioned for the next building phase. It was an encouraging sound; the massive concrete skeleton outside was beginning to grow. Khayef held out his hand, took the bag from Eddie, and placed it on the desk. He steepled his fingers either side of it and savored the moment. He had worked so hard to get the British treaty, taken so many risks, spent so much money…but now he had in his possession the authentic Sardinian copy. He smiled. Such were the ironies of life. It had cost him nothing…and he would be free from any allegations of having the stolen British treaty. It couldn't be better.

Khayef pulled out the decorated ivory canister and weighed it in his hands.

"The top pulls off but it's fairly tight," warned Eddie.

"You've not touched it?" demanded Khayef.

"No. Just checked it was there."

Khayef pulled off the top and gently fingered the brittle edge of the parchment. He put the top of the canister back thoughtfully. *How the hell will anyone be able to unravel it to determine whether it is actually the Sardinian treaty?* He set his lips into a hard line. There was still work…

He was interrupted by a knock on the door.

Khayef placed the canister back into the plastic bag and called, "Come."

Andrew Carter, looking incongruous in a suit and an orange hard hat, stepped inside. He took off the hat as if it was something smelly and put it on a shelf.

"How do we know this is the treaty?" demanded Khayef without preamble.

"I've got the story from the girl about how it was found. I must say, she's been extremely resourceful—very clever indeed. There's little doubt that it is the treaty."

Khayef banged the desk with his fist. "But how do we know?"

"We unravel it." Carter sat himself in a chair with a sigh. "It turns out that Ms. Anderson has worked for two years at the Melbourne museum and knows what it takes to unroll an old parchment."

Khayef sat himself on the edge of the desk. "Hmm. What a useful little lady she is proving to be." He turned to Eddie. "How do you see this working?"

Eddie had been standing as silent as a sentinel with his arms folded in front of him. "She has two uses. We use her as bait to get Bidjara, and we use her to open the document." He might have been talking about using a can opener.

"It will, however, take some time," warned Carter. "She estimates that the process will take about four weeks."

"Where can we keep her secure, away from prying eyes, and equipped with what she needs to unravel the treaty?"

"I've been thinking about that, sir," replied Carter. "She doesn't need very much in the way of equipment or space, so I thought she might be...er, accommodated on your boat." He shrugged. "It could be moved to an offshore mooring in Pittwater where she would be very secure."

"You bloody idiot. Might I remind you that I live on my boat because I've had to sell my house to help pay for the next stage of this development." The memory of having to sell his twenty-five million dollar harbor-side house continued to rankle—but he still had his boat. It was his pride and joy. He would never sell it—except to get a better one. He growled, "It would be the first place the police would search if someone reports the bitch missing."

"Oh, yes. Of course. Sorry."

"The concept is sound, though." He pointed to Carter. "You go sailing with your boyfriend, don't you? Doesn't he keep a boat in the next bay to mine at Pittwater?"

"He's away in Europe on some stock exchange business at the moment."

"But he lets you sail it in his absence. You told me that you did."

"Er, yes."

"Describe the boat."

Carter looked uncomfortable and rubbed the back of his neck. "Well...it's a McGruer fifty-four foot mahogany ketch—about twenty tons displacement."

"Don't bore me with the details. I want to know if it's big enough for Anderson to do her work...and for you, Eddie and a relay of other men to live aboard?"

Carter swallowed. "Ah, she's pretty comfortable. Perhaps a bit old-fashioned now—she was built in the seventies. She can sleep six." He rubbed his chin. "We could put Ms. Anderson in the fore-peak, I suppose. It has no windows, only an outside hatchway that can be locked. It has two berths and its own heads."

"Heads?"

"Toilet."

"Could she use one berth as a workbench and sleep on the other?"

"I suppose so."

"Suppose?"

Carter cleared his throat. "Yes. She can."

"Then do it." Khayef turned to Eddie. "Fix it."

Eddie nodded.

"Make sure she has everything she needs to sort out the treaty. Keep her comfortable but frightened. Don't harm her…at least, not until she's finished."

Felicity wriggled in her seat trying to ease the muscles in her limbs. The ride had been interminable. She'd been able to see through the windscreen from the back of the van and knew she was somewhere in Sydney, somewhere west of the city. Her wrists had become badly chafed as a result of her testing the plastic tie that held them together.

The last twenty-four hours had been a nightmare. Eating; going to the toilet—everything had been done with her hands tied together. No concessions had been made. Her clothes were now sweaty and foul. She'd wept her tears in the first ten hours, angry and frustrated with herself at being so easily forced into the van. They'd done it so quickly and efficiently that even though it had happened in broad daylight, nothing would have appeared amiss to anyone watching. Two men, both smiling, had come either side of her and taken her arm. One of them had grabbed her trolley bag. She and her bag had been lifted into the van with an efficiency that spoke of practice.

The smiles did not continue once she was in the van. She was hit across the face and forced into a seat bolted to the rear floor of the van. A black bag was put over her head, and her wrists were strapped together.

After a short ride, the van stopped. One of the men took the bag off her head. She saw enough to know that the van was parked in a garage or underground car park. There wasn't much time to take stock as the man pressed the muzzle of an automatic pistol against her temple. She'd shrieked in fright. He slid the muzzle of the pistol slowly down her cheek, down her neck, and then snaked it across to her cleavage where he rested it between her breasts. "Don't do anything stupid, okay?"

The passenger door opened allowing one man to get out and another dressed in an expensive overcoat to slide in and take his place. When he turned around, she was amazed to see that it was Andrew Carter.

"Good morning, Ms. Anderson. I believe you might have something we want."

He grilled her about the details of her trip overseas and whether she'd got the treaty. When she started to prevaricate, The man in the driver's seat turned and slapped her hard...then told her in detail how he was going mutilate Benjamin in order to get the details from him. The terror she experience at that point broke her. She confessed to having the treaty.

The man opened her bag, found the ivory container, and opened it. He touched the inside of it with his finger and then showed it to Carter. He'd inspected it briefly before closing it, wrapping it in one of Felicity's shirts, and putting it in the glove compartment.

Felicity realized she was in real danger. The fact that none of the men appeared greatly worried at her seeing their faces was not a good omen. She'd cried out that the treaty was incredibly delicate and needed to be handled with enormous care. She should know because she had worked at the Melbourne Museum for two years. One of her roles had been to help conserve old documents. Felicity was stretching the truth a little. In reality, she'd only spent a week working with the conservators, but it was long enough to sound convincing.

"The collagen fibers in the vellum need to be rehydrated carefully and gradually after so many centuries of desiccation. If you don't, you'll end up with nothing but crumpled fragments and dust."

"You'd be able to restore the document, then?" asked Carter.

"Given some basic equipment, yes."

"And you'd be able to do it without sophisticated equipment, with material readily available?"

"Yes."

"You said the process would need to be done gradually. How long would it take?"

She desperately wanted to buy Archie, Benjamin, and Marjorie as much time as she could, but daren't ask for too much. "Four or five weeks, I expect."

Carter stroked under his chin for an agonizing minute. Eventually, he'd turned back and said, "Then Ms. Anderson. We'll just have to keep you alive and well for four weeks, won't we."

"But now, I require you to write a note. Your hands will be untied briefly to allow you to do it." He gestured to the man with gloved hands. "Eddie enjoys violence. I suggest you comply."

She wrote the note in a swirl of emotions, hoping that Benjamin would understand its truth, its lies, and its secrets. It was her one chance to warn him…and explain—to truly explain. She released the clipboard reluctantly as Carter pulled it from her hands. He read the note, nodded, and got out of the van.

She spent the rest of the day locked in the van. They allowed her to lie on a mattress in the back, but one of the two men was always sitting in the front seat watching her. Then, a little before midnight, both men lifted her into her seat, climbed into the front… and they began driving again.

An hour or so later, the journey ended. No one said anything.

She could feel the warmth and humidity of Sydney permeating the parked van. The man detailed to watch her from the passenger seat now had trickles of sweat running through the stubble on his face.

Suddenly, the passenger door opened. The man got out, and Carter sat in his place.

Carter turned around. "Now, Ms. Anderson, tell me exactly what you would need to reconstitute the treaty and make it readable."

Felicity had been preparing for this question for the last twenty-two hours. She didn't hesitate. "I'd need two plates of glass, about half a meter square; a wooden box able to contain the vellum, and an ultraviolet lamp."

"Why?"

"The glass is simply for keeping the vellum flat and safe once we've opened it. The lamp box with the ultraviolet light is where we put the vellum each night so that the UV-light can kill off any mold. Sydney's humid climate is bad for mold. We can't afford for any of it to grow on the treaty. Mold loves calfskin."

Carter nodded. "What else?"

"I need to be able to make steam and feed it with a hose into the box. The vellum needs to sit on a Teflon coated cake rack." She tried to sound as professional as she could. It wasn't easy with her hands tied and feeling so bruised and disheveled. "I'd need a ten percent solution of urea in ethanol; a good quality misting bottle plus tweezers and spatulas."

Carter took out a notebook and jotted down the details. When he finished, he nodded to the other man, who started the engine. Soon, the van joined a stream of traffic threading its way through the city heading north over Sydney Harbour Bridge.

They arrived in paradise. It was bewildering. The van door opened and Felicity was hustled down a small pontoon onto a rigid inflatable speedboat. Around her, boats bobbed at their moorings on a perfect blue sea. Gulls cried and squabbled overhead. Offshore, a sailing boat was heeling to the wind—and a little metal dinghy, a tinny, with an outboard motor buzzed across the glittering sea. Felicity thought she must be somewhere in the Hawkesbury Estuary, probably Pittwater. Expensive houses peeped out from the heavily wooded shores of the harbor.

Their speedboat sped across the sea curving around the headlands and bays in which more boats were moored until it slowed down and edged up to the stern quarter of a beautiful, white hulled ketch. Green awnings had been rigged over the length of the deck to keep the boat cool. She caught sight of the name painted on her bow, *Excelsior*.

Eddie hauled Felicity into the yacht's cockpit. As he did, he held her to himself. She felt his sexual tension. Hard and hungry eyes bored into her. He whispered, "I'm going to enjoy you, bitch." His hand moved up to her breast, "There will be pain, I promise."

The terror and intimidation was shocking, mind-numbing and disorientating…but Eddie had pushed too far. Felicity knew she had nothing to lose. She would be killed, probably horribly, once she was no longer useful. She lifted her chin and spoke loudly enough for all three men to hear. "Eddie, if I ever feel that I have nothing to hope for except torture, humiliation, and death, I will crush the manuscript into a million fragments, do you hear?"

He drew back a hand to strike her.

Carter tapped Eddie on the arm.

He froze, in mid strike. No one moved. She stared at him. "Let me assure you that I will work hard and well at restoring the manuscript, but it will not happen unless you respect me and provide for my basic needs."

It was a terrible gamble.

Silence.

Carter eventually broke the impasse by pushing past and unlocking the hatchway doors into the saloon. She breathed out slowly, giddy with relief. It was a victory, of sorts.

Felicity climbed down the companionway steps into the main saloon. It had wood paneling everywhere and looked very luxurious.

Carter became business-like as he led her along the corridor at the far end. "I'll be in the cabin on the left. Eddie will be in this one on the right. Another, er…crewman will be in the main saloon." He pushed open a door at the end of the corridor. "You're in the fore-peak. There are two berths and a toilet. You'll find it under the step in front of the chain locker." He rapped on a door just outside the forepeak. "There's a shower unit in here which you will be allowed to use once a day. Meals and any laundry will be brought by boat daily." He moved aside to let Felicity pass into the narrow confines of the forepeak.

There were no windows, only a hatchway in the deck above them. It had a clear polycarbonate cover allowing it to act as a skylight. Disturbingly, she could see that it was locked shut with a padlock.

Carter passed Felicity's trolley bag through to her. "You'll be locked into the forepeak at all times except for your daily shower." He stretched his neck and continued. "I'll be taking the boat to a wharf once a week to take on fresh water and have the sewerage pumped out. Eddie will sit with you during those occasions." Carter furrowed his brow as if trying to think of something else to say. "Now, give me any clothes you want to have washed. I'll get it sorted. I'll also collect the equipment you need to restore the document. It may take a day or two, so I suggest you make yourself comfortable."

Chapter 18

Benjamin could see the family likeness immediately. Dr Michael Anderson was short, dark, and looked very fit. He stood at the front door of his house in bare feet, jeans, and a faded blue pullover. It was evident that when the good doctor was not doctoring, he liked to kick back and relax. He was holding a toy dart gun.

"Is that loaded?" asked Ben.

The doctor looked at the gun and smiled apologetically. "Roughhouse time before bath and bed for the kids. How can I help you?"

"I'm Benjamin Bidjara." He indicated Archie standing next to him. "And this is Archie Hammond. We're friends of Felicity. She's contracted us to help build her bull-nosed verandas."

The doctor nodded. "Of course. You're the one who rescued Flick when she got into trouble."

Benjamin nodded.

The doctor looked at him appraisingly. "She's, aah…spoken of you quite a lot. Come in, please. I'm Michael, by the way."

Benjamin and Archie stepped inside. "Michael, I don't want to take up your time, but I do want to show you a note we received from Felicity earlier today to see if you can make sense of it."

Benjamin dug the note out of his pocket. "Archie and I have been, er…helping her with some of her historical research and were due to pick her up from the Melbourne Museum to take her home when we were given this note." He shrugged. "It was left at the reception desk." Benjamin handed the note to the doctor.

As he read it through, the doctor's brow immediately furrowed with concern. He looked up and said, "You didn't have a row or anything?"

"Not at all. Things were going, ah…pretty well, and she was happy. That's why we're here. We want to know if she's contacted you."

The doctor shook his head. "Nope. Not at all." He tapped the letter against his jeans. "I've got to say…this is way out of character for Flick. It doesn't even sound like her, let alone fit in with how she behaves."

Benjamin nodded. "That's what we think. There's only one other possibility we can think of, and that's her involvement with a guy who came to see her the other day from the Khayef Group. Felicity told me he'd left her his card. I'd like to contact him, if you think that's okay, to see if Felicity is with him discussing a research grant or something."

The doctor raised his eyebrows. "I suppose so." He didn't sound convinced.

"Would you be able to look around Felicity's desk and see if you can find the guy's business card?"

"Sure. Wait here a moment, and I'll have a look."

Squeals could be heard over the sound of water splashing into a bath.

The doctor came back three minutes later. "Here. This must be it." He glanced at the card. "Andrew Carter." He handed it to Benjamin.

Benjamin took a pen out of his pocket, wrote the number down on his hand, and gave the card back. "Thanks, Michael. I'll investigate it and get back to you if I still feel there's reason for concern."

The doctor took the card and nodded. "I'd be grateful." He glanced at Benjamin. "You know, Flick's been pretty fired up and happy these last few weeks...ever since she's known you." He tapped the card onto his hand. "I don't want her hurt."

Benjamin dropped his head. "Believe me when I say the very last thing I want to do is to cause Felicity pain." He looked up. "I'd rather die."

Benjamin could hear Phoebe's measured breathing on the other end of the line as he gave her Andrew Carter's mobile number and voiced his concerns. "So, that's my fear. I don't think there can be any other explanation."

"Thank you, Benjamin," said Phoebe, much as a sergeant major would dismiss a report from a corporal. "I'll investigate things and get back to you. Please, may I speak with Mr. Hammond?"

Benjamin handed the phone to Archie. He couldn't help feel as if he was a child being banished from grown-up talk. He walked over to the bench where the panels for Marjorie's tapestry box were being clamped together by sash cramps.

He undid the cramps and began to mark the panels with a setsquare, so they were ready for cutting. He'd cut them to length tomorrow morning and then dove-tail the ends using a router. Both the radial arm saw and the router were noisy machines. It would be unkind to use either of them at this time of night.

His eye fell on the length of stinkwood sitting under the bench. It brought back a fresh wave of anxiety for Felicity. *Four weeks to die.* It was shocking, numbing, and unbelievable. He had to do some-thing physical with his hands, or he feared he would go mad. Benjamin chocked the small log in the woodworker's vice and used a handsaw to dock the ends. Then he picked up a pencil and began to draw the dimensions of a coolamon dish. It was men's work. A coolamon was something men made for their women—and so he would make one for Felicity. It was his act of defiance.

Archie forestalled any further work. "Benji, boy, we need to talk," he said as he slipped his phone into his pocket.

Benjamin reached for a stool and sat down. He leaned on the

bench with his head in his hands. Archie slid into the other stool and studied him from under pale eyelashes. "How 'ya feeling, mate?"

"Bloody angry... Terrified for Felicity..." He rubbed his forehead, "...weary of being helpless and pathetic."

Archie nodded. "Would you be ready for a bit of action, then?"

"Yes," he said immediately. "Anything to help Felicity. What did you have in mind?"

"I'd better warn you, it will probably be dangerous, certainly very physical...and we'll be operating within a legally gray area." Archie drummed two fingers on the bench top. "And, we need to start now. I don't think Felicity has anything like four weeks before she finds her life threatened."

"What! Why?"

"Because nothing's guaranteed. We need to find her as soon as possible."

Benjamin nodded.

"Phoebe will ring back at any moment with a fix on the location of Carter's phone. If he's got it switched on, it'll be pinging the local cell towers, so ASIO will be able to locate it. If it stays centered in one area, I'm prepared to act on it in the expectation that Flick will probably be nearby."

"What can I do?" It was such a simple question, but it caused energy and hope to begin seeping back into Benjamin's heart.

"I want you to make a phone call and leave a message for the boss of the Khayef Group, inviting him to come down and talk with you. You'll need to meet somewhere safe and public. Almost certainly, you won't keep the appointment, but we need to see what gets flushed out by your invitation—so we have a chance of getting evidence of their involvement."

"Payphone or mobile?"

"They'll already have your number, mate, so use your mobile. Let 'em know they're not staring you down." He tapped on his phone. "I've got their number here...and the name of the head honcho is Doran Khayef, so address your message to him. If it isn't Khayef, he'll ask around his associates and pass it on." Archie smiled. "It's time to disturb the ants' nest. If you call now, it will simply be a message left at reception for the boss, so you won't have any awkward questions to field."

Four minutes later, Benjamin made the call. "Mr. Khayef, my name is Benjamin Bidjara. You or one of your senior associates is trying to get hold of me. I suspect you have someone I'd very much like to see again, and I am prepared to sign a waiver of any claim you think I might have on your business. But in view of your recent behavior, you will only get one shot at this before I go to higher authorities. So, I want to meet with you, or the associate leading Khayef's interests concerning me, in three days' time—this Wednesday at the *Giddy Tuna* café in Port Fairy. Let's meet at 8am. Please sit at an outside table with…" Benjamin paused. "…a red carnation in your button hole." He rang off.

Archie raised an eyebrow. "A red carnation?" He shook his head. "Hackneyed…and a little cruel…but probably useful."

"Mate, you've no idea how cruel I'm feeling right now. What do we know about this Khayef guy?"

"Phoebe has given me a bit of a run down. He's doing this big building development on Sydney Harbour; owns the biggest gold mines in Victoria; and is being investigated for all sorts of dodgy deals with union officials, biker stand-over merchants, and politicians." Archie rubbed his beard. "We knew most of that already. But what I've also been told is that he's sold his waterfront home and is currently living on his two million dollar motor launch—poor bloke. He's parked it at The Quays Marina in Pittwater."

Benjamin studied the photo. The curving lines of the boat were accentuated by a continuous dark glass window running the length of the deck cabin. He closed his eyes and leaned back trying to get a mental picture of a person who would choose to own such a thing. *Ambitious…prideful…fragile self-esteem…impatient. Probably ruthless.* Could such a person be behind Felicity's abduction?

Easily, he decided.

He stared at the boat, seeing everything it represented…and hated it. "What can we do to bring this bastard down?" he asked hoarsely.

"Whoa. Hold on, buddy. First we've got to check that he's involved with Flick and the treaty thing."

Benjamin nodded, but he already knew. "What else can you tell me?"

"The Khayef Group is in thick with the Saracen motorbike gang."

"And?"

"The Saracens are running forty kilograms of meth-amphetamine—ice—from Adelaide to Melbourne in a semi-trailer. The police are planning to stop and raid it at Beaufort on the Western Highway. Evidently, they've had someone working under-cover—they've been planning this raid for over two years."

"Forty kilograms of ice. Sounds a lot."

"With a street value of a little under a million dollars per kilo-gram, it certainly is."

Benjamin whistled. "But how does that help us?"

"No idea. I'm just giving you the info Phoebe's managed to get. Needless to say, we can't breathe a word of it to anyone." Archie looked up at Benjamin. "You can't use it as a bargaining chip to get Flick back. So don't even think about it."

Benjamin had already thought about it—and discarded it. It would put Archie in prison for a lifetime. But his mind continued to swirl with ideas, passions, and fears. Forty million dollars' worth of drugs…and a luxury motor yacht. How could this information be used to destroy Khayef?

"When are they moving it?" Benjamin asked.

"In three days' time. It's an overnight run. Evidently, the gear will be in a container full of fertilizer bags on the back of the semi."

Benjamin looked out of the window to where a streetlight was shining across the road. The wind was rising, causing leaves to skitter across the pavement. He could hear the squeak of the wind-vane on his neighbor's garage. The tin cockerel was complaining again as it see-sawed in the face of the wind.

An idea began to form in his mind. It was outrageous…

Archie's phone rang. Benjamin could only hear a little of the muffled conversation. He watched Archie reach for a pen, make a brief note, and then end the call. He looked up at Benjamin and said, "Benji, fire up your computer and look for McCarrs Creek near Pittwater, Sydney. Mr. Carter's phone is currently located somewhere near its headwaters."

"What on earth is at McCarrs Creek?"

"A sailing boat belonging to a guy who is currently overseas on business. Seems he's in Frankfurt and isn't due back for another two months. Carter must be using his boat in his absence."

Benjamin nodded. "It would be a perfect location to hide someone. Can we go and investigate it?"

"Are you up for it?"

"Yes but what will it involve? How will we do it?"

Archie picked up a metal ruler from the bench top and held it upright in front of his nose. "Sword drill, mate. Sword drill."

Benjamin got down from his stool and rolled his shoulders to ease the tension he was feeling. The idea of actually doing something was hugely attractive. The question was, could they do more? He took a deep breath and decided to broach his idea. "Um… Archie, I don't think it's a coincidence that Khayef's boat and this other yacht are both in Pittwater. Do you suppose we could, er… combine two operations into one?"

"What's on your mind, mate?"

Benjamin told him.

When he had finished, Archie rubbed the back of his neck. "Benji boy, you certainly have some outrageous and morally questionable ideas."

"Is it worth considering?"

"Maybe. But it's high risk."

"Too high?"

"Well, it just so happens that I once trained for an exercise pretty similar to this." He smiled. "It was a blast."

"Sword drill?"

Archie nodded. "We'll do a swift exercise now to see if it's even remotely feasible, and then do it again in more detail if we reckon it's a goer."

Half an hour later, Benjamin looked at his watch. "It's nine o'clock. If we want to make any phone calls tonight, we probably shouldn't leave them any later." He leaned back and stretched. "One of the big questions we have is whether we can get a boat. Why don't I ring Felicity's brother? The Shark Cat would be ideal."

Archie nodded, and Benjamin made a call to Michael Anderson. "Hi Michael, it's Benjamin Bidjara here. We've just received a bit of information that might tell us where Felicity is. Are you able to come over to the workshop for a few minutes? Fine. Thanks. See you in a bit."

Ten minutes later, Michael knocked on the workshop door. He was dressed as before but had slipped his feet into a pair of sheepskin ugg boots.

Benjamin pointed to the computer and showed him a satellite image of McCarrs Creek. He pointed to the headwaters. "This is where the phone of the Khayef guy who contacted Felicity is. It may mean nothing, but Archie and I would love to check it out discreetly."

"Can it be done discreetly?"

"I probably should have told you—Archie is ex-SAS."

The doctor stared Archie up and down. Archie said nothing and continued to masticate his matchstick. Michael pushed himself back from the bench. "You two got Flick's car back from her ex-husband, didn't you?"

Archie nodded.

The doctor sucked at his teeth. "I've had a few run-ins with Nick on Flick's behalf. He's a hard-nosed, intimidating bastard, so pulling that off persuades me you must be fairly capable. But why did you want me to come over tonight?"

"Because we'd like to borrow your boat," said Archie.

"The Shark Cat?"

"Yeah."

"And tow it a thousand kilometers to Sydney and back?"

Archie nodded. "We could probably get a boat locally but this would make things less complicated."

"My ute's pretty old," said Benjamin. "But its got a 3.2-liter engine, so it should be able to pull it okay."

"You'd still have to go carefully. It's a big boat. When do you want it?"

"Three days' time," said Archie.

"Do you know how to operate it?"

"Yeah, but I'd like you to show me any idiosyncrasies and run through the procedures."

"Okay."

Outside, the wind-vane squeaked as it turned backward and forward.

The doctor nodded. "Bring the ute to the slipway at 10am tomorrow. We'll take the boat for a brief spin. If I'm happy that you can handle her, and if your ute can pull her out of the water on her trailer, you can borrow her—and any other gear I've got that's helpful."

"Thanks," said Benjamin. "That's great."

The doctor got down from his stool and made for the door. He paused as he took hold of the doorknob. "Please find Flick," he said, and was gone.

Archie rubbed his hands together. "I can get the rest of the gear we need from some people I know in Sydney. I'll contact them tomorrow."

"Is there anything more we can do tonight?" asked Benjamin.

"Yeah. You need to make another phone call. But first, let me tell you some technical stuff I've just learned from Phoebe."

When Archie had finished sharing, he looked at his watch. "It might be a bit late to call him, though."

Benjamin shook his head. "No. A late call will add to the sense of drama. It's a good time." He made the call.

"Hello Marcus."

Chapter 19

Doran Khayef was furious. He strode from the lift, barged through the glass doors into his office, and barked at the receptionist behind the paneled counter, "No one comes into my office or disturbs me until I say so."

He slammed the door of his office before the receptionist could reply. After placing a plastic bottle of kerosene on his desk, he reached down to pick up a stainless steel waste paper bin. For a moment, he splayed his fingers on the desk, leaned over, and swore savagely. Then he pulled out his phone and made a call.

Carter answered. "Good morning, sir."

"Blast the bloody morning. Now tell me this, how sure are you that the document you've got is the real Sardinian copy of that bloody treaty?" There was a pause. "Come on, man, I need to know."

"What seems to be the problem, sir? Has anything happened?"

"Just answer the bloody question."

"Ah, well…Ms. Anderson has begun working on softening the document but she's only been working on it for one day. She says it will take some weeks to fully unroll it. She's just started working on it again this morning."

"Can we be sure?"

"I think, sir, that if you take into account how the document was found, where it was found…and link it with the disclosures in the PhD thesis, there can be no doubt that this is the document. The only question is how readable it will be once we've opened it up."

"What do you mean?"

"Ms. Anderson says that the writing ink may have faded over the years, but it will still show up under UV light—or some other band in the electromagnetic spectrum. One way or another, it will be readable. She's actually got a UV light here already. She uses it overnight to kill off any fungi trying to grow on the vellum."

"And you've scared her enough to ensure total compliance? The document is safe?"

"She is co-operating fully, sir."

"So, you would stake your life on the document being the treaty and it being readable?"

"Er…yes sir. But may I ask why?"

"Because you might have to," he spat.

"But sir…"

Khayef interrupted him. "I'll tell you bloody why. It's because the bloody English have tagged their copy of the treaty with some new, hush-hush, high-tech aerosol. That's bloody why!"

"Perhaps you could…um, tell me about it."

Khayef passed a hand over his hair. "They've got a thing called a taggant which has been engineered as a result of research into quantum physics. Tiny quantum dots of powder have been put in an aerosol that can be sprayed on to bloody parchments."

"But sir, you've had it examined and tested by the very best…"

"This technology is only a few years old and still being developed. No one has ever heard of it being used on documents before, so no antiquarian could possibly know about it—damn it!" He sighed. "The tiny particles absorb and emit light at specific wavelengths. I don't know the details. All I know is that when they're illuminated with an ultraviolet laser, the bloody spray can be detected by infrared cameras. Batches of the stuff are engineered to have distinct spectral signatures."

"Oh, I see, sir."

"I damn well hope you see because I'm about to destroy the English treaty. That's why I have to be bloody sure that the Sardinian document is the real thing."

"It is, sir. It has to be."

Khayef grunted and ended the phone call. He paused, then stabbed the intercom button. "Get me a hammer from maintenance and bring it me, pronto."

He threw himself into the high-backed office chair and considered the next complication that had come his way: Benjamin Bidjara. The impudent upstart had demanded to see him in two days' time in Port Fairy. His audacity rankled. *Red carnation indeed!* Khayef compressed his lips. By the time he had flown to Warrnambool, driven to Port Fairy…and then come back, it would be over half a day. He was not in the habit of giving that amount of time to anyone he disdained.

Should he go, or should he just send Eddie to sort him out? He pondered the question for the umpteenth time. Certainly, Eddie had to be there, one way or another. Khayef sighed. There was a certain thrill at seeing a man face-to-face, knowing that you were going to kill him. It was a childish pleasure, but he enjoyed it. More importantly, he needed to learn from Bidjara exactly how much he knew. The fact that he and the Anderson woman had pieced enough clues together to go searching for the treaty in Sardinia was disturbing… even if it had eventually turned out well for his own plans. He tapped a finger on the table. *Yes*, he resolved, *I'll keep the appointment.*

There was a knock on the door.

"Come," he said.

"Here's the hammer you asked for, sir." The receptionist handed it to him and withdrew.

Khayef laid it on the desk and went to the end wall. He pushed at a piece of paneling. It moved back, allowing him to slide it to one side and reveal a wall safe. He dialed the combination and heaved the door open. The English treaty lay between two pieces of glass on the top shelf. He pulled the glass-plated treaty out and carried it to his desk. Moments later, a few taps of the hammer reduced the plates to shattered fragments at the bottom of the waste paper bin. He doused the treaty and the shards of glass in kerosene and carried the bin through the sliding door to the balcony. He stared at the ancient parchment for a few seconds, momentarily grieving the expense and trouble he'd gone through to obtain it. To destroy it now was galling.

He lit a match and dropped it.

Felicity knew she was probably going to die very soon, much sooner than she'd thought. She was horrified. *It couldn't be.* What she'd discovered was shocking and bewildering.

She stared at the outside section of vellum that had been steamed and brushed with a urea-ethanol solution for the last four hours. The process of restoration was bringing about results that should not be possible. It was going far too well. The vellum was already softening—and that shouldn't be possible.

She sat back on the wooden step between the two bunks. It was the only thing that passed for a chair in her cabin. The mattress of one bunk had been removed so the bunk could be used as a work-bench. Felicity had set up a gas camping stove at one end and was boiling a kettle with a tube running from the spout into a wooden box. The roll of vellum lay in the bottom of the box on a cake rack.

She had been using a blunt pair of tweezers to test the rigidity of the vellum's edge. Unbelievably, it had moved slightly. Felicity rubbed the back of her hand across her brow and tried to think how this could be possible. Calf-skin that had desiccated for over five hundred years simply didn't behave this way, not even when it was stored in the darkest, coolest, and driest of conditions. She looked back into the box and tweaked the edge of the vellum again. Perhaps she had cracked it and hadn't noticed?

No. The edge of the vellum bent demurely into a healthy curve.

She sat back again and looked around. The walls of her wooden prison seemed to close in on her. In the distance, she could hear the low thrum of the diesel generator; it was started up every morning to provide electricity. Being cooped up in the forepeak meant there was little air movement. Her cabin became hot with the heat of the day, a heat that was made worse because she had the camping stove running for so many hours. She'd insisted that the rear of the hatch above her be opened a few inches to allow some of the airflow from the air conditioner to reach her through the louvered doors. The fore-hatch could be opened a little way, but it was firmly secured by a steel rod that was locked in place with a padlock to prevent it from being opened any further.

She gazed up at the fore-hatch willing it to open and let her fly free, to allow her to escape the nightmare. But it remained above her, translucent and gray—a permanent cloud between her and the sunshine.

What did the riddle of the vellum mean? What should she do? She moved across to her bunk, drew up her knees and hugged them as she thought. Tears welled up at the frustration of life and its cruelty. She longed for hope; for someone to show kindness…for Benjamin.

What would he be doing now? Had she done enough to help him find her? KF—Khayef—wasn't much for him to go on. She lowered her head and found herself praying. *Dear God, there's so much that I don't understand. Please help me.* She waited for the chilling inner voice to mock her hypocrisy and tell her she was a fool…but it didn't come.

That was strange.

She thought again of Benjamin. So much had changed since she met him. Love, heady love—a love that was total and made her feel safe. She remembered how his arms had first wrapped around her, leading her up toward the surface of the sea; how he'd helped her take off her wetsuit—her breasts pressed innocently by his forearm —and she affecting to take no notice.

No notice? Yeah, right! She rested her head on her knees. It was electric—even back then.

She glanced at her watch. It was past midday; lunch would be soon. The food had been surprisingly good. Although it was served in plastic takeaway cartons, it was obviously prepared by excellent cooks, probably at a nearby restaurant. Once a day, the speedboat buzzed away to pick up the meals and the laundry. Even after the food had been reheated in the microwave, it was excellent.

She'd hardly seen Eddie. He'd opened the door once to allow her to have her morning shower and whispered, "I'm a patient man, bitch." She affected to ignore him, but inside the cramped shower cubicle, she held on to the taps and whimpered in terror until Carter had knocked on the door and reminded her that their water supplies were limited. Carter was always the one who gave Felicity her meals and he used these occasions to review her progress.

Progress? She daren't make any progress—or at least, not much. Felicity swung her feet off the bunk, stepped over to the tiny gas stove, and turned it off. Fear prickled through her. Somehow, she had to buy time to afford Benjamin and Archie the maximum opportunity to rescue her—if, indeed, they could. Would she be able to spin things out for four weeks? She very much doubted it. One thing she was now very sure of: the vellum lying in the bottom of the steam box was not the treaty signed between Henry VII of England and John II of Portugal. A detached, historical part of her heart felt crushing disappointment over this. She'd been so certain that it must be the missing Sardinian treaty. What else could it have been? The circumstances in which it was found could mean that it was nothing else. And yet…

Felicity peered into the steam box once more. The vellum remained very brown, dry, and brittle. After two days of work, it was still rolled into a cylinder shape. And yet, the edge had already started to soften. She touched it gently with a finger. Felicity closed her eyes and tried to imagine what she would conclude about the vellum if she knew nothing of its provenance. She came to a conclusion without much difficulty. All the evidence indicated that the parchment in front of her could not be much more than one hundred and fifty years old—nothing like five hundred years.

Felicity bit her lip. She couldn't stall Carter for many more days; he was far too intelligent. The trouble was, he would only need to see a few inches of the vellum unrolled before he knew that what he had wasn't the Sardinian copy of the treaty.

And when that happened, there would be no reason for her to be kept alive.

———————

Benjamin woke to the musical chortling of magpies outside his window. He eased himself out of his swag and glanced across the workshop to where Archie was also stirring himself. He'd moved himself inside for the last two days—but it hadn't been easy for him. Benjamin had heard him cry out with night terrors on the first night. On the second night he'd moved his swag closer to the open window. The workshop was chilly. The pot-belly stove had died out some time in the early morning.

He went outside to the toilet and took the opportunity to inspect the carpet of snail shells and the spider's web. No visitors.

After a cold shower, he sat down with Archie and worked his way through a cooked breakfast.

"I've got some gear being brought up from Melbourne. It should be dropped off about lunchtime," said Archie, as he cupped a mug of tea between his hands.

"What sort of gear?"

"Dive gear, mostly—a semi-closed nitrox rebreather unit." He took a swig of tea. "Think of them as scuba tanks, but ones that leave no bubbles. They make divers hard to see."

Benjamin raised an eyebrow. "Sounds like pretty sophisticated stuff."

"Nah, not really. This one is fairly low tech, but fine for what I need. It'll give me 160 minutes dive time at five meters. I won't be going deeper than ten. The unit is actually lighter and more comfortable than a scuba tank. Your air stays warm and moist so your mouth feels less dry."

Benjamin shook his head. His old life had been shattered in the last month. He'd discovered both agony and ecstasy. The agony of anxiety…and the crushing fear that he might lose Felicity. And the ecstasy of having found her…of feeling love…of being complete… of being significant to another…of being captivated by the giddying, disturbing power of her sexuality. She looked fantastic. Her smile, her…

"Mate, bloody pay attention!"

Benjamin realized that Archie had been speaking. "Er, sorry. What were you saying?"

"I've also got ten cans of temporary car-art paint coming. It's black. Your job this afternoon is to spray-paint your ute." He tapped the end of a match on the bench top. "It doesn't have to be too professional, but it does have to be black. Think you can manage it?"

Benjamin nodded. "Yes. The only job I'd like to finish today is to put the last two coats of Scandinavian oil on Marjorie's blackwood box."

Archie put the match into his mouth. "Well, take it easy today, mate, because tomorrow the balloon goes up."

Chapter 20

The next day, very few words were spoken. Archie lifted up a bag that Benjamin had never seen before. He heard a faint metallic chink as he settled it on his shoulder.

They walked together into the town center, now busy with early morning trade, toward the café where Gabrielle worked. Benjamin carried Marjorie's box under one arm. The final coat he'd applied to it was still a little tender, even though he'd placed it in front of the stove overnight.

They walked down a side road and turned into the service track that went to the back of some two-story apartments. The door to number two was open, and they made their way upstairs. Archie immediately went to the old sash window, opened it, and looked across the road to the café. Seemingly satisfied, he said, "Keep well back from the window and stay out of sight."

He then dragged a heavy desk to the center of the room, put a rug over its surface, and lifted a chair on top of it. Archie climbed up into the chair and checked that he had a clear view to the café. He got back down and opened his shoulder bag. Its contents were as sobering as Benjamin feared. Three minutes later, the various sections of a collapsible rifle had been assembled, complete with telescopic sights and a silencer. It was a grim looking thing.

"Is that really necessary?" asked Benjamin.

"Relax. I only plan to use the telescopic sights."

"The silencer?"

Archie sniffed. "I'm being a good boy scout." He climbed up into the chair and settled the rifle across his knees.

Benjamin was careful to keep back from the window, but he found he could see a little if he stood on the bed. There was only one small table on the pavement in front of the café. A large elderly woman was sitting at it, knitting.

The two men waited.

The building they were in had once been an old bank. Someone had since renovated it and divided it into a number of holiday units. The room he was now in had all the modern conveniences but had been allowed to keep its old-fashioned ambience. Benjamin approved.

Forty-five minutes later, Archie murmured, "They're here."

Benjamin took out his phone, called a number, switched the phone to speaker mode, and placed it on the desktop.

Archie had the rifle up to his shoulder and began to give a commentary. "Black hire car...parked on the opposite side...two men...one getting out...short...gray suit...black hair...it's Doran Khayef...walking across the road...Gabrielle on doorstep...slipping her phone into her apron pocket...she's putting on long, black theater gloves...looking dramatic. Stay quiet now."

The ensuing conversation could be heard through Benjamin's phone.

"Good morning, sir. Coffee? We serve the best coffee in town."

"I want to sit at a table outside."

"Sure. I'm just putting the tables outside. If you give me a hand, we'll put one outside for you."

"What bloody time do you get up and going in the country? It should all be set up by now."

"Ah, sir, it's been a bit chilly. But the sun's out now. It'll be lovely out here. Can you take the edge of this table and give me a hand?"

Indistinct grumble. Scuffling noises.

"Now, sir, what can I get you?"

"A skinny chai latte. And I need another chair. I'm expecting someone."

"Certainly, sir. What about a Melting Moment? I recommend them."

"Oh, I suppose so. One of those too."

Time passed.

A fly flew in through the window and started to buzz around Archie's head. He didn't flinch or acknowledge it in any way. Benjamin crept forward and swatted it away.

Ten minutes later, more conversation could be heard on the phone. "Here you are, sir. I hope you enjoy it." Clunk. Clatter. "Are you here on business or having a holiday?"

Pause. "Business…with one of your locals." Pause. "I hope he's out of bed because he's twenty minutes late."

"Oh, who would that be, sir? I know a lot of people around here."

"Mind your own bloody…no, well perhaps you might. He might have already been here. I was a bit late. Perhaps you can tell me. His name is Benjamin Bidjara."

"Oh, Benny."

Benjamin winced.

"Yes, I know Benny. He's been here a few times. He's a bit… well, slow, socially. Can't pick it when a woman's cracking on to him…and he eats with his mouth open."

"He hasn't been here this morning?"

"Nah."

"Damn and blast." Pause. "He's late." Scraping noises. "Bloody man. I'm not going to wait any more."

"I'm sorry, sir. Benny's a wood-turner, an artist…and they're a strange lot. It can sometimes be difficult to get them to pull their head out of their arses to see what's right in front of their eyes."

"Well, tell him…tell him he's had his chance."

"Yeah. Sure."

Archie continued his commentary. "Khayef crossing road... getting into car...slamming door...car moving off."

He dropped the rifle from his shoulder and began dismantling it. "Right, we're clear. Let's pack up and go." Benjamin walked over to the window. The large woman who had been knitting was now holding a large black garbage bag open as Gabrielle dropped the clear, plastic table top cover into it. Gabrielle glanced up at the window as she tied the neck of the plastic bag into a knot. Benjamin gave her a thumbs up.

Gabrielle grinned and extended her middle finger at him, rudely.

Fifteen minutes later, Benjamin and Archie were crossing the old wooden footbridge over the Moyne River to the eastern bank. The sun glinted cheerfully on the water as it lapped against the mud and sedges. The tranquility of their surroundings was at odds with the savage business they were about to engage in. Benjamin was no longer carrying Marjorie's box but was now holding the black bin liner. It contained nine unused clear plastic table coverings and one used one.

Once across the bridge, they turned right and walked down Griffith Street toward the slipway. It wasn't long before Benjamin saw his ute, looking unfamiliar in it's black livery. It was hitched to the double-bogey trailer carrying the Shark Cat.

They packed their bags with the rest of the gear inside the boat and got into the ute. Benjamin took a deep breath. His role had been fairly passive thus far but this was no longer going to be the case. For better or for worse, he was now fully involved.

***

The ute had its back pressed well down by the heavy, and occasionally bucking, boat trailer. Benjamin drove at a stately pace north to Hamilton, then on, past the rocky ranges of the Grampians to Horsham. After three-and-a-half hours driving, he turned in to a caravan park where the two of them booked a cabin.

Benjamin and Archie unhooked the boat trailer and carried the luggage from the Shark Cat into the cabin, where it could be kept safe. By the time all the gear was inside, there was very little floor space left. The only piece of luggage they didn't carry inside was a large plastic storage bin. Archie lifted it out of the Shark Cat and strapped it onto the tray of the ute.

"Will that be big enough?" asked Benjamin.

"It has a sixty-liter capacity. Should do. Let's grab something to eat. Then I need to make a phone call."

Benjamin didn't find the next three hours very easy. He was seething with anxiety, questions, and self-doubt.

Archie was inspecting his phone. He had just finished speaking with Phoebe and was now checking the weather forecast. "We'll have a bit of light. There's a half-moon. No rain."

"What did Phoebe say?"

"The truck's been loaded and is due to leave Adelaide at 4:30pm. It's a red Kenworth semi-trailer. It's got *Night Rider* stenciled on the bonnet spoiler. She should be pretty easy to spot. We'll wait for it on the Adelaide side of Horsham and then tail her."

"And Phoebe's sure the police won't be tailing it?"

Archie nodded. "They've got watching points along the way at Horsham, Ararat, and Ballarat. They won't be tailing them in a car. The last time they did that, the truck driver noticed, pulled into a truck stop, and did a runner. The police won't start tailing the truck until it gets near the Westgate Bridge outside of Melbourne. They're planning the drug bust when it arrives at the warehouse."

"What are our chances?"

"About fifty-fifty. We've got a lot of points at which we can bail out." He shrugged. "If the traffic won't let us get alongside the truck before one of the rest stops, we won't even try."

Benjamin closed his eyes and leaned back on his bed. They only had a fifty-fifty chance of pulling it off. He felt sick. And if they did succeed, they were only at the beginning of what was required to attack Khayef. Benjamin continued to fret. "We know that the truck is carrying bags of fertilizer on pallets but how sure are we that we know which one the drugs will be in?"

"We're not." Archie grinned. "That's what makes it so exciting."

Benjamin shivered and again wondered at the extraordinary psyche required by the SAS. One thing he was very sure of, he couldn't do it.

Archie continued. "All we've got is logic. That tells me that the drugs will be in the third or fourth pallet they load. It will probably be on top of the first two pallets. That way, the bags carrying the drugs are less likely to be crushed and damaged. By putting them in against the end wall of the container, they lessen the chances of detection. Anyone wanting to inspect the cargo will have to remove all the other pallets in order to get to them." He glanced at Benjamin from under his pale eyebrows. 'relax, mate. Doing bold and arsey things doesn't mean we don't put a priority on safety. If we don't find the drugs in the end pallets, we bail out. Okay?"

Safety...yeah. Benjamin could think of a better definition of 'safety' than the activities they were contemplating.

Chapter 21

"How far ahead is the next rest stop?" Benjamin consciously eased his grip on the steering wheel and tried to relax. He was holding it too tightly. Both he and Archie were dressed in black wetsuits and were wearing reinforced diver's gloves.

Archie looked at the GPS map on his phone. "About two kilometers."

Benjamin checked his rear view mirror. His heart started to pound as he heard himself say, "Traffic's pretty light and there's a dual carriageway just ahead. This might be our opportunity."

"Okay. Make up ground on the truck—as if you're keen to overtake."

They had already passed one rest area because of congested traffic. Benjamin was slightly ashamed at feeling a sense of relief: perhaps they would have an excuse not to continue their madcap plan. The decision had been made to abort the mission if they couldn't make use of the first three rest areas. These areas were primarily designed to allow truck drivers to pull over and sleep if they were close to exceeding the length of time they could legally drive. Car drivers also used them to rest and revive. Because the Adelaide to Melbourne run was only eight hours, drivers from

Adelaide rarely stopped in these bays. At night, they were invariably deserted—in theory.

A double set of truck tail-lights glared at them from two hundred meters ahead.

"Make ground, buddy," urged Archie. "Get a move on."

Benjamin flattened the accelerator.

The tail-lights drew closer.

Archie opened the glove compartment and pulled out a black automatic pistol. It looked brutal and sinister—an impression in no way diminished by the silencer screwed onto its end. Benjamin shuddered as Archie cocked the gun and chambered a bullet into the breech.

"Get up to the drive tires and then ease back for a few seconds. If we blow one of those, they'll have to stop pretty quickly. With a bit of luck, a single shot will blow out a double set."

Benjamin nodded dumbly.

The road suddenly widened into dual carriageway. He swung the ute out and began to overtake the semi-trailer. The trailer had a row of orange lights along its length. Slowly, they went past: one… two…three…four. Then the first of the twin sets of drive wheels approached. They were huge and thundered just one meter from Archie's open window. Archie barely appeared to raise the gun. It coughed twice in quick succession. "As fast as you can now," ordered Archie.

Benjamin was dimly aware of a flopping noise and the truck rapidly falling behind them as he sped ahead. From the corner of his eye, he saw a sign on the side of the road: *Rest Area—500 meters*.

Archie continued to give directions. "About fifty meters from the rest area, switch off your lights and pull in. Brake to a stop using only the handbrake. Park near the entrance under the trees. Leave the engine running."

"Okay."

And suddenly, there it was: the slipway to the rest area was up ahead on the left. Benjamin took his foot off the accelerator, switched off the headlights, and pulled on the handbrake. The ute shuddered and threatened to fishtail. He fought the car back under control with one hand while continuing to pull on the handbrake. They rumbled along the graded dirt until they came to a stop beside some trees.

Archie and Benjamin donned diver's masks, then got out and crouched down behind the ute.

They didn't have very long to wait. Benjamin watched with terrified fascination as the snarling truck swung its bluff nose off the highway, onto the slipway leading to the rest stop. It growled its way past the ute, losing momentum until it came to a standstill with a hissing of brakes. Dust from the dirt surface billowed out from under its wheels.

For a moment, no one moved. The drivers in the truck's cabin stayed where they were. They had left the headlights of the truck switched on as if they were undecided.

"Go!" Yelled Archie.

Benjamin and Archie sprinted through the dust toward the cabin of the truck. Archie leaped onto the running board and smashed the passenger window with the butt of the pistol. As he jumped back down to the ground, Benjamin sprang up behind him and threw a shoebox into the cabin before leaping back down.

Almost immediately there was a howl and a curse. Two drivers hurled themselves from the cabin, one from the passenger side and the other from the driver's side. They were followed by a cloud of angry wasps. A sawn-off shotgun fell from the passenger seat onto the ground beside the truck. The man who had been holding it was now bent double, swatting at the wasps.

Benjamin trusted Archie to take care of the man on the driver's side. He pulled out the taser from the haversack slung around his shoulders, and shot it at the man in front of him.

Four minutes later, both drivers had their mouths and eyes taped with gray duct tape.

Benjamin stood guard over them as Archie climbed up into the cabin. After brushing the shoebox containing the papery wasp nest onto the ground, he revved the truck's engine, doused the lights, and released the brake. The prime mover hissed air, revved again, and lurched forward. Archie turned the truck hard right and then killed the engine. The cab, with its fiberglass wind deflector, now obscured the end of the container from the road. Benjamin was also grateful for the line of trees that helped obscure the truck from passing motorists.

Archie climbed down and handcuffed the two drivers' hands onto the trailer's tie rail.

Benjamin shook his head to remind himself he wasn't in a dream and forced himself into action. He climbed on top of the turntable coupling and stood up behind the end of the metal container. He reached up but couldn't touch the top of it. Below him, Archie was pulling at the starter motor of the petrol-driven demolition saw. Brrr…brrr…brrr.

Please start! Please start!

The saw roared into life. Once it had settled down into a burble, Archie handed it up to Benjamin.

The weight of the demolition saw was appalling. Benjamin would only be able to hold it above his head for short moments at a time. He pressed the trigger. The large cutting blade started to spin as the engine howled angrily. It made a terrible noise. He hefted the saw above his head and eased the blade into the metal. The unit bucked, and sparks squirted away to his right. The big blade cut through the thin metal almost instantly. It was just as well; holding and controlling the saw above his head was almost more than he could manage. He needed to rest four times before he had cut horizontally across the end of the container.

Benjamin then put a second cut across the container, two meters lower. His forearms and shoulders screamed for mercy as the heavy saw again juddered its way through the metal. Cutting down low was easier but even so, he was almost whimpering with fatigue by the time he had finished. He let go of the trigger and rested the heavy saw at his feet. Sweat was running down the inside of his wetsuit in the places where it wasn't compressing him. His facemask was beginning to mist up. Seconds counted. Two cuts to go, both vertical.

Benjamin hauled the saw above his head again and began to cut downward. Sparks showered toward him—blinding him, and bouncing off his facemask. He could feel tiny needle pricks as the sparks found the small area of unprotected flesh around his mouth. With huge relief, he discovered that the saw was easy to control at this angle. He cut down to the lower horizontal cut in just a few seconds.

After resting briefly, Benjamin began the final cut. As he sliced toward the bottom, it occurred to him that a plate of steel measuring over four meters square was likely to fall on top of him. To his relief, Archie climbed up beside him and took hold of the thin steel plate with his reinforced gloves, as it began to twist forward.

"Drop the saw and jump!" Archie yelled.

Benjamin did so. Heedless of its well-being, he dropped the saw and vaulted down to the ground. A second later, Archie yelled, "Look out!"

A large panel of container steel dropped onto the turntable with a bang and somersaulted on to the ground.

Dust hung in the air.

Benjamin picked himself up from the ground and retrieved the demolition saw. Surprisingly, it was still working. He killed its engine and lifted it into the ute, nestling it between some spare tires.

He returned to the truck and looked up inside the container. Plastic bags of fertilizer were stacked on four pallets two on top of two. Archie was unable to reach the top layer of bags. They were still hidden behind the steel wall that Benjamin hadn't been able to reach and cut out. He was, however, pulling at the second-top layer of bags. He'd gained a purchase on it by slashing it with a knife so that it spilled much of its contents. Fertilizer pellets cascaded down around him.

Benjamin's job was now to watch, nothing more. It was just as well: he was exhausted. He and Archie had worked out earlier who would do what tasks so that the physical demands were shared.

Trucks and cars hummed past them on the other side of the line of trees, their headlights staring ahead, all apparently innocent of what was going on.

It was surreal.

Benjamin looked back to the pallets of fertilizer. The edges of three bags per layer could be seen. It was, as Archie had previously explained, a pattern that allowed the center of a pallet to contain anything and remain invisible from the outside.

Archie continued to burrow away. Bags of fertilizer now fell out quickly. Some fell to the ground, others fell onto the turning bed and had to be kicked onto the ground. He worked his way down one wall of a pallet until he'd gone half way.

There was nothing.

Without stopping, he began on the pallet beside it.

Cars and trucks continued to speed by. Half of Benjamin's mind noticed that there seemed to be a lot of trucks traveling tonight. He caught himself reasoning that it was a Thursday night. Many trucks would want to make the eight-hour night run so that they could unload on Friday morning—before the weekend.

The other half of Benjamin's mind was terrified.

He glanced at his watch. It was impossible. They had only taken nine minutes.

Thump. Another bag fell to the ground. *Thump.* Yet another.

The absurdity of Benjamin's situation dawned on him. Here he was, dressed in a diver's wetsuit, raiding a semi-trailer somewhere in the middle of the Victorian Wimmera.

"Hey, mate." Archie interrupted his thoughts. "We've got something here." He took the torch hanging around his neck and shone it into the hole he'd excavated. Then, reaching in, he pulled out a bag. It was very much smaller in size than the fertilizer bags. Benjamin could see the glint of crystals in the torchlight through the layers of clear plastic.

"Come here and grab it," said Archie. "Watch you don't twist an ankle on the fertilizer bags." As Benjamin took the bag that was handed down to him, he felt its contents crunch slightly. He carried it to the storage bin in the back of the ute and dropped it in.

Three minutes later, eight packages had been secured inside the plastic bin.

Benjamin climbed into the front seat of the ute as Archie walked over to the two truck drivers to check on their well-being and ensure their handcuffs remained secure. Archie patted one of them on the shoulder before walking back to the ute.

As soon as Archie climbed in, Benjamin shifted the ute into gear and drove out onto the highway. He continued along it for ten kilometers before turning off onto a small paved country lane. Moments later, they were parked by a farm gate. The hoof prints of cattle and cowpats pockmarked the earth around them. It was a gate used by dairy cattle—cattle that would be milked again in the morning. Their footprints would trample all signs of them ever having been there.

Archie and Benjamin got out of the ute, filled two buckets from plastic jerry-cans and began to wash the temporary car-art paint from the utility. Gradually, its original white paint reappeared. Once they'd finished, they washed themselves in their wetsuits and then changed back into their normal clothes.

Curious cows watched them from over the fence.

They drove back to Horsham using the back roads. It took a long time, not least because they stopped every forty kilometers or so to change a rear wheel. First one, then another was rolled into the bush beside the road and a second-hand wheel put on in its place. It was an hour-and-a-half before they got back to their caravan park.

Archie chivvied him along for the next two hours as they repacked the packets of drugs. It seemed to Benjamin that he'd been wearing gloves of one type or another forever. As he finally pulled off his latex gloves, he couldn't help but feel that he was shedding his innocence. No fingerprints. Anonymous. Who was he?

He sighed. At the very least, he was a man who was prepared to break the law in order to destroy those who threatened people he loved. The enormity of what he and Archie had just done appalled him. He looked at his hands. They were shaking.

Archie glanced at Benjamin and put on the kettle. "I prescribe tea…with four spoons of sugar." He pulled two mugs out from the cupboard. "It helps with shock." Archie tore open some sachets of sugar and tipped their contents into the mugs.

Benjamin nodded his thanks as he accepted his mug of tea. It was a challenge even to reach out and hold it. His forearms had become stiff, and his hands felt clumsy.

Archie selected the music function on his phone and chose an easy-listening playlist. Benjamin laced his fingers together and bent them backward to ease out their stiffness. The music was therapeutic for Archie, too, even if he wasn't inclined to think about it. What Benjamin really wanted, though, was...what? To hear a voice...

Felicity...I just want to hear your voice...Where are you? Are you okay? More than anything else, I just want to hear your voice...

Not possible. The desperate ache.

Benjamin began to feel the stirring of an idea. It demanded attention—like an itch. The sensation surprised him. It was an insistent conviction that he should call Marjorie. He reached out and took hold of his phone.

His call was answered almost immediately. "Hello Benjamin."

Marjorie's voice didn't sound tired, even though it was nearly midnight. Benjamin was relieved. She continued, "I was having a wretched night and couldn't sleep. I hoped someone might call."

"Oh." A million questions immediately suggested themselves. He ignored them. "I...um, know Archie rang Phoebe earlier but I just...felt the need to call. It's...been..." He trailed off.

"Shocking?"

"Yes."

"Bewildering?"

"Yes."

"Confronting?"

"Yes."

"And it was something you did for love."

"Um...yes."

"You've bitten the apple, Benjamin. But not all apples are bad. Some strengthen you."

There was silence for a long while.

Eventually, Benjamin said, "I tried to pray, you know. But I wasn't very..."

"What was the voice like, that tried to stop you?"

"How…How do you know?"

"What was it like?" Marjorie insisted.

"It was chilly. It jeered."

Marjorie sighed. "I'm afraid that's something you'll have to get used to."

Benjamin didn't understand, but he pushed on. "Marjorie, how do I know that your Christian faith isn't just a Western cultural thing? After all, I'm part Aboriginal…and we have a different spirituality."

"Do you, Benjamin? Do you really? Don't you have a supreme Creator, a single higher being whom your people know is the ultimate source of life and creation?"

"Er…yes."

"Well, when you discover his love for you, you will discover your full identity."

"But aren't other ways of expressing spirituality just as valid?"

"All spiritualities are searches for a God we instinctively know exists. It's just that our attempts to define him have resulted in some rather odd ideas." She paused before continuing, "It was an impasse that God solved by coming to us."

"Coming to us?"

"Mmm. He came to pay the price for our sins that separated us from him."

"Marjorie, I've broken more laws in the last five hours than most people do in a lifetime."

"I know, dear. Life's complicated."

Benjamin could hear that Marjorie's voice was getting weaker. He chastised himself for wearying her. "I'd better go. Thanks for… speaking to me. I…I needed to hear…"

"So did I, Benjamin." Marjorie's breath labored for a while before she continued. "Just one more thing."

"Yes."

"Thank you for my lovely blackwood box. It's beautiful."

Benjamin searched for the right words to say. In the end, he gave up and settled for, "You're welcome."

Chapter 22

B enjamin had seriously underestimated the effect that towing a heavy boat on a tandem trailer would have on petrol consumption. Archie always insisted on paying, and he did so with cash. When Benjamin questioned him about it, he was evasive. "I've got an expense budget. It's not massive, so we need to be careful." He grinned. "And I need to keep the receipts."

His comment made Benjamin shake his head. He could picture the receipt:

COST:

Several hundred dollars.

PURPOSE:

1) Raiding a semi-trailer of forty million dollars' worth of drugs belonging to a motorcycle gang

2) mounting an attack on a major commercial operation

3) ...and, please God, *finding Felicity*

Felicity...What would she be thinking right now? Was she safe? Would she know that he and Archie were coming for her? Benjamin dare not allow the anguish over what she might be going through to overwhelm him. He couldn't bear to picture it; knowing he would be totally debilitated by it. Yet the monster was always there, threatening to crash over him and drown him in despair. He forced himself to relax and retreat to a place within his heart—a still place where questions were sometimes answered.

Outside, the Wimmera plains spread out before him. Benjamin grieved at what he saw. Vast tracts of land had been cleared of trees to make room for farms. Huge fields bordered by crooked gray posts cut from native timber stretched into timelessness. Its emptiness shrieked at him. Once there were stringy barks and mallee trees. Now, only remnants remained.

Inside his heart, he traveled deeper and deeper into that quiet place—and when the path faded into peace, he knew he had arrived. He sat down and waited.

There was a stand of buloke trees, so loved by the red-tailed cockatoo.

Inside, he continued to wait.

A zephyr of wind warmed his cheek—a caress. It was nothing, nothing at all…except that it was a comfort.

It was enough. Benjamin allowed himself to float slowly to the surface, to meet his conscious mind as it searched the Wimmera landscape.

Archie shifted in the seat beside him. His eyes were half-closed.

Benjamin risked making a comment. "I'm not sure that getting rid of the rear wheels has done us much good. If the police search us now, they'll find forty kilograms of methamphetamine, a power saw, and two wetsuits."

"Yeah, mate. If we're stopped now, we're gone for all money. But my concern is what happens next week when this little mission is over. We need to be squeaky clean by then." He closed his eyes. "Police investigations usually take a bit of time. That's why we need to move quickly while we can."

Benjamin nodded. "I've been thinking a bit about that."

Archie raised an eyebrow.

"The absolute priority in this Sydney trip is to find Felicity and secure her safety. Nothing else we do must be allowed to jeopardize that."

"Your point?"

"If we do find Felicity, I don't want her compromised by our being in possession of a stack of illegal drugs. So, ideally, I'd like to ditch the drugs first. The trouble is, that's bound to be risky—and I don't want us getting caught before we find Felicity."

"So, what do you have in mind?"

"If Felicity is in the sailing boat, how confident are you of being able to get her out?"

"Pretty confident."

"Could you do it on your own?"

"Yeah."

The certainty of Archie's reply was slightly disturbing. Benjamin swallowed and continued. "Let me place the drugs while you are nowhere near. Then, if something goes wrong, you can slip away on your own and still rescue Felicity."

Archie nodded. "Sounds reasonable. But if you're going to place the drugs, mate, there're a few things you're going to have to learn…and a few things I'll have to do to set you up."

They headed east along the Wimmera Highway through Bendigo, then across country to Seymour. By the time they had climbed onto the Hume Highway and were heading toward Sydney, a plan of sorts had taken shape. Benjamin thought the sheer audacity of what they were contemplating was appalling. The only thing that kept him focused was his determination to destroy the evil that threatened Felicity. Anger, he discovered, was a great motivator.

Archie grunted as he looked at the screen on his phone. "Phoebe's sent me a picture and a plan of Khayef's boat. Take a look."

Benjamin glanced at it quickly. He saw again the sweeping shape of the luxury yacht. Its curving windows of black glass made it look as though it was wearing too much mascara.

Archie gave him the details. "It's a sixty-nine foot Ferretti luxury motor cruiser capable of thirty knots. It has three double cabins, all with en suites, and one crew cabin with its own bathroom."

"Doesn't sound too shabby."

"It's got one fore-hatch, which we have to assume will be locked. The only access to the cabins is via a staircase by the main driving console. There is no way to get to it without going through the main saloon."

"So we'll have to do all we want to do outside her?"

"Yeah. But it'll take balls. You sure you're up for it?"

"What can you tell me that might help me get through it?"

Archie glanced at him appraisingly and said, "Rule one: The most ballsy missions require the most patience. You've got to out-wait what people normally expect. Being patient under pressure isn't easy."

Benjamin nodded.

"Rule two: Get comfortable. Take it slow and conserve energy. Then, when you need it, you've got it. Don't be heroic and expend energy until you need to. That is particularly the case when you're working underwater. Anything underwater takes twenty times more energy and ten times longer."

Benjamin wasn't sure Archie's wisdom was much comfort.

It was a deceit that gave the illusion of some civility: Carter always knocked before he unfastened the bolts and opened the door into the forepeak. Felicity was expecting him as the speedboat had returned only a few minutes earlier. It would have brought their lunch—invariably hot and generous in its portions. She chose to foster the illusion by responding to Carter's knock, saying, "Come in."

In reality, she wanted to scream, to hit him, to do anything that might help her escape her imprisonment. Being confined in such a small space for so long was beginning to wear her down. Clouds of melancholy and despair rolled over her—never leaving her alone for long. She'd set in place a routine that helped her deal with them, but each day, it was getting harder. Felicity began her routine by thinking of Benjamin and imagining what he might be doing to find her. He would be doing all he could to find her. She knew with abso-lute certainty that he would be doing all he could. Hour after hour, day after day, she instructed the neural pathways in her brain:

Benjamin will not rest until he's found me…and he has the resources of a formidable team to help him. The second thing she did was to put herself through a punishing exercise routine. Her confined space meant that her options were limited. Squats, sit-ups, and push-ups constituted the core of her regime but each day she tried to introduce a new exercise to ensure variety. She exercised for ten minutes every two hours.

Felicity sometimes found herself pondering the serenity of Marjorie even in the face of death. She envied her.

Knock, knock.

Felicity sat up on her bunk and straightened her blouse. "Come in."

Carter came in and handed her a silver foil container. A plastic fork was balanced on top of it. In his other hand he held a hemp shopping bag. He nodded to her. "Miss Anderson. We have risotto today." He turned around to Felicity's makeshift workbench. "How are you progressing?"

Very formal; surreal. *You are planning to use me and then kill me.* "Quite well. Here, I'll show you." She stood up and bent over the box with the vellum at the bottom of it. "I've managed to unroll another five millimeters. That's good progress." *Win his confidence. Show compliance.* What she didn't say was that it was her practice to spend a few minutes desiccating the vellum with her hair drier every few hours so that the solutions she applied to it would have minimal effect. As she leaned over, she stretched the fabric of her blouse and showed as much cleavage as she could.

She took a pair of tweezers and bent back a corner of the vellum. "See?"

Carter peered inside the box, his nose just inches from her breasts. He didn't even blink.

Oh dear, she thought. *That's not going to work, then.*

She stepped back and sat down on her bunk. "This is such a beautiful boat. How did you come across it?"

Carter furrowed his brow. "It belongs to a friend."

"He must be a very generous friend."

"Oh, he's…never mind."

But Felicity had seen it, the softening of the eyes—for a fraction of a second. *They're lovers.* Her mind worked feverishly, trying to decide what she might do with this information. She drew in a breath and said, "This boat is designed for...well, I think it's designed for pleasure, maybe even love. How can you bear to see it used as a prison, as a place of threat...even murder?" She shrugged. "You're a refined man, how is that possible?"

Carter compressed his lips. "Miss Anderson, don't try and worm your way into my conscience. Any refinement you see in me is an illusion. Nature, as you must know, is inherently predatory. Pleasure is the only thing that makes sense."

"But pleasure without loving relationships...well, surely that's a lonely sterile thing."

"Oh, I've experienced love." He laughed bitterly. "That was particularly predatory." He stared at her, then stretched his neck. "You won't talk about these things with me ever again, or I will allow Eddie to indulge his particular expressions of love. Is that clear?"

Felicity didn't trust herself to say anything. She hung her head and allowed her hair to hide her face. Terror prickled the silence.

Carter's tone then changed completely. "I've brought something that I want you to tell me about." He reached down, picked up the shopping bag, and pulled something out of it.

Felicity stared at the object Carter was holding. She had been totally unprepared for what she saw. Carter was holding the Atlantis stone.

Felicity fought down an impulse to snatch it from him. *Please, please handle it carefully. It represents the breakthrough of a lifetime...and it's my link with Benjamin.*

"Oh, that," she said, affecting a normalcy she did not feel. "I wondered where that had gone. I was quite pleased to have found it, but I haven't had the chance to examine it carefully or tell anyone about it yet."

"What is it?"

"I'm not entirely sure. I found it in the silt while I was diving off Warrnambool. There's a chance that it may be Portuguese. If it were cleaned up a bit more, we might be able to tell. It would certainly strengthen the theory that the Portuguese discovered Victoria in the early sixteenth century." Felicity reached up and ran a finger over the engraving. "Get me a shallow basin and some hydrogen peroxide, and I'll finish cleaning it for you if you like."

Carter was silent for a while before eventually nodding. "Yes. Please do that." He placed the stone on the makeshift workbench and turned to leave the cabin. Without looking around, he said, "Your co-operation is appreciated and will be rewarded with…at least a degree of…comfort. Enjoy your meal."

Once he'd locked the door, Felicity reached over and picked up the Atlantis stone. She clutched it to her chest, rolled into a fetal position…and began to cry.

Chapter 23

Benjamin nosed his fiberglass kayak between the strange aerial roots of the mangroves. He stared through the clear water to the millions of mysterious holes that pockmarked the mud below him. A tiny crab with large pink claws scurried out from one of them. It was all so unfamiliar. The untidy tangle of roots at the base of the mangroves gave the impression that the trees were huddled together, preparing to set out like spiders to wander across the beaches.

Archie continued to instruct him how to propel himself properly. "Pull the paddle through the water...and as you lift it free, twist your wrist so that the other blade drops in vertically."

After fifteen minutes of instruction, Archie pronounced himself satisfied that Benjamin was competent enough to venture along the coast. They were both wearing large floppy hats and had daubed their nose and cheeks with white zinc cream, ostensibly to ward off sunburn. When sunglasses were added, they were unrecognizable.

They had parked the ute with the Shark Cat in the Gibson Marina car park and then hired two canoes from Paddlecraft Canoe Hire.

"We only need to paddle five klicks…and we've got nearly three hours to do it, so take it easy," said Archie.

Benjamin nodded and followed Archie as he paddled with economical strokes out into Maybanke Cove. They headed north to clear the end of a long private jetty that reached out into deep water from a luxury house. Benjamin found the display of wealth around him disturbing. The beautiful houses on the foreshore all had private jetties. Hundreds of boats were moored just beyond them, all of them waiting for exercise. In the mean time, they advertised their owner's wealth. Benjamin shook his head and couldn't escape the gnawing suspicion that he was diagonally parked in a parallel universe. He just didn't fit here. The thought worried him. *Am I an inverse snob?*

"Bloody keep up, Benjamin."

Benjamin applied himself to the task.

Scotland Island, with its fringe of jetties, sat on the other side of the channel. It looked gentler than the harsh display of wealth on the mainland. Perhaps it was the trees. They paddled past the Bayview Yacht Club and headed across to The Quays Marina. Benjamin's mind was now fully on the job. He inspected the marina ahead of him. The smaller boats were housed in the berths nearer to the shore. They stuck out at ninety degrees from the pontoon with their sterns tethered to the walkway and their bows moored to posts in the water. The bigger boats were moored on the outside pontoons—and the biggest of them all was the luxury cruiser belonging to Doran Khayef. It was conspicuously moored between two pontoons in a prime position.

They took their time and chatted as they paddled up and down the rows of boats. Benjamin saw that the large pontoons had a cement-board walkway that was kept afloat by a series of floating tanks. He could see spaces between the tanks under the walkway.

Archie said, conversationally, "Stay here and poke about while I explore around the other side. I'll be about ten minutes."

Benjamin would have normally enjoyed pottering around the boats if he wasn't so anxious. As it was, he found waiting difficult.

When Archie returned, Benjamin noticed that his tee-shirt was wet. "What happened?" he asked.

"Fell in."

Benjamin didn't believe it for a moment.

Archie nodded up ahead. "Let's have a closer look at Khayef's boat."

Trying not to look both guilty and conspicuous, Benjamin followed Archie around the line of yachts toward Khayef's boat. It was almost the last boat in the line. Two people were standing on the rear deck. Archie stopped paddling and murmured, "The fat bloke is Khayef." Then he began paddling again.

Benjamin trailed behind in his canoe. He watched, appalled as Archie's canoe glided toward Khayef's pontoon. Archie yelled out in an exaggerated Australian accent, "Hey, mate. Didja know two of ya bloody fenders 'ave gone flat? Ya might wanna do somethin' about it if ya wanna keep ya bleedin' paintwork good." Archie didn't wait for a response. He sketched a wave, turned his canoe around, and paddled back to Benjamin. Archie grinned at him. "Time to get back, Benji. But don't rush. Smell the roses."

As they paddled back along the coast, Benjamin asked, "I suppose you might know something about those two fenders going flat?"

Archie stopped paddling and leaned back in his cockpit. "As it happens, I do. The vinyl seating around one of the valves is busted, and the other fender has a small split." He shook his head. "It's the Australian sun. Bad for plastics."

"And can I ask why the Australian sun has been particularly harsh today?"

"Well, hopefully, the marina's CCTV will soon have excellent film of them changing the fenders."

Benjamin would have smiled had he not been so concerned about what he would shortly be undertaking.

It was Sunday, and there was plenty of activity on the water. A fleet of sailing boats was beating its way south into a freshening breeze off Scotland Island, and motorboats were skimming across the water. They even passed a pod of canoeists creeping their way around the coast. Benjamin gave them a friendly wave.

An hour later, the kayaks had been returned to the hire people, and they were eating meat pies in the front seat of the ute. "Now what?" asked Benjamin between mouthfuls.

"We go shopping."

"What do we need?"

Archie grinned. "Funnily enough, we need two large fenders." He looked at the piece of paper sitting on the dashboard in front of him. "Two air-filled F4 Polyform fenders with a thirty-liter capacity, to be exact. We also need an Aztek Compact 4:1 pulley system from a rock-climbing shop…and some lever-action suction handles for carrying glass." Archie burped and patted his chest with his fist. "And then, Benji boy, you're going to spend all of tomorrow practicing…while I try to catch some fish."

That night, they again slept in their swags on the floorboards of the Shark Cat—only partly sheltered from the elements by its canopy. It didn't take long for the mosquitoes to find them. Benjamin spent a troubled night hiding from their torment.

Dawn came reluctantly, heralding an overcast, humid day. The cloud leached the color from what had yesterday been a beautiful scene. Today, it was depressing—like a fairground on a rainy day.

They launched the Shark Cat and motored north to Towlers Bay, where they could anchor and prepare for the evening without attracting too much interest.

Archie divided his attention between dealing with the two new fenders and fishing. Rather surprisingly, he caught three mullet.

Benjamin spent much of his time in the water getting used to the various pieces of apparatus they had bought the previous day. Archie set him a punishing series of exercises. "Never mind, Benji Boy," he promised when Benjamin protested. "You'll be able to rest all day tomorrow."

As evening approached, Benjamin took the wheel of the Shark Cat and motored sedately past the western side of Scotland Island to The Quays Marina. He was acutely aware that beneath the boat, in the narrow gap above the water between the two hulls, two fenders tethered to suction handles were being towed along, invisible to the outside world. The handles could supposedly hold one hundred kilograms, but Benjamin didn't want to test them unduly—particularly as the fenders now weighed considerably more than when they had bought them.

Benjamin threaded his way through the moored boats, throttled back and edged toward the pontoon that led to the marina buildings onshore. Khayef's boat was ten meters away on the other side of the pontoon. As the boat nudged the pontoon's fender, Benjamin leaped forward to secure the boat to a cleat. As he made it fast, he saw Archie slip himself over the side into the water and begin to clean the accumulated salt off the sides of the boat with a sponge.

Everything had to appear normal. The marina was well-monitored by security cameras; Archie had plotted the position of each one during their expedition in the canoes. Benjamin walked down the pontoon to the marina offices in his hat and sunglasses. A heavily sun-tanned young man was behind the desk. He was dressed quite smartly but had bare feet. Benjamin smiled; he seemed to perfectly embody the Pittwater culture.

Benjamin asked if he could have a temporary berth for two nights. The young man asked whether the boat was registered and had insurance cover. Benjamin said that the boat belonged to a friend, and he wasn't sure about the insurance. The man was apologetic but did invite Benjamin to use the Marina Café. "It's open for breakfast and lunch."

"Thanks."

When Benjamin returned to the boat, Archie was throwing a bucket of water over the foredeck and wiping it down with a sponge. Benjamin climbed aboard, turned the starter key, and backed the boat away from the pontoon. Archie joined him at the wheel and put a hand on his shoulder. "Now it's time to find our other little rabbit."

Once Benjamin had cleared the moored boats and was in the main channel, he opened the throttle. The Shark Cat skimmed its way past Church Point out into the wide headwaters of McCarrs Creek. The creek was dotted with moored boats. Up ahead, Benjamin could see some houses built on the heavily wooded western side of the creek. Many of them seemed to be standing on tiptoe, high off the ground on piles, as if trying to peer through the treetops to the waters below. These houses could only be accessed by water and were a great deal more humble than their Pittwater neighbors.

Just offshore, old wooden boats with rotting gray wood and peeling paint held on to their mooring lines. They lifted their gull-like sterns out of the water like Victorian women trying to keep their dresses out of the wet. The boats rocked gently, nodding at memories of bygone days. They reminded Benjamin of the weathered faces of old men seen late at night in the firelight. Their faces had a dignity and a knowing that was a little sad. It was as if they wanted to whisper a warning but knew that no one was listening.

The wind was rising steadily, and the Shark Cat began to pound. Spray sizzled past the sides of the cabin. Normally, Benjamin would have found it exhilarating but not today; his eyes were searching hungrily among the crowded boats for one particular vessel. The thought that Felicity might only be a few hundred meters away was causing waves of anguish to wash over him. He was desperate for hope, for action…desperate to hold and feel her love.

"There it is, matey," said Archie.

"Where?"

"I won't point to it. Someone may be watching. Fine on the port bow, on the far side of the creek. The big bugger."

Benjamin saw her. She was almost the last vessel in the creek before the open water—a beautiful white-hulled ketch with a green awning stretched above her decks. A rigid inflatable was tethered alongside.

"Stay in the main channel," ordered Archie, "and head to the far side of the creek. When you get there, throttle back, and creep past the jetties. I'll tell you which one to moor up to."

Benjamin did as he was told.

The wind was now growing in strength. Dark, roiling clouds were bringing the daylight to an early close.

"That one. The first one," said Archie pointing.

Benjamin throttled back and nosed the boat into the tiny jetty. "Why here?" he asked.

"No one at home. See the house up through the trees? Its blinds are drawn. So, let's behave as if we own the place."

Drops of rain started to freckle the wooden floorboards of the jetty as they tied up. Benjamin made his way along the jetty and climbed the steep, winding path through the gray gums and Sydney red gums with their striking roots that flowed around their bases like larva. He mounted the steps to the house's veranda, pulled out a notebook, and scribbled a note.

G'day,

We tied up on your jetty to dodge a storm. Sorry, couldn't ask—no one at home. Hope you don't mind. Have a beer on us.

Benjamin placed two bottles of beer by the front door and tucked the note underneath.

Rain was now falling heavily. Gusts of wind shuddered the veranda and dashed rain against the windows. The trees thrashed and swayed around him, nervous at the thunder rumbling in the distance. It matched his mood exactly. He turned and looked through the trees at the view across the water. The white ketch was almost the closest boat moored to them. It was rocking and pitching at its mooring like a live thing, trying to break free. Felicity might be there. The thought was tantalizing. He clenched his fists and hooked an arm around a veranda post to steady himself.

When he had regained his composure, he headed back out into the rain.

Doing nothing for a whole morning was sheer hell. Archie seemed to be content fishing from the small jetty to which the boat was tied.

He had his hat and sunglasses on, and was sitting on a portable icebox. From time to time, he delved inside it to produce a beer bottle. No one watching would guess that they only contained water. "We need to look harmless…and anyone watching needs to get used to us being here," he explained.

Benjamin grumbled and fidgeted as he fished with his hand-line. Eventually, Archie told him to head up to the veranda of the house with his swag and get some sleep. "I don't want to see you for four hours. Then we'll eat mixed beans for tea—lots of low-GI carbohydrates. You'll need them. But for now, rest." He pointed up to the house. "Go."

Benjamin did as he was told. He climbed up to the house, rolled out his swag, and lay down. For a long while, he listened to the rich, echoing call of the currawongs. Once or twice he also heard the distinctive call of the aptly named whip bird. He couldn't remember where he'd learned their sounds.

An oppressive humidity was the only legacy of the electrical storm that had raged most of the night. The sky was now blue, and the sea was at its sparkling best.

Dappled light filtered and flickered through the tree canopy, and a cooling breeze blew across the veranda.

Benjamin slipped gently into unconsciousness.

Chapter 24

Doran Khayef's favorite place on his boat was the flybridge. He sat down on the padded bench behind the driving console and drew heavily on his cigar. He liked seeing things from a height: his boat was the highest in the marina. It was certainly the biggest, and that's how he liked it. But there was always the gnawing ache for more. The marina, good as it was, wasn't anything like the luxury marinas of Europe and America. It was small beer—and he wanted bigger things.

He'd had to sell his harbor-side home but this was only a temporary setback. Once the massive redevelopment on Sydney's foreshore was finished, he would have his own penthouse suite and a private berth for a boat very much bigger than this. His current boat only had a crew of two, one of whom was the cook. The other helped with odd jobs like changing the fenders, as he'd done yesterday. He hired a third whenever he put to sea because he was not an experienced sailor. Money could buy anything.

Cigar smoke curled into the air. He'd learned to like cigars. Initially, he'd hated them, but they were a necessary prop. He smiled and inspected the end of his cigar for evenness of burn. It was Cuban, of course. He had cigars for different occasions. Big cigars were used in company—they looked good, but he rarely enjoyed them. They were exhausting and took too long to smoke, particularly when you were conversing with other people. If unattended too long, they went out, and required relighting. No, his favorite cigars were smaller…but not too small. He had standards. And the very best were smoked alone, like now.

Khayef reflected on the last twenty-four hours and scowled. The two policemen who had visited him at teatime had now departed. They had been polite and confessed that they didn't have a search warrant—but could easily get one if required. Would he mind if they had a quick search of the boat for a woman who had been reported missing? She'd being linked with the Khayef Group because of a research project. "Someone has suggested that you might know where she is."

Khayef had managed an appropriate level of outrage—but he'd been careful not to overdo it. "What's the name of this woman?"

"Felicity Anderson."

"Sounds familiar, but I can't place her."

"She was being sounded out by your company to do some historical research on the mahogany ship near Warrnambool."

"We fund a lot of philanthropic works. I'm afraid I don't know the details of each one. I can find out if you like." He knew he was stretching the truth. The fact was, his company funded almost no philanthropic works. Money was tight—at least for the moment.

But he'd acquiesced easily enough and shown the boat off like a salesman. The police had been impressed. *As they bloody well should be.*

The one thing he really needed was a massive financial injection into his projects—something that his newly acquired gold mines should supply. If his lawyers could make his tax-free claim stick, he would reap billions more. And that would set him up for his next project: politics, where the real power lay. The business perks of having insider information would be huge.

Meanwhile, he had to get the treaty unwound and authenticated. He sniffed. Carter had reported that the restoration process was going well. *It damn well better be.* Khayef was glad that Eddie was permanently on hand to ensure that it was. But what about Bidjara?

Every day Eddie spent with the Anderson woman was one day longer Benjamin Bidjara stayed alive.

And Khayef didn't like that. He threw the stub of his cigar over the side. He hated loose ends.

———————

Navigation buoys winked their green and red lights across the inky water. These, together with the lights of the various settlements around the harbor, turned the bay into a fairyland. Even at this hour, there were still a few boats stealing their way across the water, heading in for a late dinner.

Benjamin and Archie were dressed in black wetsuits. The mood was subdued. Archie guided the boat past Church Point and on toward The Quays Marina. Benjamin patted the equipment that was strapped onto the outside of both legs, ostensibly to check all items were present and correct—but in reality to assure himself that what he was doing was real.

"Time to get your mask and fins on, Benji. I'll drop you ten meters off the pontoon."

Benjamin nodded and gave voice to his thoughts. "Archie, no heroics, right? If this goes pear-shaped and you don't hear from me, head straight back and get Felicity. She's the priority, okay?"

"You've made that crystal clear, mate. You just concentrate on taking it slow and doing exactly what we practiced."

The marina slid toward them. Benjamin donned mask and fins, and began breathing deeply to ventilate himself in readiness for his dive. The water at the back of the boat began to boil as Archie operated astern propulsion, slowing the boat to a standstill. Benjamin rolled over the side and immediately duck-dived below the surface of the water. He could hear the propellers of the twin Mercury engines hiss in the water as Archie pushed the throttle open again.

A ten-meter swim at a depth of two meters was no great challenge, but it was a novelty to be doing it at night. Experienced as he was at free-diving, he was nonetheless glad to reach the underneath of the pontoon. He bobbed up between two of the pontoon's flotation tanks and exhaled quietly. Once he'd got his bearings, he dived again and swam toward the larger of the two pontoons alongside Khayef's boat. Again, he allowed himself to drift to the surface between the flotation tanks. Archie had tethered two boat fenders and a diving bag full of equipment in one of these spaces—but which one? Everything was so disorientating at night.

Easy does it. Slow your breathing down. Take time to relax and notice what's going on around you.

Benjamin forced himself to relax and look around him. A shoal of small fish had gathered around one of the posts anchoring the pontoon. He could see them silhouetted against the lights of the marina.

He dived down and swam to the space between the next two tanks. As he did so, he felt his head bump up against something large and slippery. There was a moment of panic until he realized it was the rubbery side of a boat fender. He felt around and discovered that they were clipped onto the handles of suction caps. They'd been fastened to the side of the flotation tanks, just as Archie had described.

The massive fiberglass hull of Khayef's boat sat two meters away. Benjamin was relieved to see that the lower half of the hull was in shadow. The object that particularly attracted his attention was the large boat fender hanging down its side. He swam toward it and peeped up from the narrow gap of water between the pontoon and the hull. There was no noise to indicate anyone was nearby. Archie's voice came clearly to mind. *Wait, Benji boy. Wait and listen. You need to be more patient than anyone else who might be around.*

So, he waited.

Nothing. Just the faint smell of cigar smoke. Though out of sight, someone was on deck. He would need to be careful.

Time to go to work.

First, get comfortable.

Benjamin unclipped a suction handle from his leg, sank under the water, and fastened it onto the boat hull beside the fender, just below the surface. He secured another handle about an arm's width away and tied a rope loosely between the two of them. Benjamin then positioned two suction handles below the waterline to use as foot-holds.

Even doing these simple tasks was exhausting. He drifted back under the pontoon and floated there for three minutes to get his breathing and heart rate back under control.

Take it slow and stay focused.

Benjamin reached into the equipment bag and pulled out the Aztek 4:1 rock-climbing pulley. He was careful; he'd learned that it needed little excuse to become horribly tangled. Benjamin clipped the end of the pulley onto one of the fenders floating under the pontoon beside him. He allowed the other end to swing below the fender out of harm's way. He would need it later to hoist the fender, now weighing twenty-five kilograms, out of the water and above his head.

Now for the moment of truth.

Benjamin took off his fins and clipped them out the way onto one of the suction caps. He reached for one of the heavy fenders floating beside him, freed it from its tether, and tugged it behind him. Then, taking a deep breath, he ducked under the water and squeezed himself between the rope harness and the boat hull. His feet fished around on the side of the slippery hull. *Where are the footholds? Aah. Got them!*

He stood up, testing their strength. *Firm. Good.* Benjamin was now tethered to the boat and able to use both hands. He reached above the fender hanging from the boat and tied a small loop of cord onto the rope using a prusik knot. Then he turned around and fished for the end of the pulley system floating beneath the other fender floating in the water behind him. He found it and hooked it onto the loop of the prusik knot.

Slow. Slow.

Benjamin made himself breathe deeply. He felt across to the top of the fender hanging from the boat. Archie had reported that the fenders were secured to their ropes with bowline knots. They were easy to undo—in theory.

Mercifully, they were. Benjamin undid the knot and eased the fender down until he was able to push it under the pontoon. Then, as quickly as he dared, he began to tug on the pulley rope until the thirty-kilogram fender containing twenty-five million dollars' worth of drugs had been hauled up the boat's side to the prusik knot. Once it was there, he reached for the fender rope hanging down the ship's side, fed it through the eye of the replacement fender, and secured it with a bowline.

Nearly finished.

Benjamin's fingers were becoming stupid with fatigue.

He freed off the pulley and allowed the fender rope to take its weight. Finally he de-rigged the pulley and ducked back under the pontoon to catch his breath.

Phew. One fender had been replaced. It had taken hours. He looked at his diver's watch. The whole process had taken fifteen minutes. *Unbelievable.*

Benjamin took the diver's knife from the sheath on his forearm and stabbed the fender floating beside him. It deflated with a sigh. Benjamin took his time cutting it into small pieces, stuffing each piece into a string diver's bag.

Did he have the energy, indeed, the courage, to do it all again and swap over the second fender? He'd seen it hanging beside the boat about two pontoon bins away. It looked as teasing as Mount Everest from Base Camp One.

The heavy fender floating beside him nudged him gently. He would first have to ferry it, along with all of his equipment, to the space under the pontoon opposite the boat's next fender. That would take at least three trips—a great deal of energy and time.

Time is not a problem, Benji. This isn't a time-sensitive operation. Take it slow. You can even rig a sling under the pontoon and sleep for an hour if you want.

Do people actually do that? he wondered.

Benjamin reached for his fins and slipped them back on his feet. Then he unclipped the heavy fender from its anchor point and began towing it behind him.

Replacing the second fender did take more time, but not much. Once he'd got all the gear assembled opposite the fender, he was able to repeat the process without any problems. Nothing required any great effort other than the necessity for strong fingers to undo the bowline knot. Archie had planned the mission brilliantly.

Even so, Benjamin's muscles were getting tired. He'd been working slowly and carefully but the fact remained, he'd been in the water for almost an hour. Every movement was now requiring him to dig deeply into his reserves.

Wearily, he recovered all the suction handles. Those he couldn't strap onto his legs, he stuffed into the string bag containing the pulley system and the chopped-up fenders. He tucked the bag behind his diving belt after expanding it to its limit in order to accommodate the bag. However, when he tried to swim, he started to sink; he was nowhere near neutral buoyancy. He kicked with his fins to keep himself on the surface and undid his dive belt. After he jettisoned two lead weights he refastened the belt around himself and the dive bag.

After doing a final check, he swam to the end of the pontoon and pulled a mobile phone out from a waterproof bag. He switched it on, punched in a pre-programmed number, and then packed it away again.

A few minutes later, he heard the low burble of the Shark Cat's twin Mercury's. He watched with relief as it throttled back and drifted just a few meters off the end of the pontoon. Benjamin rolled over, pushed against the underside of the pontoon, and dived under the boat. He surfaced on the far side of it, out of sight from anyone watching from the shore. A rope with a loop tied in the end, was dangling over the side. He grabbed hold of it as Archie eased open the throttle and nosed the Shark Cat into a gaggle of moored boats.

Once they were among them, Archie closed the throttle and folded out the climbing ladder. Benjamin started to climb up it, slow and clumsy with fatigue. Archie reached out and hauled him on board. Benjamin fell onto the floorboards and lay there, gasping for breath like a hooked fish.

Archie stepped over him and got back to the controls.

Chapter 25

"How are you feeling, mate?"

"I want to pee."

"Not in the wet suit, you don't." Archie fished about under the counter and threw him an empty drink bottle.

Benjamin wanted to laugh—hysterically. To be bothered by things so prosaic after all he'd been through, was absurd.

Archie had moored the Shark Cat temporarily to a vacant buoy on the far edge of the group of boats. He had propped a fishing rod up in the back of the boat, just for show.

Benjamin made himself comfortable and recounted what he'd managed to achieve in the last hour. "Khayef's got about fifty million bucks worth of methamphetamine hanging down the side of his boat." Benjamin rolled his shoulders to ease the cramp. "When they find his fingerprints all over the plastic wrapper of one of the parcels, he's going to have the Saracens at his throat and the police banging on his door. Hopefully, that should end him."

"If we find Flick and pin a kidnap on him as well, he'll be totally stuffed," said Archie. "So let's concentrate on that now." He looked around. "This is a good, quiet place to go over things one last time." He switched on the cabin light and pulled out his large black equipment bag. Archie extracted a tool belt and took what looked to be a phone from one of its pockets. It sat within a thick case. He showed it to Benjamin. "This case converts a smart phone into a thermal imaging camera." He turned it over and pointed to two small lenses. "It utilizes two cameras. One is for video graphics, and the other is infrared."

Benjamin was intrigued. "How does it work?"

Archie showed him. He selected the infrared function and aimed the lenses at himself. Benjamin could see Archie's body shape in the display window, colored red and yellow.

"Impressive," he admitted.

"And it can do that through ceilings and plasterboard walls, provided a warm object is just the other side of it. If we pass it over a boat hull, we should be able to see if anyone is inside—if they're sitting close to the hull." He switched off the camera. "I've looked at the boat plan. If Flick's on board, the most obvious place will be in the forepeak. It has its own toilet and there are no windows; just a hatch that acts as a skylight."

Benjamin nodded. "I agree."

Archie looked at him. "How are you feeling now?"

"Getting my energy back. I just want to get on with rescuing Felicity."

"You've done your work for tonight, Benji boy. Now it's my turn. Your job is to stay in the boat and wait."

"What will you do?"

"I'll scan the bow with the infrared camera. " If someone's there, I'll have a look and find out who."

"How will you do that?"

"You don't have to concern yourself with the details. But, as you have asked, I'll drill a hole in the hull and take a peek inside with this little beauty." He opened up another pouch in his tool belt and produced a coil of wire with a plug in the end.

"What's that?"

"It's a 1.2-millimeter diameter camera on the end of a wire. It was developed by an Israeli mob for medical endoscopic work. Very handy."

Benjamin shook his head. He reached across and opened the next pouch in the tool belt. It contained what looked like another coil of wire.

"Be a bit careful with that, mate. That's a spiral wire saw."

"A saw?"

"Yeah. Diamond coated. The aerospace industry has been putting them into band-saws for years."

Benjamin shook his head and put the tool belt down. "But if you find Felicity, what will you actually do?"

"I'll lob in a flash-bang. It'll stun everyone…then I'll go in and get her. Routine stuff."

Benjamin couldn't help but think that what passed for routine in Archie's world would not be that generally agreed on by most other people. "You'll be armed?"

"Yes." The significance of Archie's answer was highlighted by a thoughtful silence. Archie pointed ahead. "Let's get back to our jetty. That's where I'll swim from. The ketch is only seventy meters offshore."

Archie switched on the navigation lights, started the engines and swung the boat into the main channel. Soon they were sweeping across the mouth of McCarrs Creek, passing quite close to the white ketch.

Benjamin forced himself to look straight ahead and not at the yacht as they swept past. What he did see up ahead was that someone was on the jetty they'd been using. A 'tinny'—a small aluminum fishing boat with an outboard on its back—was tied up alongside it.

Archie had also seen it. "We might have to find another jetty, Benji boy."

Benjamin watched a tall woman with a dog running around her heels walk out along the jetty. He closed his eyes and brought to mind his impressions of the house. What did it tell him? He had seen a birdbath outside and some potted plants. The person who owned it was someone who cared about others. The dog confirmed it.

"No," said Benjamin, "It would look suspicious if we suddenly operated from another jetty or mooring. Let's go and say Hello. We'll lose nothing and, at best, it'll give us good cover." He looked at Archie in his black wetsuit. "But we would look more convincing if we took our wetsuits off."

Archie nodded, throttled back, and began to strip off his wetsuit, swapping it for a tee-shirt and shorts. Benjamin did the same. Once they had changed, Archie opened the throttle and motored toward the jetty.

As they drew near, Benjamin called out, "G'day. Just wanted to confess that we tied up to your jetty last night to dodge the storm—and to say thanks. We'd planned to do some night fishing. Trying again tonight."

The woman was now in the tinny, preparing to lift out a cool box. The dog started barking and wagging its tail. It looked to be some sort of terrier. "Oh, that was you, was it?" she said. "I read your note by the front door." She hefted the cool box onto the jetty with a grunt. "I'm pleased you made use of the jetty."

Archie called out. "Will you let me carry that cool box for you? You look as if you could use a hand."

"Well, thank you Sir Galahad. Truth to tell, I'd appreciate it." She smiled. The woman looked to be in her mid-fifties. She had short brown hair that was starting to gray and was dressed in sandals, a caftan tunic and white linen pants. "I can reward you with two bottles of beer. I'm afraid I prefer wine."

Archie brought the boat up alongside the jetty.

Benjamin stepped off and secured the mooring lines. He smiled. "Then I'll be sure to bring some wine next time." He pointed to Archie. "He's Archie. I'm Benjamin."

"Hi, I'm Kate." She pointed to the cool box. "I've got a whole week off, which I plan to spend with some good books and a Shiraz or two. I've had to bring rather a lot of shopping."

Archie climbed up onto the jetty. "Here, let me take it."

The dog stopped barking and began sniffing at Archie's feet. It looked to be quite young.

What happened next seemed to play out like a slow motion film.

Benjamin could see Archie—and the dog—and the look of horror on Kate's face.

The dog tangled itself between Archie's feet, causing him to trip. It yelped and scurried away. Archie fell headlong, dropping the box and twisting sideways to try and protect himself. His left forearm crashed against the edge of the box.

Benjamin heard the bone break.

All went quiet.

Archie moaned. He made a half-hearted attempt to reach across and hold his arm, and then lay still.

"Oh no!" exclaimed Kate, and immediately climbed onto the jetty. She pulled the cool box out of the way, told Archie to lie still, and then felt over his body to determine what, other than the arm, was broken. She spoke over her shoulder. "Ring triple zero. Call an ambulance to the Church Point ferry wharf."

Benjamin did so. As he rang off, Kate continued. "Watch him. I'm going to the house to get some cling film." She scooped up the dog and hurried up the jetty.

"Benji, mate. Sorry." Archie's face was becoming pale and clammy. He spoke between clenched teeth. "Not good. Not good at all." He squeezed his eyes shut. "Sometimes, no amount of training or planning can protect you against the balls-up factor if life is determined to get ya." He reached out toward Benjamin with his good arm. "Now listen, mate. Forget about Felicity. We'll organize a police raid on the boat tomorrow."

"If they're holding her there, they'll probably have a contingency plan to get rid of her before the police arrive."

"That's a risk we'll just have to take." Archie exhaled between his teeth. "Sheeesh."

Benjamin held his hand up. "Lie still and don't worry. I'll sort the boat out and get things straightened out at this end."

"Don't do anything silly, Benji."

Benjamin nodded and stood back to make room for Kate as she bustled back to them.

"Let's see if we can sit him up," she said without preamble. "I need to splint his arm."

Between them, they managed to get Archie seated on the cool box. Kate told Benjamin to hold Archie's right arm up out of the way while she wrapped some cling film around his torso, trapping the broken left arm to his side.

"You've done this before, Kate," said Benjamin.

Kate guffawed. "I'm actually a doctor at Mona Vale hospital. Ironic, don't you think?"

"I'm just glad you're here."

She nodded. "Let's get him into your boat. It's bigger. I'll follow you in the tinny. That way, I'll be able to get back." She tested the firmness of the wrapping. "This should also keep him warm. I'll go in the ambulance with him to the hospital."

Benjamin tried to think of something to say. "Thanks. Um, I'll tidy up here…and carry the box up to the house."

Kate leaned back on her heels. "I'm so sorry about this. I've locked Fidget up inside a bedroom, so he won't bother you." She looked up at him. "You'll find two bottles of beer in the fridge."

It took just a few minutes for both boats to motor across the mouth of McCarrs Creek to Church Point. Ten minutes later, they could hear the *whoop, whoop, wheeeeh* of an ambulance. Archie was clammy and shivering by the time it arrived. Before Kate climbed into the back of it, Benjamin exchanged phone numbers with her. "Call me when you know something."

She grimaced. "Saturday night at Accident and Emergency can get a bit busy. Getting him sorted may take a while."

The ambulance drove off, leaving Benjamin in a storm of anguish—both for Archie as well as for Felicity. What on earth should he do now? What could he do? He tilted his head back and breathed in the night air, calming himself and forcing himself to think. The drama of the ambulance's arrival had attracted the attention of the people dining under the awning of the Waterfront Café. He needed to get away as soon as he could and find solitude.

Benjamin made his way back to the Shark Cat and motored slowly across to the wide headwaters of McCarrs Creek. He passed the white ketch. It was just fifty meters away. So close. The rigid inflatable was no longer beside it, but there were some lights on, indicating that people were aboard. He checked his watch. It was only 8:30pm.

The question that he kept mulling over was: could he investigate whether Felicity was on board the ketch? Did he have the skills? More importantly, could he affect a rescue if she was there?

He moored the boat alongside the jetty and carried the cool box up to the house. It was heavy. No wonder Kate had been grateful for their help. The front door was unlocked, and the lights were on inside.

The dog barked.

Benjamin busied himself putting things away. He unpacked the cool box and put the perishable things into the fridge. He also emptied the contents of two shopping bags that Kate must have carried up earlier. After putting a bowl of water into the bedroom for the dog—and being licked enthusiastically for his trouble—he walked back down to the boat. The shrill screech of cicadas could be heard all around him. They were deafening. The males were calling for a mate.

And so was he.

He climbed on board the Shark Cat and switched on the cabin light. His attention was immediately drawn to Archie's tool belt, sitting on the table.

He picked it up and weighed it thoughtfully in his hands.

Chapter 26

Benjamin felt like a stuffed turkey. He had put Archie's wetsuit top on because of its large size. The extra space was to allow him to slip a pair of fins down his front. They had been trimmed slightly to make them fit alongside two suction handles.

He had switched the cabin lights off twenty minutes earlier, and Benjamin's night vision was now fully established. It was time to go. He checked that Archie's waterproof tool belt was secure for the third time. Any further delay would only allow his misgivings and fear the chance to scream at him again.

He rolled over the gunwale and into the water. When he surfaced, he peered around the stern of the Shark Cat to check his bearings. The ketch was just seventy meters away. He dived and kicked out through the inky blackness. He had put on his long free-diving fins in order to give him as much speed as possible. Surface stops had to be kept to a minimum; the last thing he wanted was to be spotted as he surfaced to catch his breath. The starlight twinkling in the wave-tops above him was the only thing giving him any perspective of depth. He kicked on into the unknown.

Benjamin surfaced for the fourth time in front of the bow of the ketch. He resisted the urge to hang on to the mooring chain. The slightest pressure on it could change the motion of the boat and be felt by those inside. He edged as near as he dared to the bow where he was least likely to be seen, and caught his breath.

Take your time. No heroics. Get comfortable.

The first thing to do was free himself of the mask and fins inside his wetsuit. He fastened a suction handle to the hull below the waterline, well back from the bow. Then he unzipped the top of his wetsuit, withdrew the fins and mask, and clipped them to the handle. Three minutes later, his own fins and weight belt were also hanging from the handle.

Benjamin was now more buoyant and able to float easily. He fished inside the tool belt for Archie's infrared scanner and removed it from its waterproof bag. Tentatively, he switched it on. The screen blinked. He selected the infrared mode and watched as the screen color changed to deep blue. As he passed it over his arm, it showed red. It was working. *Thank God.* He held it above him between finger and thumb and began sweeping it over the surface of the hull, making his way slowly back from the bow.

From inside the hull, Benjamin could hear what sounded like a film being played, perhaps on a computer. Lots of noise. *Good.* However, he still needed to be quiet and only allow his finger and thumb to run over the surface of the hull.

He swept down a third of the length of the boat and dared not go closer to the main cabin. Nothing. The temptation to despair stabbed at him, but he kept it at bay by staying busy. He kicked his way back to the bow and around the other side, where he repeated the process.

About four meters from the bow, the screen's blue-black face changed to yellow. Benjamin swept again. Yellow-orange. His heart started to pound. Was that Felicity? The thought of her possibly being just inches away, was almost more than he could bear. He wanted to pummel and rip his way through the hull to see her.

Impossible. *Settle.*

Benjamin reached inside his wetsuit top and retrieved the last suction cap. He fastened it just above the waterline. Then he unclipped his weight belt, extended its length, and clipped it around himself and the handle. Gradually, he allowed the belt to take his weight. *No sudden movements.*

All good—so far.

He felt into his tool belt and retrieved the tiniest hand-drill he'd ever seen. The drill bit was already in place, protected by a cork. *Cold hands. Don't drop it.* He let the cork float free. Then, reaching up to where he judged the person's head most likely was, he turned the handle and began to drill a two-millimeter hole into the perfectly finished mahogany hull. The drill bit was obviously very sharp, probably titanium. It was amazing how easily it cut through the wood. He turned the handle slowly. *Keep it quiet.*

The drill bit suddenly nudged forward. It had broken through. Benjamin withdrew it carefully and dropped the drill into the water. Its job was done. He put his hand on the suction handle and pushed down on it slowly, causing his head to rise to the level of the hole. For a brief moment, he saw a pinprick of light. He put his lips to the hole and blew.

It might have been a kiss.

He had not been able to make the tiny endoscope camera work on the Shark Cat, so he'd abandoned it, greatly frustrated at his lack of technological competence. There was only one thing for it. He put his lips to the hole and whispered as loud as he dared, "Felicity."

The noise was puzzling. Felicity opened her eyes and listened. The faintest of grunching sounds was coming from somewhere very close. Her world had become very small during the week of her imprisonment; she was acutely aware of everything going on within it. She put down her book and listened. The sound was coming from the hull, right beside her ear. She turned around just in time to see the end of a tiny drill bit break through the wood. It withdrew as quickly as it had appeared. She would have dismissed it as an optical illusion except for the fact that the hole was still there. As she watched, a tiny puff of wood dust blew into the cabin. She held her breath. What did it mean? She put her ear close to the hole and listened.

And then she heard it: "Felicity."

She was in shock. *At last! Rescue!* And not only rescue but Benjamin himself. How was that possible? The yearning she had suppressed for so many days suddenly broke out. She placed a hand against the hull, trying to feel him, and whispered, "Benjamin."

Too loud! Keep quiet, for goodness' sake! She bit her lips and listened in terror for any response from Carter or the odious Eddie.

Silence. Just the gentle slap, slap, slap of the wavelets against the hull and the sound of a film being watched in the saloon. *Thank God.*

Felicity pressed her ear against the tiny hole and heard two taps on the hull. She tapped once in return. Then she heard Benjamin's voice again: "Escape hatch. Escape hatch."

She tapped once and whispered, "Padlock. Padlock. Padlock."

Two faint taps.

Pause.

Another two taps—barely audible from even a few inches away. She pressed her ear closely in time to hear, "Saw. Saw. Saw."

What could he mean? There was no saw. Felicity closed her eyes and clenched her fists. It was unbearable. How…"Ouch!" She felt the prick of something sharp poke her ear lobe. Jerking her head away, she turned to see a long piece of wire being poked through the hole. She tentatively took hold of it and felt it rasp between her fingers.

It was a saw! Somehow, this piece of wire was a saw. Extraordinary. With rising hope, she pulled the wire through. It slid through the hole with a faint 'zip' sound.

Felicity looked up at the padlock anchoring the security bar across the hatch entrance. If she cut the steel tang with the saw, it would cause too much noise, and she would be found out.

She heard footsteps…and froze. Felicity had become an expert in identifying the footsteps of Carter and Eddie. These ones belonged to Carter. She looked at her watch. Yes, Carter would be going into the main cabin for his evening shower. It was part of his routine. Eddie showered in the morning after the speedboat arrived with the other man who stood guard for the day.

With her heart in her mouth, Felicity called out, "Carter."

The footsteps stopped. "Yes?"

"I'm going to be cleaning the stone for a while—scraping it with a spatula. Tell me if the sound disturbs you too much."

Pause. "Oh. Right. Thank you."

She heard Carter open the door into his cabin.

The padlock hung above her, teasing her. Somehow, she had to cut its steel tang without causing the hull to vibrate like a drum. She needed to deaden the sound. What could she use? She glanced around.

Nothing.

Then her eye fell on the rubber tube running from the spout of the kettle to the box containing the vellum. She disconnected it, cut off a thirty-centimeter length with a pair of nail clippers, and wedged the rubber between the padlock tang and the U-bolt to which it was fastened.

As she sat down to survey her work, she heard the rhythmic pulse of the water pump delivering water to Carter's shower. There was no time to lose.

She threaded the wire saw across the tang and started to pull it back and forth. It was a mistake. Within a few seconds, her fingers were raw. She needed a handle for each end of the wire saw.

Felicity cut off two small lengths of rubber tubing and wrapped each of them around the ends of the wire saw.

Much better.

She applied herself to the job once more, being careful to keep her sawing erratic, as if she really was scraping the Atlantis stone.

After five minutes, she had barely cut through a quarter of the metal. Disturbingly, she heard Carter's shower stop. She would have to be even more careful now.

Felicity reasoned that Benjamin would have his ear pressed to the side of the hull and be hearing everything. How long could he wait? She had no idea. Anxiety washed over her. She fought to keep it under control, and reapplied herself to the job.

Her arms were now getting very tired. She thanked God that she had maintained her fitness. Even so, she needed regular breaks during which she lay down on her bunk. When she did, she listened for Benjamin through the hull—but heard nothing. He was being very quiet. Was he still there? She desperately hoped so.

Felicity gave herself a longer rest when she had reached halfway, and then another when she had cut through three-quarters of the metal. She had to retie the rubber tubing a few times, but she now felt she was on the home straight.

The agonizing minutes dragged by. Then, suddenly, she broke through. She had done it!

Felicity undid the rubber tubing, eased the broken tang sideways, and removed the padlock. It was a good feeling. She placed the padlock and the retaining bar under her pillow, then crossed over to the tiny hole and knocked twice.

A faint answering knock came back immediately. How was that possible? She looked at her watch. The cutting of the padlock had taken thirty-five minutes. How could anyone stay in the water with their ear pressed to the side of the hull for that length of time? She wanted to laugh, to cry out, "I did it! I did it!" But instead, she said, "Done. Done. Done…I love you."

There was a pause. She heard something but couldn't understand it. She pressed her ear closer.

Then she heard it.

"Marry me. Marry me. Marry me."

She put her hand to her breast and caught her breath. *Did he say…? Yes, he did…he really did.* Her head began to spin in a dizzy whirl. Benjamin was crazy. She put her hand on the hull wall in an effort to reach him…to tell him what she felt, that he had transformed her life, that she had never felt so loved and honored, that he was so extraordinary, so special…so beautifully, uniquely special. Without stopping to think, she put her lips to the tiny hole and whispered. "Yes, yes, yes. A thousand times yes."

There was a moment's silence.

"Wait, wait, wait."

Uggh. Horrible words. Hateful words. She slapped the hull in frustration. Her eyes welled with tears. She rolled over and pressed herself against the hull, visualizing him on the other side, aching for him…and listened.

Felicity felt the slightest of lurches, as if a wave, bigger than the other waves, had nudged the bow.

But all she heard was silence.

Benjamin pushed up on the suction handle and gripped a stanchion that held up the wire guardrails. He pulled himself up, slid under the lower wire, and lay flat against the foredeck. A flickering of light through the front windows of the main saloon told him that a film was still being watched. He glanced up. Fortunately, the canvas awning over the deck was keeping the foredeck in front of the main mast very dark. It was unlikely that he would be seen. He edged over to the wooden coaming of the forward hatch. Could it be true that Felicity—his fiancée!—was just underneath it? He closed his eyes. The thought felt wonderful. Above all, it felt right.

But, time enough for that later—if indeed there was to be a 'later'—for they were both still in real peril.

Benjamin reached over, held his breath, and pulled open the Perspex hatch cover. It opened with a squeak of its rubber gasket.

And there she was, looking up at him. Smiling. Love dancing in her eyes. She reached up to him.

Benjamin put a finger to his lips then swung himself over the hatchway and lowered himself to the floor.

Her arms were around him instantly.

Benjamin held her to him, desperately trying to make himself believe she was really in his arms. He entangled his fingers in her hair as she tilted her head and searched for his lips. A small mewing sound escaped her as they kissed. Her lips were warm and moist. "Yes," she whispered again, as he drew back and searched her eyes.

She felt so good. The love and feminine sexuality she exuded were electric. Benjamin shook his head in bewilderment that anyone like her could love him. His hands ran slowly down her neck, caressing her shoulders, then down her side, following her contours until he was holding her waist.

She held him behind his neck, arched her neck back, and pressed him to her breasts.

A small sob escaped him as he felt her warmth. He moved his hands, feeling her…protecting…discovering. She loved him. It was more than he could bear.

Slowly, the reality of their dire situation ebbed back into Benjamin's consciousness. He lifted his head. Felicity pressed a finger against his lips and whispered, "Two men. One psychopath… armed…in the saloon. The other…in the main cabin."

Benjamin stood up and nodded. He unzipped his wetsuit top and handed it to her. For a moment, she ignored it and reached out to put a hand on his chest, feeling its wetness. Smiling a secret smile, she took the wetsuit top. Felicity began to strip off her blouse and jeans. Benjamin's instincts for propriety caused him to turn away.

When he turned back, she was standing there, dressed only in bra and pants, facing him, waiting for him to see her.

It was too much. Benjamin sank to his knees, reached for Felicity's waist, and drew her to him. He felt her fingers stroke his hair as he pressed his cheek against her.

The moment lasted only a few seconds. Then Felicity stepped away and began zipping herself into the wetsuit top.

Benjamin took out the black waterproof bag holding the infrared scanner and whispered, "Put anything you want to take with you in here."

Felicity dropped in her passport, credit cards, and bank notes.

As he folded the bag away in his waist belt, Benjamin whispered, "Mask and fins are waiting outside. When I lift you out, lie flat on the foredeck. I'll join you and close the hatch. Then we go over the side, you on the left, me on the right, so we don't rock the boat. We do everything slow and gentle…and together. We'll meet at the bow. Don't hold the mooring line."

She nodded. "Then swim for the shore?"

"Underwater as much as possible, although you don't have a weight belt, which will make it difficult."

"I think I can solve that." Felicity leaned across to the bunk and picked up a flat-looking stone. It took a moment before Benjamin realized what it was. It was the Atlantis stone! She unzipped the wetsuit and pushed it inside. "Now I'm ready."

Felicity put a foot into Benjamin's cupped hands and reached for the hatch coaming. When she nodded, he heaved her up through the hatchway. After switching off the cabin lights, he hoisted himself up through the opening and joined her on the foredeck. He closed the hatch, nodded to Felicity, and began crabbing sideways toward the guardrail. Felicity began moving in the opposite direction, mirroring his movements. A glance told him that Felicity was beginning to slide herself over the edge. He began to do the same. However, the bottom wire of the guardrail snagged his tool belt. He froze and plucked it free. *Had anyone heard?*

Nothing.

Benjamin took hold of the base of a stanchion and swung himself over the side. He paused briefly to feel the motion of the boat.

There was no unusual rocking. Felicity had done well.

He let go of the stanchion and slipped into the water.

Be patient and take it slow.

Benjamin located the suction cups under the waterline and put his fins and weight belt back on. After collecting Felicity's mask and fins, he unfastened both suction caps and let them sink into the depths.

Silently, he swam to the front of the boat.

Felicity was there, lying on her back, sculling with her hands to keep herself afloat. She looked comfortable. He thanked God that she was a seasoned diver.

Benjamin handed Felicity her mask and fins. No words were said. Once they were in place, she signaled she was ready.

They duck-dived and struck out toward the shore.

Chapter 27

The Shark Cat burbled its way quietly across the harbor. Felicity was lying under the foredeck, changing into some of Benjamin's spare clothes. Once they were abreast of Church point, she stood up behind him, wrapped her arms around his waist, and rested her cheek against his back. It was the most delicious feeling he had ever experienced. Nothing, he vowed, would ever threaten her again.

As he pondered Felicity's safety, it occurred to him that she could easily suffer further grief if he and Archie were found to be in possession of items associated with the heist of fifty million dollars' worth of methamphetamines. He handed the wheel over to Felicity and began jettisoning objects over the side into the inky black waters of the harbor. The dive bag containing the pulley and chopped-up sections of fender was the first to go, followed by the heavy demolition saw. It was probably very expensive. Benjamin didn't care.

He looked around him. As beautiful as Pittwater Harbour was, he wanted to get away from it as soon as possible. He pulled out his phone and put a call through to Kate to inquire about Archie.

"Kate McCauley speaking."

"Hi Kate, Benjamin here. How's Archie going?"

"He's being attended to now. X-rays show a broken humerus. It's a clean break, thank goodness."

"When do you think I'll be able to pick him up and take him home?"

"Tomorrow lunchtime, I expect. They'll operate tonight, then put him in a cast. He'll need time to get over the anesthetic."

No, no, no, thought Benjamin. *Archie has to get well away.* "Thanks, Kate. Er, what will you do tonight?"

"I'll probably stay here in one of the doctors' accommodation units."

Benjamin was relieved. He didn't want Kate anywhere near the sailing boat once those on board discovered Felicity had escaped. "That sounds wise. You've been through enough tonight. Thanks, Kate, for keeping an eye on Archie." He rang off.

What to do? Benjamin looked at his watch. 10:15pm—not too late. He needed to make a second call but not now. The slipway at Bayview Park was approaching, and it wasn't easy to see in the dark. He was relieved to discover that the tide was high. It meant that the ute could stay on the slipway and did not need to go on the sand where it risked getting bogged.

Felicity took charge of the procedure of loading the Shark Cat onto its trailer. It quickly became evident that she was well-practiced at it. As she tied the boat down, Benjamin made his second call.

Phoebe answered. "Marjorie's phone. Hello Benjamin."

"Hello, Phoebe. I need some advice—fairly urgently."

"Right. I'll put you on speaker so that both Marjorie and I can listen." There was a brief pause. "Okay, go ahead."

"The good news is that we've found Felicity and rescued her from the yacht in McCarrs Creek. Her captors don't know we've got her yet."

"Oh, well done, dear. Are you all safe?" Benjamin could hear Marjorie's voice. It was very weak but warm like a mother's.

"We're safe. But I want to get as far away from here as I possibly can. We've got the boat on the trailer, and I'm about to move off, but I don't know where to go."

"Isn't Archie with you?" asked Phoebe.

"No. That's just it. He's in Mona Vale hospital getting a broken arm fixed. He won't be ready to be picked up until tomorrow at the earliest."

Marjorie's voice came back straight away. "Don't worry about Archie. He'll look after himself. I take it, then, that you managed Felicity's rescue without his help?"

"Yes." Benjamin hurried on. "I need to get away from here as quickly as possible, but there are two things the police need to be aware of straight away."

He paused to marshal his thoughts. How much should he tell them?

Phoebe's no-nonsense voice broke in. "Tell us what they are."

"Ah…right. The first is that there are currently two people aboard the yacht where Felicity was held. One, at least, is armed and very dangerous. The police really need to raid the yacht before morning—before they discover that Felicity is missing. Once they discover she's gone, they'll run."

"I'll see to it. The second thing?"

"I…I'm pretty sure I overheard one of them speak about a shipment of drugs they'd just received. They spoke of it being hidden on the boss's boat. Do you suppose that might be Doran Khayef's?"

There was silence. Had Benjamin overplayed his hand? He sweated.

"Do you suppose it might be on his boat?" asked Phoebe enigmatically.

"I reckon it could be."

"Then we'll organize some action on that as well. Anything else?"

"Where do I go now?"

"I think I would be happier if you were under the jurisdiction of the Federal police rather than the State police, as ASIO has a good relationship with them. Can you drive to Canberra? Both ASIO and the Federal police are based there."

Benjamin thought quickly. That would be a four-and-a-half-hour journey with the boat. They would arrive in Australia's capital city at 3am. "Yes," he said. "But what happens when I get there? I have Archie's equipment…and hardware to dispose of."

"You'll be supplied with accommodation. Don't worry about the equipment—ASIO will take care of it. You must expect to be interviewed at length by the Federal police tomorrow. I'll call you with the details once I've organized it."

"Thanks Phoebe."

"I'll get on to it right away. Now I'll leave you to say…goodbye to Marjorie."

A few seconds later, Marjorie's voice could be heard. It was breathy and very faint. "Benjamin."

"I'm here, Marjorie. How are you feeling?"

"Time enough for that…later, dear."

He could hear her labored breath.

"Benjamin, I…I'm so glad to have met you."

There was silence. Benjamin furrowed his brow, trying to understand. He stammered, "Me too. You, er, have been a mentor and…" What word could he use? There was only one word that fitted, but he hesitated to use it. He consulted his instinct, and felt peace. "You have been a mother to me."

After a lengthy pause, he heard faintly, "You have…made me very happy, Benjamin."

It was time to die.

A relief. She was ready.

For the last few days, Marjorie had been holding on. Consciousness and dreams had become blurred. Only one thing drove her to stay alive—one burning desire: and that was to see Benjamin safe… and found.

There were tears, kisses, and the holding of hands when things became too sacred for words. Phoebe's presence at this time, her closeness and her love, were the most beautiful gifts she could give.

Now all was done.

Death, that final test of faith, was knocking at her door. It was time to surrender herself to the love of the one she had always known, not as a theory but as a person. He who held truth and love together; he who had shown that death was not a terminus but a door leading to the fullness and rightness of things—now waited for her with a smile.

The words of the twenty-third Psalm came to her. "The Lord is my Shepherd…"

A tear escaped her eye.

Felicity opened the door to the bedroom, where Benjamin was sleeping, and watched him. She had been awake for only a few minutes before she'd thrown the coat he'd given her over her shoulders and crept through to his bedroom—just to check on him.

Their accommodation suite was on the fifth floor of a gray concrete building, of which there seemed to be so many in Canberra.

She watched the steady rhythm of his breathing and his tangle of dark curling hair. It called to mind the night she had first hugged him after that first meal he'd cooked for her—all so long ago now. She remembered the smell of wood-smoke in his hair. It was delicious, and the feel of…

There was a knock on the door.

Felicity looked down to her bare legs and called out, "Hang on." She went to her room, pulled on a pair of Benjamin's shorts, and returned to open the door.

Archie was standing there with his plastered arm in a sling. His face was pale, but his sardonic grin was in place. He looked her up and down. "We might have to find you some new clothes, girl."

"How are you feeling? And how on earth did you manage to get here so quickly?" asked Benjamin, who was now standing at the bedroom door.

Archie looked at his watch. "I flew in half an hour ago. Evidently, there's a bunch of people fairly anxious to speak to us." He made his way to a kitchen chair. "And I feel bloody awful, if you want to know." He sat down. "You are aware that it's nearly 1pm, aren't you? I've been asked to rouse you out and tell you that a car will be picking us up in thirty minutes to take us to the police station." He fingered the sachets of instant coffee in the bowl in front of him with distaste. "Any decent coffee?"

Felicity ignored the question. She pointed at Archie. "I've been waiting to speak to you."

"Oh?" said Archie, leaning back in his chair.

"Don't act so innocent. The treaty—the one we found in Cagliari—that wasn't what you put inside the ivory canister, was it?" She slapped the table. "So where's the real treaty?"

The hum of traffic could be heard through the window.

"Is that true?" asked Benjamin as he came out from his bedroom and stood beside Felicity.

Archie nodded. "Yeah. Sorry about that."

"Sorry!" Felicity exploded.

"Hear me out," said Archie, holding up his good hand.

Felicity bristled. "This had better be good."

"Relax. The treaty is in the safe hands of the Australian government who, I might say, have access to the very best resources for restoring and preserving old documents."

Felicity was about to protest when Archie again held up a restraining hand. "I posted the real treaty to the Australian embassy in Rome…and from there it was carried in a diplomatic pouch to Canberra."

"Posted!" expostulated Felicity.

"Very safely, mate. By the time I'd finished packaging it, it would've stayed safe even if you'd played football with it."

"But why the charade? Why swap it?"

"I wanted to check no one else knew about the treaty and was trying to get their hands on it." He sighed. "It's just that my ruse worked a little better than I'd anticipated."

"You bet it did, buddy. It nearly got me killed."

"Yeah. I told Benji that we wouldn't have much time to spring you before they tumbled to it."

"Um, you didn't let me know any of this," Benjamin pointed out.

"It wouldn't have changed anything if I did—except panic you into premature action. I would have told you otherwise."

"Then what was written on the piece of vellum that I had?" asked Felicity.

Archie smiled. "Absolutely nothing. It was an old piece of stuff that no one actually got around to writing on. That's why I could use it. Evidently, the manuscript was found during the renovation of Old Government House in Parramatta."

A knock on the door spared Archie any further interrogation. Benjamin opened it to two policemen. They asked with official brusqueness if all three of them would accompany them to the police station.

They were each interviewed individually. After an hour of questioning, they were asked to wait, presumably while their reports were compared and analyzed. Felicity felt exhausted and emotionally drained. When she pointed out that she hadn't eaten since the previous night, she was given a sandwich. Two officers—a male and a female—sat with them as they waited.

Eventually, Felicity could take it no more. She turned to the female officer. "Please excuse me but I want to go shopping for some basic clothing and toiletries." She forced a smile. "And, after being confined for over a week, I need to have a walk in the fresh air."

"I understand," said the officer. "I'll just check."

Two minutes later, she came back and invited them to follow her. The officer led them into a large office. A balding man in his late forties entered just behind them and introduced himself as Detective Inspector Ingpen. "Sorry to keep you waiting." He sat down at the desk and said without preamble, "I have three pieces of information for you."

His comment succeeded in deflating Felicity's mutinous spirit.

Detective Ingpen went on. "This morning, we raided the boat on which you, Miss Anderson, were held prisoner. Unfortunately, we found it empty but we have retrieved Miss Anderson's belongings." He looked at Felicity. "Crime Scene have them for the moment." He picked up a pen and began tapping it on the pad beside him. "What is more concerning is that we found the body of Andrew Carter floating in Pittwater. He had drowned." The detective stabbed the pad with his pen. "And there have been no sightings of the man called Eddie." He looked up. "So you will understand why we needed to keep you here until we found some answers." He glanced at Felicity and Benjamin. "Establishing the time of Carter's death has now put you in the clear regarding his murder."

Felicity was shocked. "Us? Murder?"

Ingpen smiled a smile that didn't touch his eyes. "Sorry miss, we have to check everything."

"What's the second piece of news?" asked Archie.

"The second piece of news is that we also raided Mr. Khayef's boat this morning and, er…found some substances on it that will be the subject of further investigation." He leaned back. "So, thank you, Mr. Bidjara, for your information. It was useful."

Felicity turned to Benjamin, mystified. "What information?"

Benjamin shrugged. "I reported a comment that I heard through the louver doors of the forepeak just before I got out."

"Oh." Felicity thought it unusual that Benjamin hadn't shared this with her earlier. She glanced at him. He gazed back steadily. She saw the peace in his eyes…and felt reassured. He would tell her later if it was important.

The detective cleared his throat. "Finally, I've been asked to pass on to you some news that you might find distressing." He averted his gaze from them all and picked up his pad of paper. "I regret to inform you that Miss Marjorie Eddington has passed away." He looked up. "Evidently, she had some connection with you through ASIO. They asked us to let you know."

Chapter 28

Felicity had washed away most of the weariness of the twelve-hour drive to Port Fairy in a long hot shower. With the Shark Cat now safely parked in her brother's driveway, and with most of the questions regarding her well-being answered, Felicity began to relax. It felt good to be dressed in clean clothes at last.

She was alone in Benjamin's workshop. He and Archie had walked into town to buy some takeaway food to bring back. Both had expressed the need for exercise.

Felicity walked among the woodworking machines and breathed in the smells of the wood. It was a resinous, sweet aroma that conjured images of craftsmen working wood through the centuries.

She smiled as she picked up a log of wood lying on the bench. It was surprisingly light. Benjamin had shown it to her before he left. "That's what I'm using to make my next gift for you," he'd said, almost shyly. "Every blackfella makes a coolamon for his girl." Felicity picked it up and sniffed it. It smelled quite pleasant, despite Benjamin telling her that no one ever dared burn it in a fire. "It smells really bad when it's burned," he'd warned.

The same books she'd seen during her first evening in the workshop were resting on the drill press. She fingered them sadly.

Benjamin hadn't had much time to read in the last few weeks. She'd so enjoyed listening to him talk about his love of books on that first night. There was one phrase she particularly remembered: "Books have the power to still busy people and point them to better versions of themselves." It was a beautiful sentiment. Benjamin used words well. She wished she could have read the essays he'd written during his final year at school. It was such a pity he hadn't continued to use his talent for writing.

She shivered. Technically, summer had just begun, but there was still a chill in the evening air. Felicity stood by the potbelly stove, seeking its comfort.

Her thoughts were interrupted by a knock on the door.

She kept the door on the safety chain as she opened it and peered through the crack. It was Marcus. He was stony-faced.

"Oh, hi Marcus," she said, unlatching the door. "What's the matter?"

The door was suddenly kicked open. Felicity stepped back, narrowly avoiding being hit in the face. Marcus was pushed through the door by a figure who stepped in behind him.

"Hello, bitch. Did you miss me?"

It was Eddie. A vicious backhanded slap sent Felicity sprawling to the floor. Eddie stepped over her and pulled out a silenced pistol from a shoulder holster. He pointed it around the room, then strode over to the door of the shower cubicle and kicked it open.

Marcus's face was stricken as he helped Felicity get to her feet. "I'm…I'm so sorry, he stammered. I didn't…"

"Where's your bastard boyfriend?" Eddie grabbed Felicity by the hair and wrenched her to her feet so that her face was centimeters from his own.

"He's not here," she replied, trying not to scream in pain.

"I can see that, bitch. I asked where he is." He shook Felicity's head, making her scream.

"Hey, hey," protested Marcus.

Eddie ignored him and looked around the workshop. He started at the workbench and began to laugh. Felicity knew why. He'd seen the odd assortment of cutlery that she'd laid out on the bench in readiness for their meal. "So, we're expecting company, are we?" He smiled unpleasantly. "Then we'll just have to wait for them won't we?"

"They're coming back with quite a lot of company. You can't kill them all."

He rounded on her. "Oh, yes I can, bitch." He slapped her again. "I can kill anyone I like."

Felicity staggered sideways.

"Hey. Don't do that. You never said..." Marcus got no further. Eddie pistol-whipped him on the side of the head. He collapsed to the floor.

"No, no!" cried Felicity. She bent over Marcus's inert form, sprawled behind the door, and checked his vital signs. His breathing came in shallow rasping breaths. She grabbed him under the arms and dragged him away from the door, over toward the stove. Her mind was working feverishly. Felicity rolled him into the recovery position and said over her shoulder, "We've got to keep him warm." She hooked open the door of the potbelly, reached up to the bench to collect the log lying there, and put it in the fire.

Please God. Please God.

She turned to see Eddie aiming the gun at her head.

She screamed at him, "Shoot me, then, you bastard!"

He stepped across to her in a few strides, grabbed her hair, and pulled her head back. "Oh, I will, I will. But I want to make your boyfriend watch. Then I'll kill him too."

Felicity started to flail at her tormentor.

Eddie stepped back and kicked her in the stomach.

She collapsed onto the floor.

Searing pain pierced what little was left of her consciousness. He stepped over her and took out a roll of masking tape. Eddie taped around her head and mouth several times, dragged her across the workshop floor, and dumped her beside the door like a rag doll. He squatted down, grabbed her breast, and squeezed it hard. "You're a hot bitch. Do you know that? I wish I could spend more time with you." He put his face close to hers. "Now stay quiet, or I'll use you to keep me warm right now."

It felt surreal to be walking through Port Fairy in the cool of the evening. Everything was so quiet and peaceful, totally at odds with the drama and violence of the previous week. Benjamin was tempted to think that recent events had all been a dream. Only Archie's broken arm gave visual proof of what had transpired. *Will I ever really be able to feel the peace of this town again?* Benjamin wondered. He very much hoped so. It was a lovely town—although not one he'd engaged with much in the past. He smiled. Since knowing Felicity, all that had changed.

The warmth from the Chinese takeaway seeped through the carrier bag. He could feel it against his leg. The prospect of eating it with Felicity in his workshop filled him with warm anticipation. It had been a long day.

The evening was still. Only the occasional car passed as they made their way along Bank Street. It was as they turned left heading down the street to his workshop that he first smelled it. At first, he thought that someone's septic tank was badly in need of attention, but as he got nearer to the workshop, he was very sure of what it was he was smelling: it was stinkwood.

How many logs of stinkwood could there be in Port Fairy? *Only one.*

Could Felicity have burned it by mistake? Even as Benjamin thought about it, he knew it wasn't possible. Felicity had been charmed by his idea of making her a coolamon. She'd stroked the log, smelled it, and replaced it on top of the workbench. It was nowhere near the firewood bin.

Would Felicity have allowed anyone else to burn it? Again, Benjamin shook his head. *Never.* It was special to her. It could only be burning because something was dreadfully wrong.

He placed a hand on Archie's shoulder. Archie stopped and shot him a questioning look. Benjamin nodded toward a large pine tree and steered Archie into its shadows. His mind was working furiously.

"What's up, mate?" asked Archie.

"I think Felicity could be in trouble. She's burning the stinkwood log I was starting to make her coolamon from."

"Is that the shitty pong I can smell?"

"Yeah. It's sometimes called shitwood."

Archie pulled a face. "Good name for it."

"Seriously, Archie. The wood was special—and Felicity knows it. This can't be a mistake."

Archie's face hardened. "Then, Benji boy, we need to find a way of getting inside and giving whoever is waiting for us a bit of a surprise. What possibilities are open to us?"

Benjamin's mind began to race.

After a moment, he asked, "Do you still have a gun?"

Archie nodded.

Felicity could smell the stinkwood even though the potbelly was supposedly a sealed unit.

She was now bound and gagged with masking tape. Marcus's hands had been similarly secured. He was lying beside her, still unconscious.

Waves of desperation overwhelmed her. She turned her head and pressed an ear against the wall, resolving to bang against it with her head and feet as hard as she could as soon as she heard Benjamin and Archie return. Eddie would shoot her, but she might be able to give them enough warning to at least put them on guard.

The night was still. Somewhere across town, a dog started to bark...then all was quiet. Only the occasional hum of traffic on the A1 could be heard. Felicity waited for death, in whatever form it chose to arrive.

Suddenly, the quiet was shattered by a splintering smash that made the workshop shudder. Felicity looked with astonishment as the twin flaps of a trapdoor in the floor flew open. She saw the bolt that had secured it spin through the air...and caught sight of a heavy ax being pulled back down below the floor.

Felicity immediately kicked out at Eddie's legs.

He cursed and spun around, aiming his gun at her.

At that moment, the ostensibly comatose Marcus became animated. He lurched up and threw his body across Felicity.

Eddie shot him in the back.

Felicity felt the shock of the bullet's impact through her own body. Before she could scream, Archie erupted through the trap-door, holding a gun.

Everything seemed to happen in slow motion. Felicity saw the look of astonishment on Eddie's face as he saw Archie.

Archie paused for the tiniest moment—a mere instant. Felicity thought he might not fire. Eddie's gun was still pointed at Marcus. It was just a split second. Archie's eyes hardened…and he shot Eddie in the heart—twice.

The bark of the gun was shocking. The death it brought, brutal.

All went quiet.

———

Benjamin dropped the ax and pushed up past Archie who was keeping his gun trained on Eddie. He leaped across to Felicity and began pulling Marcus off her. "Are you alright, Felicity? Are you alright?" he yelled. He searched her body for any signs of wounding.

Relief flooded through him as he saw Felicity nod vigorously. But she was kicking and making mewing sounds, trying to say something through her gag. What was she trying to make him understand?

Marcus.

Benjamin turned to Marcus and saw the small hole in the back of his coat. Blood was seeping around it. He eased Marcus onto his side and checked his vital signs.

There was barely a pulse, and his breath came in shallow gasps. Marcus coughed and blood began to trickle from the corner of his mouth. His eyes were screwed shut, and his lips were twisted, trying to make a sound.

"I…I'm sorry."

"Lie still, Marcus. We're getting an ambulance."

Benjamin could hear the rattle in Marcus's chest. It didn't sound good. He bent down to check Marcus's pulse.

Archie climbed out from the trapdoor hole and stood beside Benjamin. "How is he?" He knelt down and felt for Marcus' carotid artery. "There's barely a pulse." Archie rocked back on his heels. "This bloke took the bullet that was intended for Felicity."

Benjamin looked at Marcus in astonishment. Then he knelt down and whispered, "Thanks, mate."

He was amazed to hear Marcus grunt through tortured gasps. "Told Khayef about you," he coughed. "Wanted a story." Marcus fought for breath. The gurgling reached the top of his throat, and he couldn't cough any more. The sinews in his neck strained bar-tight as he choked, "Sorry." Then his head lolled sideways.

Benjamin felt for a pulse.

There was none.

For a long while, Benjamin didn't move. He was appalled. Slowly, he reached out and began stroking Marcus's forehead. "Tonight," he whispered, "you became the hero of your own front page."

He looked across to Felicity. She was safe. Thank God!

A tidal wave of emotion broke the dam wall…and he began to weep.

Chapter 29

Q ueen Street in Melbourne's city center was not a place in which Benjamin felt comfortable. Towering office blocks turned the road into a canyon of cement and glass. He felt hemmed in, despite the street being wide enough to allow cars to park along the center strip rather than along its edge. It looked to him as if someone had turned the road inside out.

Benjamin found the building he was looking for and took the lift to the solicitor's office on the eighth floor.

As he rode up in the lift, he reflected on the previous month. So much had happened. He and Felicity had attended two very different funerals.

Marjorie's funeral had taken place at St Hilary's Church in Kew. The old church had been tastefully modernized with new extensions. It was just as well; the place was packed. State dignitaries, indigenous Australians, and the community of St Hilary's filled the place. The funeral was very much a thanksgiving service. Whilst there was sadness, the level of hope and thanksgiving was palpable.

Marcus's funeral, however, was soul-crushingly sad. The service, held in a funeral parlor, was entirely secular. It offered little other than sentimental clichés.

The door of the lift opened, and Benjamin was led to the office of Albert Carstairs. When he entered the room, he was surprised to see Phoebe sitting in one of two chairs facing a mahogany desk. The florid man behind the desk rose to his feet and introduced himself. He was overweight, and only just managed to look dignified in his dark suit. After Benjamin shook the man's hand, he bent down and spoke quietly to Phoebe. "Phoebe, your relationship with Marjorie was very special. I can't imagine what you're feeling. I'm so sorry."

Phoebe's bosom heaved in what might have been a sob. "Thank you."

Carstairs cleared his throat as Benjamin took his seat and began to explain why he'd asked Benjamin and Phoebe to attend his office. "As I said in my email, it concerns the disbursement of Miss Eddington's estate." He looked at Phoebe and smiled. "You, Phoebe, are already aware of the substance of Miss Eddington's will because we both recently signed as witnesses to it."

Phoebe nodded.

"Then you will recall that you will inherit some items of a personal nature, such as paintings and books." Carstairs looked down at a document in front of him. "Evidently, you insisted that it was all you would accept. Miss Eddington has made a comment to that effect and…" He smiled. "…she upbraids you for your self-lessness."

Phoebe sniffed. "I have more than enough at my stage of life to live very comfortably, thank you."

Carstairs turned to Benjamin. "Miss Eddington has instructed me to give you a letter, Mr. Bidjara, which she has asked you to read before we proceed any further." He handed an envelope across to Benjamin and rose from his seat. "I'll leave the two of you alone whilst you read it." He turned to Phoebe. "Perhaps you could remain on hand to answer any questions Mr. Bidjara might have."

"Of course," said Phoebe.

Carstairs walked to the door. "Let reception know when you are ready to proceed."

Benjamin was not at all sure what was happening. He tapped

the envelope on his hand, trying to work out how it could be significant. Nothing came to mind. He drew a deep breath, opened the envelope, and started to read.

My Dear Benjamin,

I am so pleased to be able to write this letter. For many years, I thought it might not be possible.

Let me explain by telling you a story.

Many years ago, I was engaged to be married to Terrance Stanthorpe. He was a missioner and health worker who worked among the Aboriginal communities of the East Kimberley. One night, he was ferrying an Aboriginal woman in labor to the clinic as she was having difficulty giving birth. It was the wet season, and the creeks were in flood.

The situation of the Aboriginal woman was desperate, so Terrance tried to drive his truck across a flooded creek. It was a mistake. The truck was swept sideways and rolled over in the water. Terrance was knocked unconscious. The husband of the pregnant woman managed to get his wife out of the truck to the safety of the creek bank. He then went back to get Terrance.

Sadly, both were drowned.

The man who tried to save my fiancée was your father, Jimmy Bidjara. You were the baby that was born later that evening.

For many years, I was beside myself with grief. But by God's grace, I moved on and have lived a life that I've found as surprising as it has been fulfilling. One of the areas that life swept me into was genetic anthropology. I did a PhD that helped uncover European physiological features in Aboriginal communities on the west coast of Western Australia. As a result of this work, almost all the genetic data from Aboriginal communities throughout Australia found its way to my computer in one form or another.

Some years ago, I was thinking, as I often did, about the man who had died trying to rescue my fiancée. I typed his surname into the computer and discovered your name. I also discovered your rather unique genetic heritage. You have, as you now know, a gene sequence that could only have come from Portugal.

This background may help you understand why I have organized my affairs as I have.

My heart's desire, Benjamin, is that you really discover who you are. From what I have observed, you are well on the way to doing so.

You are a remarkable young man. I count it a privilege to have known you, and have my life entwine with yours.

God bless you.

Marjorie

Benjamin looked dumbly at the words that now began to swim in his vision. What an extraordinary story—both sad and heart-warming. He leaned back and blinked back the tears that were threatening. Marjorie had completed the story that Jabirrjabirr had begun to tell him in the Kimberley. He and Marjorie were connected. *Remarkable!* Benjamin closed his eyes and brought her to mind. She swam into focus and smiled at him.

He lowered his head, wishing that he had known her for longer.

"Any questions?" asked Phoebe brusquely.

Benjamin fought to find his voice. "Um, probably. But none that I can articulate now."

Phoebe nodded. "I have something to give you before Mr. Carstairs comes back." She removed her coat from what Benjamin had assumed was a traveling case.

It wasn't. It was the blackwood box he had made for Marjorie.

Phoebe laid a hand on it, as if not daring to touch it and said, "Marjorie learned that no one had collected your father's bones from his funeral platform. Willful as ever, she collected them herself, wrapped them in linen, and has kept them safe until she could work out what to do with them. Your box contains your father's bones."

Benjamin sat in silence, shocked…barely comprehending.

Phoebe continued. "Marjorie suggests that you might like to contact Peter Jarijari. He's an elder of the Gunditjmara people— your people." She reached into her coat pocket and pulled out a card. "He might help you decide what to do with them."

Benjamin felt very content in Felicity's company as he drove from the outskirts of Warrnambool toward the coast. He followed the Marri River until he arrived at a small tourist car park that had been carved into the low-lying scrub. It was late in the afternoon, and he relished being alone with Felicity after having worked all day at her house with a gang of workmen.

Felicity got out of the ute, took Benjamin's arm, and tugged him along the path that led down to the beach. The wind took her hair and whipped it across his face. It stung deliciously. "I hope you realize that the sightings of the mahogany ship were all in this area," she said, giving his arm a shake.

"Hmm." Benjamin breathed in the sea air and the smell of the scrub. "That ship has been responsible for quite a lot, recently." He smiled. "It brought us together."

Felicity came to a halt. "I suppose it has." She let go of his arm and yelled into the wind, "THANK YOU, MAHOGANY SHIP!"

Benjamin laughed, reclaimed Felicity's arm, and led her down to the track.

They could hear the roar of the surf well before they saw the long curving beach. The sea, when it came into view, presented an impressive spectacle. Serried ranks of waves were marching toward the shore—the place of their destruction. Benjamin shivered. It was a savage place—a place where ships could die.

Benjamin watched as a wave heaved itself up from the ocean, growing in grandeur and menace—higher and higher, rising and curling forward. Light shone through its turquoise back, spume flew off its crown until the wave tripped over its arrogance and fell with terrible force. The pounding seemed to shake the very ground on which they stood. All that remained was the mist of a thousand mysteries—and the hint of a rainbow.

A rainbow.

Yes, Benjamin reflected, *the time is right*.

He dug into his coat pocket and pulled out a package wrapped in a piece of wood shaving. "For you," he said, handing it to Felicity. "You burned my intended wedding gift to you. This is its replacement."

Felicity opened her mouth in surprise, took the parcel and, without a word, unfolded it.

Inside was a wooden pendant. A dark, curving shell cupped a white wooden pearl.

"You made this?" she asked, lifting it out.

Benjamin nodded. "I heard a parable once of a man finding a pearl so beautiful that he sacrificed everything to obtain it." He shrugged. "It made me think of you."

Nestled in the strip of shaving under the pendant was a twist of brown paper. Felicity unwrapped it, and extracted a white gold ring crowned with a princess-cut solitaire diamond.

"I didn't make that," Benjamin confessed.

Felicity took him by the hands and stood on her toes to give him a lingering kiss. "That," she said, "was in case my answer to you earlier wasn't clear enough."

"Hmm…message gratefully received."

They walked along the white sands, arm in arm.

"Tell me everything that happened to you yesterday," said Felicity. "I've been dying to ask you, and you haven't said a word about it. Was it…okay? How are you feeling about it?"

Benjamin furrowed his brow. How could he explain what had happened yesterday? The feelings he had experienced were beyond words. He drew a breath. "Well, as you know, I went to visit Peter Jarijari, an elder of the Gunditjmara—my mob." How strange it was to say that. *My mob.* Benjamin laughed. "He was only twenty minutes drive away. That's local, isn't it? I mean…" He trailed off. Benjamin had been so close to his roots all this time and not known it. Strange.

He continued. "I found the address and when I stood in front of the house, I could smell the sweet fragrance of wood-smoke. I didn't even think to knock on the front door. I just followed the smell and walked down the side of the house to a big open area out the back. Five blokes were there sitting around a fire." He shook his head, almost in disbelief. "I walked up to them and said, 'My name is Benjamin Bidjara. I'm Jimmy Bidjara's son.' Which was all wrong because our lot are not too keen on mentioning the name of those who are dead."

The surf pounded the beach as the sun edged closer to the horizon.

"What happened next?" Felicity jerked Benjamin's arm, jolting him out of his reverie.

"Well...no one said anything for a while, then a bloke, who I later found out was Peter, said, 'You been gone a long time.'" He turned to Felicity. "Can you imagine that?" He tried to laugh, but it was more like a sob. "I...I was thinking, 'Yeah, a lifetime,' but I kept quiet. Well, anyway...this bloke, Peter, pointed to a space by the fire and said, 'Sit down.' It was as simple as that."

"I don't understand," said Felicity.

"I was home." He paused. "Peter introduced me to two of my uncles and an auntie who was in the house. It turns out that Peter is also some sort of pastor to the community."

Felicity nodded.

They were both quiet for a long time as they watched the sun sink to the horizon and throw a shimmering path across the sea to where they stood.

Benjamin felt that it would be safer emotionally to turn the conversation to things more immediate and practical.

"We need to get back. Gabs is coming around tonight with a bottle of homemade wine after dinner." He shook his head. "Goodness knows how she and Archie are going to get on when they meet each other."

Felicity smiled. "Who knows?"

"Who knows, indeed?" They turned and made their way back along the beach.

He squeezed her arm. "How's the budget for the rebuild going?"

"Disastrous, thanks to you."

Benjamin raised an eyebrow.

Felicity shook his arm. "Don't pretend innocence. You've been crazy this last month. Totally irresponsible, actually."

"Oh?"

"You know full well. You've insisted on double glazing; insisted on insulating behind the weatherboarding; insisted on putting insulation film over the panes of glass in the old shop window." She waved a hand. "You've persuaded me to opt for an expensive kitchen, and to use bathroom tiles that are beautiful but hideously expensive. I don't know what's got into your head."

"You, actually," Benjamin said, drawing her close.

"Well, the reality is, I can't afford both you and the house. I can't see any option but to sell it so I can pay off the debts."

Benjamin started to laugh.

Felicity pummeled his chest crossly. "Seriously."

"Would it sell easily?"

"A three bedroom house with a study in a desirable location, and an upstairs view to die for—I should say so."

"Then you're happy that you haven't over-capitalized?"

"No," Felicity admitted. "I'll walk away from it with a handsome profit." She lowered her head. "But I had so wished that…" She corrected herself. "…we could have lived there."

"If someone offered you the right price, you'd sell it?"

"Yes, I suppose so. I'd be silly not to."

"Then I'll buy it."

"What?" Felicity swung around and stood in front of Benjamin, blocking his path. "Just what are you saying, Benjamin Bidjara?"

Gee, she looks good when she's mad. "Ah, well…it appears that Marjorie's house in Kew, conservatively valued at two point four million dollars, is up for sale. That, coupled with her other assets, brings her estate to almost three million dollars." He shrugged. "It seems I'm the sole beneficiary. I've been trying to find a good time to tell you."

Felicity stood with her mouth open. "Then, then, " she stammered, "you could…"

"Yes," interrupted Benjamin, "we can finish our house." Benjamin began to smile—but a distant cloud of emotions caused him to drop his head.

Felicity reached out, lifted his head, and searched his face. "What's the matter?"

Benjamin tried to laugh but failed, then looked at her with

desperation. "Felicity, I'm not a millionaire type of bloke. What on earth am I going to do with this responsibility?"

Behind them, the surf continued to boom and pound, causing mist to drift across the beach like smoke from a battlefield. Benjamin looked for the rainbow but couldn't find it.

"What's your passion in life, Benjamin? What really matters to you?"

"Besides you, you mean?"

"Seriously."

Benjamin rubbed his forehead and tried to identify the feelings that were swirling within him.

A wave crashed on the beach with a boom and a shudder.

"I'm angry at the lack of hope for Aboriginal kids," he said at length.

"What do you think would help them the most?"

"Meaningful jobs. Jobs they can relate to."

Felicity nodded. "Have you considered funding a scholarship program for apprentices?" She smiled. "I've seen you teaching Archie. You could even take on an apprentice yourself. You're a natural teacher."

Benjamin enfolded Felicity in his arms and buried his face in her hair. "Will you help me, Mrs. Bidjara?"

Felicity lifted her head. "Mrs. Bidjara. Hmm, I like that."

"We'll get married the moment your decree nisi comes through." Benjamin spoke through the muffle of her hair. "Peter has agreed to conduct the wedding."

Chapter 30

Benjamin wasn't used to flying, far less being greeted at the airport by someone holding a card with his name on it. Felicity and Archie walked with him across the arrivals hall to meet the man holding the card. None of them had to wait to collect luggage, as this was only a day trip to Canberra.

Their driver whisked them along dual carriageways toward the city center. At one point, they were able to see up the avenue to Australia's war memorial, held to be sacred by so many, and across Lake Burley Griffin to Parliament House, held to be rather less sacred.

They arrived at a driveway next to a multi-storied building. The driver showed his pass to an armed guard who opened the electronic gate for them. A few minutes later, all three of them were escorted inside to a small conference room.

Benjamin nodded his thanks as a secretary handed him his coffee. As she left, a slim man in a light gray suit came into the room and introduced himself as Mr. Johnson. He didn't give a first name. Johnson pushed his spectacles up his nose and sat himself down. "Thank you all for coming this morning. I realize that it has meant an early start for you." His gray eyes flicked over them.

Benjamin had the impression that it didn't take very long for Mr. Johnson to appraise anyone.

"I've called you together in the hope of bringing to rest the issue lying behind the Doran Khayef affair. I refer to the issue of the sixteenth century treaty signed between Henry VII of England and John II of Portugal."

Benjamin interrupted. "With respect, Mr. Johnson, the Khayef thing was a little more than an affair. It involved murder and kidnap. My interest in agreeing to your request to come here this morning was to get some assurance that Felicity, indeed all of us, are now quite safe."

Mr. Johnson looked at Benjamin without expression. "Perhaps we should begin there." He leaned back in his chair. "Mr. Khayef is currently remanded in custody. His lawyers have been playing merry hell and are trying every trick in the book to get him out. But, because of the attack on you by his late bodyguard, there is no chance of him being granted bail."

Felicity was chewing her lip. "Is the case against him likely to stand up in court?" she asked.

"His lawyers will try to distance him from the actions of his bodyguard, but it isn't a convincing argument." Johnson shrugged. "Nothing is certain. Big business, politics, and the judicial system can be…well, they can look after each other's interests. Let's just leave it at that."

Benjamin didn't want to leave it at that. "That doesn't give us much assurance."

"I wish I could give you more. What I can say is that Khayef is ruined financially. His creditors have foreclosed on him, and he is about to be declared bankrupt. He's in a great deal of debt—a fact that probably motivated him to take some, er…saleable assets from the Saracens."

Archie was chewing on his matchstick. "I'm guessing you mean drugs."

Johnson didn't answer. Archie continued. "How certain are you that he was behind the theft of Saracen assets?"

"The case for that is fairly compelling. We have fingerprints and

CCTV." He held up three fingers and said, "He had the means, the motive and the opportunity." Johnson folded down his fingers sequentially as he spoke.

Archie nodded. "So, our Mr. Khayef is not going to have a very comfortable time on a number of legal fronts."

Johnson nodded. "Correct. He is being seen to be what he is—an unprincipled megalomaniac. Very few will want to associate themselves with him now." He compressed his lips into a thin line. "What will happen to him will depend on what sort of hold he has over people in high places. Everyone is keeping their heads down at the moment because they know we're watching to see who comes into play."

Benjamin had the impression that with people like Mr. Johnson around, people were wise to do so.

"Would Khayef's plan to claim tax free status for his gold mining activities really have succeeded?" asked Felicity. "It sounds pretty fanciful to base a claim on a sixteenth century treaty."

Johnson turned his attention to Felicity. It was like seeing the barrels of a gun swivel. *Ready…aim…talk.* "Khayef had rather more faith in his claim than our lawyers do. Nonetheless, his claim was not without merit." Johnson drummed his fingers. "It's a legal gray area. The danger to Australian taxation laws comes from the fact that the treaty was signed by an English monarch." He smiled. "Things would be a whole lot easier if Australia was a republic. As it is, we are still legally headed by the British monarchy—and this treaty has never been revoked."

"Then why have you asked us to bring…" Benjamin almost said 'the Atlantis stone.' "…the Portuguese stone with us?"

Johnson manufactured a half-smile. "Because we like to be sure."

Felicity responded immediately. "If I give it to you, it will mean that you could destroy it if it was in Australia's interests." Benjamin could hear her resentment. She hadn't allowed anyone other than herself to carry the stone on their journey to Canberra. Even now, she was hugging the shoulder bag that contained it to herself.

Johnson said nothing.

Benjamin cleared his throat. "Mr. Johnson, not only have our lives been put at risk, but we have also needed to fund the costs of finding the Sardinian copy of the treaty and mounting a rescue operation to free Felicity. These costs have been borne by Archie and the late Miss Eddington."

Archie interrupted. "Actually, it was all funded by Marjorie." He shrugged. "She thought that funding it through conventional ASIO channels might be too unwieldy."

Johnson began drumming his fingers. "Do you have the receipts, Mr. Hammond?"

"Yeah."

"If you give them to me, I'll credit the expenses to Miss Eddington's estate."

Benjamin suddenly realized that he would be the beneficiary of this, which wasn't what he had intended at all.

Felicity broke in. "There remains the small issue of you wanting me to meekly hand over the greatest historical find I'm ever likely to make in my life…one that is important to all Australians."

The drumming fingers stopped. "I am aware that I'm asking a great deal of you, Miss Anderson. But, you will not find us unappreciative."

"What exactly does that mean?"

Mr. Johnson pushed his glasses up his nose and stared at her, taking aim. "I understand that you are an historian who has ambitions to be a writer. Is that so?"

Felicity nodded.

"Are you a good writer?"

She stammered, "I…I think so."

"Then it might interest you to know that the Australian Government is commissioning a book series on the history of Australia. If you had that commission, how do you think you would go about writing it?"

Felicity's mouth dropped open. She paused, evidently struggling to pull herself together. Eventually, she said, "I'd want to write the facts in everyday prose…and make it read like an adventure. Three volumes should do it, and none of them should be too big."

Bravo, thought Benjamin.

Mr. Johnson stared at her without blinking. "If you make application to write this series, I can assure you it will be viewed very sympathetically."

Felicity nodded her understanding. She then shocked Benjamin by saying. "I accept, provided my fiancée writes the series with me. That way, you'll be sure to get an indigenous Australian perspective." She lifted her chin. "Presumably, you have the treaty close to hand, perhaps even in this building. You also have the Portuguese stone. And you have Benjamin." Felicity pulled the Atlantis stone out from her shoulder bag, unwrapped the bubble plastic around it, and pushed it across the table to Mr. Johnson. "You do realize that when all three of these things come together, Benjamin could make a claim on all the gold mined in Victoria."

There was silence for a long while.

"You are a writer, Mr. Bidjara?"

"He is," answered Felicity on Benjamin's behalf.

Mr. Johnson sighed and pushed himself back from the table. "Then we'll see what we can do."

Archie elected to stay on in Canberra to sort out some affairs with ASIO. Benjamin suspected that he might finally be retiring from their service. Who knew where the future would take him? Benjamin very much hoped that he would keep in touch.

He leaned over to Felicity in the aircraft seat beside him. "You have some explaining to do, young lady."

"What do you mean?" she protested.

"You and I both know that the stone you gave Mr. Johnson wasn't the Atlantis stone. It was a good copy, I grant you—probably made by Gabrielle—but it wasn't the Atlantis stone."

Felicity twisted her head away evasively.

"Felicity?"

She turned back. "Well, Mr. Bidjara, it so happens that my friend Gabs is making you and me a wedding present for our new house. It's a sculpture of a fish." She prodded his arm. "Because your people have deep links with fishing around Port Fairy."

Benjamin furrowed his brow, failing to see the relevance of what Felicity was saying.

She continued. "It's looking fabulous. It's held together with wire…and has shingles of wood and pieces of flat stone for scales."

"Don't tell me…"

"Yes," she smiled. "One of the pieces of stone looks a lot like the Atlantis stone."

Note from the author

Thank you for reading *The Atlantis Stone*. I hope you enjoyed it. Please consider leaving a review on Amazon for the benefit of other readers.

A lot of what you read was based on my personal experience of staying in the charming town of Port Fairy, and spending time exploring the secrets of Sardinia in the Mediterranean.

I'm pleased to be able to report that the "Stone Collection" of books is growing all the time. It includes:

The Peacock Stone

The Fire Stone

Four more are in the process of being made available.

To be kept up to date on new releases, sign up to my mailing list at www.author-nick.com. New subscribers will receive an exclusive bonus novelette, *The Mystic Stone*, a complete story, six chapters (15,500 words) in length. It is an adventure that takes place on Caldey Island off the rugged Pembrokeshire coast. I hope you like it.

What is true...and what is fiction?

Historical records of sightings of the 'mahogany ship' near Warrnambool... TRUE

The existence of a fragment of stone in South Africa with etchings of a flotilla of ships and Mendonça's name, together with the date 1524... TRUE[1]

The existence of a stone with *Ilhas do ouro*—land of gold—carved into it, together with a depiction of a two-masted, lateen-rigged sailing ship... FICTION

The alleged claim that a document was found in Canberra recording how soldiers were ordered to destroy the mahogany ship in case it compromised British sovereignty claims over Australia... TRUE

Historical details surrounding the search for lands where gold might be found... TRUE

The theory that the mahogany ship was a caravel belonging to Mendonça's flotilla... TRUE

The Portuguese artifacts found in New Zealand... TRUE

The Treaty of Tordesillas... TRUE

Historical details concerning the kings and queens of Portugal and Spain in the sixteenth century (except the treaty between Henry VII of England and John II of Portugal)... TRUE

The treaty between Henry VII of England and John II of Portugal... FICTION

The existence of Britain's National Archives at Kew... TRUE

The history of Sardinia (excepting reference to a copy of a treaty between Henry VII of England and John II of Portugal)... TRUE

The existence of Cagliari's Elephant Tower and the statue of the elephant... TRUE

The woods used for woodturning and their characteristics... TRUE

The details surrounding scuba diving off Warrnambool... TRUE

The threatened radicalization of the Aboriginal communities in northern Australia in the 1970s... TRUE

The details surrounding Australia's SAS activities in Afghanistan... TRUE

The quotes concerning mathematics, God, and Paul Dirac... TRUE[2]

The history and culture of the Gunditjmara people from around Warrnambool... TRUE

The details of a five-hundred-year-old Portuguese liturgical prayer book, one page of which has a kangaroo-like creature sketched into a decorated letter starting a paragraph... TRUE

The details of the 'Giddy Tuna' and other shops and buildings mentioned in Port Fairy... FICTION

The charm of the town of Port Fairy...and the Moyne River... TRUE

A smart phone case which has a thermal imaging (infra red) camera, powered by the case's own battery... TRUE

The micro ScoutCam 1.2mm diameter camera, developed by the Israel-based biotechnology firm, Medigus, for endoscopic diagnoses... TRUE

The existence of a diamond-coated spiral wire saw... TRUE

Notes

Chapter 13

1. The CFMEU is the 'Construction, Forestry, Maritime, Mining and Energy Union' in Australia.

What is true...and what is fiction?

1. This is true according to Peter Trickett's book, *Beyond Capricorn* (2007), p. 180, plate 11.
2. Paul Dirac was a theoretical physicist at Cambridge who worked in quantum physics. His calculations resulted in the discovery of anti-matter.

About the Author

Nick Hawkes has lived in several countries of the world, and collected many an adventure. Along the way, he has earned degrees in both science and theology—and has written books on both. Since then, he has turned his hand to novels, writing romantic thrillers that feed the heart, mind, and soul.

His seven full length novels are known as, 'The Stone Collection.'

His first novel, *The Celtic Stone*, won the Australian Caleb Award in 2014.

Also by Nick Hawkes

The Peacock Stone

A young girl comes to live in the slums of New Delhi. It is a place of danger where street gangs rule. Through the initiative of a blind beggar, she is taken to work in the home of a rich businessman. There, she observes a world of education and privilege—a world that is out of her reach.

But danger still stalks.

A kidnap attempt forces her to flee to her childhood home in the tropical backwaters of Kerala—a land of wooden boats, fishing and elephants.

Violence, intrigue and love flourish.

Whether she survives will depend on her being able to understand the significance of the pendant given to her by the blind beggar—the peacock stone.

More details at www.author-nick.com

(See next page for more)

Also by Nick Hawkes

The Fire Stone

Sebastian, a young farm hand living in the Australian mallee, is being watched by Val, a fugitive hiding in the forests on the banks of the River Murray. Val has an official document that confirms his death fourteen years ago. There is no official document that confirms his particular skill: assassin.

Pip divides her life between her musical studies at the Adelaide Conservatorium and her work as a barista. Her ordered life is shattered when bullets fired through the window of her home reduce her cello to matchwood. The violence appears all the more bewildering given that she lives with her father David an Anglican cleric and retired missionary.

A web of violence draws all four of them together.

Everything in Sebastian's life begins to change when he is given the gift of a Koroit opal—*The Fire Stone*. It begins a journey in which he is challenged by David's wisdom and confronted by Pip's love.

The four of them seek to escape the violence that pursues them by sailing across the Pacific to the islands of Vanuatu. There, in the village community of Lamap, the final drama is played out…

…before *The Fire Stone* makes an unexpected return.

More details at www.author-nick.com